"Captain, I just picked up a radar transmit less than five klicks from here. Pretty small. Looks like a battlesuit unit."

The gunship captain grinned. "Great! Let's bag it."

"On our way. Hey, I'm getting a hit on a comm frequency, too."

The scanner operator put the audio on the speaker. "Goddammit, Starkiller, turn the bleedin' radar off. You wanna get us all killed?"

The captain smiled. "Yes, I'd guess that was a rebel combat unit. Bearing?"

"Eighty-four. And I've got a target lock."

The gunner spoke up. "Permission to fire?"

The captain shook his head. "Negative. Let's find his friends first. Any luck?"

The scanner op swore. "He's heading for the base of that cliff! See that ledge sticking out of the canyon wall? There must be a cave under there. The scanners can't read through the rock."

The captain smacked an open palm with his fist. "Damn. I don't suppose we have any torps loaded."

"Negative, sir. Lasers only."

The captain sighed. "Well, I suppose if we can't dig them out, we'll have to bury them. Gunner, target that ledge and fire on my command."

REBEL MOON

BRUCE BETHKE

AND

VOX DAY

POCKET BOOKS

New York   London   Toronto   Sydney   Tokyo   Singapore

This book is a work of fiction. Names, characters, places and incidents are products of the author's imagination or are used fictitiously. Any resemblance to actual events or locales or persons, living or dead, is entirely coincidental.

An *Original* Publication of POCKET BOOKS

POCKET BOOKS, a division of Simon & Schuster Inc.
1230 Avenue of the Americas, New York, NY 10020

ISBN: 1-4165-0190-8

This Pocket Books paperback printing May 2004

10   9   8   7   6   5   4   3   2

POCKET BOOKS and colophon are registered trademarks of Simon & Schuster Inc.

Printed in the U.S.A.

To Ted, from Ted.
And to Gami, with love.

A PRELUDE TO WAR

When seeking the root causes of the Lunar Revolution of 2069, one needn't dig far. The United Nations' position of power on Earth depended on control of the food supply; control of the food supply in turn depended on control of the lunar hydroponic food factories; and the hydroponic food factories themselves were heavily dependent on the ingenuity, the sweat, the determination, and far too often the blood of the lunar colonists.

Did this revolution have to happen? Not necessarily. The Committee on Lunar Development (CLD) could have admitted the colonists' complaints were legitimate and then acted to improve the working conditions, repeal the much-hated oxygen taxes, and remove certain petty and corrupt committee-appointed colonial officials. The Peace Enforcement Command (PEC) could have admitted that its easy victory over the Idaho Christian Patriots Militia (see *The Sagebrush Rebellion*, Chapter 5) was a fluke and responded to the initial outbreak of civil disobedience with less shooting and more diplomacy. Or the Security Council could have recognized the legitimacy of the 2068 plebiscite, and granted the Lunar delegation a seat in the General Assembly. Any of these actions alone might well have defused the revolution.

But the so-called fourth possibility — that the colonists could have given up, surrendered quietly, and resigned themselves to their lives of near-indentured servitude?

That was never an option.

— Chaim Noguchi, *A History of the Lunar Revolution* (Herschelton West Mars: Cebrenia Publishing, 2201).

CHAPTER 1

The thief and the barbarian slipped cautiously through the main chamber of the Great Temple of the Dark Goddess, their long steel swords unsheathed and ready for action. The walls and pillars of the room were decorated with vast friezes, worked in silver and gold and highlighted with fistfuls of sparkling gems, showing the goddess Kharauma in all of her most obscene poses.

"Get a load of that," Finn Fingers whispered, pointing with his free hand toward a particularly lurid construction. It showed the goddess in her half-woman, half-snake incarnation, the one her devotees called the Serpent Whore, writhing with pleasure in the black-taloned embrace of the Scarlet Rider.

Icehawk the Barbarian responded with an inarticulate grunt and flexed his massive pectoral muscles as he stifled a yawn. He found himself bored by the unimaginative eroto-occult images associated with the Dark Goddess and frankly felt he'd seen more stimulating artwork on black velvet in a back stall at the Minas Tirith bazaar. But he did not seize the moment to engage the little thief in an esoteric

3

debate on lousy religious art: instead, he tightened his grip on his sword and kept his mind focused on the quest. Somewhere in this temple, the devotees of Kharauma had hidden the Key to the Great Rune, that which kept the Scarlet Rider and his hordes imprisoned forever in the Mirrored Abyss. Now Icehawk and Finn Fingers had mere hours left in which to find the Key and either return it to Ice Mountain or destroy it, in order to keep the high priestess of the temple from using it at midnight to unlock the Forbidden Gate and unleash the Lord of Hell.

Somehow, it seemed to Icehawk, his quests always ended up like this. Three months before, he'd joined a party of twenty adventurers setting out from the Wolf Isles in search of nothing more than a little mayhem and booty. They'd fought their way past draugs and drekis, played murderous hide-and-seek with orcs and Imperial patrols, had their fortunes told by the Wise Woman of the West, and been steered to the Isle of the Viprans.

And now here they were, deep in the bowels of an ancient temple, only two of them still alive, and just six hours left in which to save the world.

With a sudden start, Icehawk realized he was still staring at the frieze of Kharauma and the Scarlet Rider. He peeled his eyes off the image, looked at Finn, then frowned and pointed. "Hey, your sword is glowing."

The thief looked at his own weapon and nodded. "You know, I think you're right." As they watched, the pale blue aura surrounding the weapon grew steadily brighter, and previously unseen runes on the blade began to emerge as letters of fire.

"That'll teach you to go poking around in Va'ardish burial mounds," Icehawk said. "Boris *told* you that thing was enchanted. I wonder what those letters say."

Finn looked up, first at Icehawk, then past him, and the little thief's eyes slowly grew wider. "How about 'Look behind you'?"

In a flash of flowing blond hair and gleaming blue steel Icehawk spun around to face the frieze again.

4

"Er, Hawk?" the thief asked nervously. "Am I seeing things, or are the Scarlet Rider's eyes glowing?"

"More like blazing, my fine fast-fingered friend." Icehawk raised his sword and began to back carefully away from the frieze. "This does not bode well for us. I suggest we leave."

"And I concur. Which way?"

"Deeper into the temple. If we go back the way we came, we'll never find the Key in time."

"Gotcha," the thief said. "And if we don't find the Key, this whole party was for nothing."

Icehawk heard Finn sigh. "Okay, I'll take point. You cover my back. Let's—"

The Scarlet Rider's eyes flared a blinding crimson. There was a loud *crack* as the frieze split down the middle, the sound of a massive grinding of stones, then something oily and black spurted out of the crack in the wall and began collecting in a thick pool on the marble floor.

Icehawk faced the black pool and dropped into a *zenkutsu* fighting stance. "Run, Finn!"

"No! We stick together!"

"Wrong! I'm the muscle; you're the brains. If only one of us is left to steal the Key, it has to be *you!*" Icehawk shifted his stance slightly as the pool drew itself together and began to take definite form. "Leave the monster to me! I'll catch up with you later, if I can."

The thief made no answer, but from the sound of rapidly receding footsteps behind him, Icehawk guessed Finn Fingers had taken his advice. He shifted his grip on the golden hilt of his sword, edged sideways slightly, and focused all his attention on the thing before him.

The black pool had coalesced into an eight-foot-tall creature that combined the least appealing features of a snake, a spiny ridgepig, and a hill troll. Its eyes were fiery red and it wore a flowing crimson cape, but it wore nothing else to hide the definite fact that it was a male and apparently an excited one at that.

"So," Icehawk said, feeling more than a little nauseated by the sight, "are you a demon from the deepest pits of hell, or are you just happy to see me?"

"Beware, mortal!" The thing's voice was deep and mostly growl. "I am the Scarlet Rider, and I shall feast on your soul!"

Icehawk laughed bravely. "The Scarlet Rider? *You?* I don't *think* so! It's not midnight yet, and besides, what loser wrote your lines?"

"Blasphemer!" The beast lunged. Icehawk easily ducked under the outstretched black talons and slashed upward, his blade biting into the monster's left forearm. The thing screamed and recoiled, black ichor spraying wildly.

"You call *me* blasphemous? What about *these?*" Icehawk gestured around the temple chamber, feeling more confident as he realized that none of the other friezes had come to life. The beast roared incoherently and lunged at him again. Again Icehawk dodged the blow and slashed, but this time a spatter of the creature's thick black blood landed on the back of his neck and began to sizzle like hot acid.

"Yeow!" Icehawk slapped at the burning spot, then slapped his burning fingers against his leather pants, then noticed that his blood-covered sword blade was melting away like a plastic knife on a barbecue grill. He ducked another blow and darted to the side. "Okay, Little Red Riding Hood, I'm through fooling around with you. *Kairblema'gh!*"

The monster shuddered at the harsh sound of the Word of Change, pausing a moment in its attack. "What are you doing, mortal?"

Icehawk cast the hilt of his ruined sword aside and smiled as he felt the mighty surge of blood-power flooding through his veins. "Getting back to my roots, beast. Bet you didn't know I was a half-breed."

The thing squinted suspiciously. "Half what?"

"Well, Mom was a princess, of course. So I'm half human."

"And your father?"

"Was a Belkranagh Dragon, I'm afraid."

The beast began to mewl with fear and retreat toward the frieze it'd come from. Icehawk followed, smiling dangerously as his form began to shift and expand.

"Now, what was that you said about feasting on my soul?"

"Dalton!" a female voice called out from somewhere off to his right.

"Hang on, honey!" the mighty Icehawk yelled back. "I'm just about to kill this thing."

"I don't care. You've been saying 'Hang on, honey' for the past two hours. I'm hungry!"

"Damn," he muttered. "It's only been an hour. At most." He broke off his attack and invoked his real-time clock. It was *18:32.* Oops. "Okay, hold on, honey, I'm coming out. Just give me a few seconds to save game and tell DeShayne." He invoked the save command, then called up the real-time comm channel.

Three seconds later DeShayne Jones's coffee-brown face popped into view. Normally Finn Fingers's real-world alter ego was smiling and unflappably cheerful, but this time he wore a scowl. "Yo, Dalt. What up? Why you ditching now?"

Dalton shrugged. "It's my girlfriend. I promised I'd have dinner with her tonight, and she's getting impatient."

Another three-second light-speed lag. "Dinner? Already?" DeShayne looked alarmed. "Aw, shoot, I hosed my two p.m."

Dalton laughed. "Relax. I'm six hours ahead of you, remember? You groundhogs can never keep time zones straight."

DeShayne laughed with Dalton and looked relieved. "That's right. You Loonies are on Greenwich time, ain'tcha? Guess I can make it to my calc class after all."

"I guess you can." Dalton paused. "So what do you think? You want to pick this up again later? Say, in about two hours?"

"Sure, but make it more like three. I got that calc class at two, like I say, and sometimes it run long. The prof gets pissed if you log off before he done droning, you know?"

"I know. So tell you what: I've got a little gopher I can send you; wrote it when I was telecommuting to M.I.T. It sets up a proxy that pretends to take your place and automatically logs out when the class ends. Pretty seamless, actually."

"Hey, that'd be cool!" A note of respect entered DeShayne's voice. "Man, you never told me you graduated from M.I.T."

"Well, I didn't, exactly. Came up here to research my thesis, got offered a real job, never went back. You know how it goes."

"I wish. There are days I think I be lucky to ever get out of Chicago alive, much less find a real job. Here you taking your life in your hands just by going down to Skyway level, and forget the street or subway. At least in the games the monsters got *reasons* for trying to kill you."

Dalton nodded. "Understood. And that, my friend, is why I really think you should think about moving up here after you finish school. Granted, the taxes up here suck like vacuum, and the Colonial Office learned bureaucracy from the Russians. But the people here are real smart, we've got artificial gravity in most of the living domes now, and there's no shortage of work if you're willing to get your hands dirty. Not like down there, where you've got, what? Twenty billion people competing for two billion jobs?"

DeShayne looked unconvinced. "I dunno, man. I spent a month in North Dakota one weekend. I got to imagine the Moon is even worse. Fifty thousand people spread out across an entire planet? It'd be way too slow for a big-city boy."

The next voice was neither quiet nor light-speed lagged. *"Dalton!* Aren't you ever going to—"

"Whoops, gotta go! Call you after twenty-two hundred."

"That's, uh, four o'clock Central, right?"

"Right. Bye!" Dalton broke the connection, then pressed the button that retracted the flatscreen into the headboard of his bed. Rolling off his pillow, he winced as a shot of pain flashed through his lower back.

"Hon*ey,"* the voice nagged from the other room, "come *on."*

"I'm coming, I'm coming." Dalton found his way to his feet and worked his back and arms into a stretch at the low ceiling. "Just give me a minute, okay? I've got a bad kink in my back."

"And whose fault is that? You've been lying in bed for more than three hours. That can't be healthy."

Dalton finished his stretch, let out a quiet sigh, and tottered into the other room of his tiny apartment.

Like the bedroom, the living-dining room was cluttered by dirty coffee cups, unlabeled data disks, and computer hardware in various stages of disassembly. In the far corner sat his latest prized acquisition: a real Twentieth Century Vectrex. It didn't work, of course, but he'd located a complete scan of the original service manuals at a library site in New Guinea, of all places, and he was planning to upload them just as soon as he finished breadboarding together a power converter. It was a project he'd been puttering with off and on for the last two months.

In the center of the room, though, stood the reason why the classic system and so much else still wasn't finished: the woman who was at once both the love of his short life and the bane of his existence. A slender, sexy auburn-haired hydroponics engineer with an athletic build and a proximity-fuse temper.

Dara.

"Honey, why don't you ever let me clean this place?"

To avoid answering, Dalton picked his way through the obstacle course and kissed her.

"You look pale. Are you feeling all right?"

"Yeah."

"You were on-line an awfully long time. Who were you with?"

"DeShayne."

"Oh, him. So how's the game going?"

"Well," said Dalton, suddenly coming to life, "Fingers and I are the only ones still on the quest, since the ice dragon froze Boris and the Viprans killed Shawn. We've managed to find a way inside the temple that holds the Key, but we only have until game-time midnight to steal it before the high priestess of Kharauma uses it to unleash the Lord of Hell and—"

Dara interrupted. "And that would be bad, right?"

Dalton recognized his cue. "Yeah. Right." The flow of words shut off like a spigot. Dalton looked around, moved a box full of computer parts, and uncovered a chair.

"DeShayne?" said Dara, thinking out loud. "Isn't he that tall blond guy from Kepler we met at Myra Cakan's party?"

Dalton considered sitting down on the chair, then realized he'd been flat on his back for three hours and decided to keep standing. "No, that was Shawn. DeShayne is the college kid in Chicago."

Dara shook her head and smiled. "I don't see how you get off on those games, but it *is* pretty cool how you can play them with people all over the world. Both worlds," she corrected herself.

Dalton shrugged. "No big deal."

"I mean," Dara went on, "whenever *I* talk with people back on Earth, there's always that blasted light-speed lag. How come you can keep UNET synched and stay interactive in real time?"

"Uh . . ." Dalton froze, suddenly stricken with the sensation of being a coyote that'd just run off the edge of a cliff and was now standing suspended in midair, afraid to look down for fear that gravity would reassert itself. "It's technical. Really technical. You wouldn't understand."

Wrong answer. Dara took a step closer, put her hands on her hips, and screwed her face into a frown. "Just try me."

Dalton was saved by a sudden inspiration. "Gee, honey, I'm tired of always talking about, you know, my work. How was *your* day?"

"Rotten!" Dara said, to Dalton's boundless relief veering off onto the new topic. "You'd think the damn FAO would *test* their new genetic nightmares before they bother to ship 'em up here, y'know?"

Dalton nodded attentively and simulated the appearance of being interested. "Um . . . FAO?"

"You know, the Food and Agriculture Office—the amateur Frankensteins responsible for all the new genetically engineered crops we're supposed to be growing in the greenhouses. They sent us a beaut this week: hybrid zucchini-kudzu with termite digestive enzymes. It's supposed to grow in anything, right? Save us tons of money on biomass recycling?"

Dalton nodded again, then saw Dara's expression and switched to shaking his head. "It didn't work?"

Dara let out a snort that turned into a cynical laugh. "Oh, it *worked* all right. We put it out in G-seven dome, just to be on the safe side. Damn thing grew *two hundred meters* overnight! Took over the dome completely and was starting to digest its way through the airlock seal when we finally figured out a way to kill it." She sighed again.

"Poor baby," Dalton said sympathetically. "Rough day."

"Yeah," Dara said. "So now you owe me a wonderful night. That starts with dinner, and if I don't get fed soon, I'm going to faint from starvation. Ergo, chef, *s'il vous plaît.*"

"Right." Dalton shuffled over to the CityComm panel and thumbed a touchpad. "FoodNet, please."

There was a soft hum and a few clicks; then the calm, synthetic, gender-neutral voice of the Port Aldrin Central Computer answered. "FoodNet ready."

"Central? What dinners are available for delivery now?"

The computer digested his request a moment, then responded. "Option one: succulent roast turkey breast with mashed potatoes, gravy, and carrot coins. Option two: tangy Szechuan vegetarian entrée, with lo mein noodles and rice. Option three: traditional beer-battered cod, with English chips and no vegetables. Please order by option number."

Dalton turned to Dara to ask which she preferred, only to find her glaring at him. " 'Tangy'?" she asked, her pug nose wrinkled into a sneer. " 'Succulent'? Have you tech boys been screwing around with Central's vosynth again?"

Dalton put his hands up in a don't-hit-me gesture. "It wasn't my idea. The Nutrition Authority is trying to get people to stop cooking in their rooms and eat balanced meals, so they had us put more adjectives on the menu." He tried a weak smile on her. "Any of those options sound appealing?"

Dara switched off her mock glare and smiled sarcastically. "Let me see: the cod is actually processed neokrill, the Szechuan vegetables actually *are* vegetables, but I can't stand to look at anything green right now, and the turkey is actually a cloned tissue culture growing in a big vat over at Kepler—which means it once was part of an actual bird. I'll have the turkey."

Dalton nodded, then turned back to the comm panel. "Central? Two option one turkey dinners, please." He looked over his shoulder at Dara. "Anything for dessert?"

"Me?" she suggested brightly.

Dalton sighed, smiled, thumbed off the comm panel, and thanked his lucky stars he'd met a woman who didn't require being re-seduced on a regular basis.

CHAPTER 2

Mare Tranquillitatis, Luna
Chaffee Memorial Launch Control
24 October 2069
21:30 GMT

An alarm bell chimed softly. Lars Hendrickson, senior cargo launcher supervisor, grade 3, swore a mild oath, then took one more sip of his coffee before setting the cup down on the computer console.

"Nine-thirty already? Jeez." He took a last look at the crossword puzzle that lay unfinished in his lap—the eight-letter word for "subvert" starting with *s* was still eluding him—then sat up straight, tossed the puzzle onto the console beside his coffee cup, and grabbed his electronic smartpad.

"Stupid UNSHA safety rules," he grumbled to himself, as he knew he was alone in the launcher control center. "Every hour on the hour, manually check the flinkin' readouts." Lars stood up, hitched up his sagging pants, then plodded off on the first leg of his rounds. "The readings never bounce. They never will. So who's to know if I'm half an hour late?" He paused before the first telesense console, gave it a quick eyeball, and nodded approvingly, then started scanning the readings into the smartpad by passing his hand over the console. "Everything is always perfect. A chimpanzee could do this job. In his sleep."

"Input complete," the smartpad said, indicating it had accepted the scan and was digesting the data.

"I mean, heck of a challenge for a retired master sergeant, innit? Twenty years with the Peacekeepers, only to wind up here?"

"Invalid command," the smartpad said.

Lars ignored the response. "Baby-sitting this pile of junk. Sucking up to twerps from UNSHA and UNCLD and every other pack of half-wit New York bureaucratic twits. And then I had to fire that damn Limey, Britt, yesterday and take his shift myself!"

"Invalid command," the smartpad repeated.

"I mean," Lars said to the pad, "wasn't much of a choice, huh? Sneaking six days off just this month for a bunch of stupid political meetings?"

"Ready for the next entry," the smartpad suggested.

Lars gave the smartpad a backhanded slap. "You want politics? *I'll* give you politics! You little punk protesters are unhappy? Out the airlock! Don't like the way the UN runs things? Out the airlock! Let's see how smart you talk when you're sucking vacuum!"

"Please move on to the next entry," the smartpad asked politely.

Lars took a deep breath, then deflated, sighed, and shuffled around the corner.

The four strangers clustered around the interociter matrix generator immediately got his attention. Especially as they seemed to be taking it apart. "Hey! *You!*" Lars bulled in, waving the smartpad like a weapon. "This is a secured area! How did you—"

Lars stopped cold when he noticed the strangers were carrying *real* weapons. Pistols. H&K LP-7 Mark Fives: laser pistols, to be precise, military-police issue.

An instant later he registered that the men were also wearing hologram hoods to hide their faces, and their black coveralls carried forged dome identification badges.

Lars Hendrickson, UN-PEC master sergeant (retired), stood frozen in his tracks.

"We're rerouting control of the launcher," one off to the left side of the group said in a voice that was barely more than a hoarse whisper. "Don't interfere and you won't get hurt."

Deep in the back of his mind some part of Lars's brain started screaming, *Retreat, dummy!* But a lifetime of master sergeant authority was still in control of his voice and his hands, so he thumped a fist on the smartpad and shouted louder, "Rerouting control? Impossible! Not without written authorization from— Where's your authorization? I demand to see your authorization!"

A moment later he was staring into the main collimator lens of an LP-7 Mark Five. It looked much bigger than he remembered.

"Here's my authorization," the man holding the gun said. "Now, much as I would enjoy vaporizing that lump of fat you call a brain, I'd prefer it if you'd just politely step aside."

Something in the timbre of the man's voice triggered a matchup from Lars's memory. *"Britt?"* Through the eyeholes in the hood, suddenly familiar blue eyes went wide, and this time it was the gunman's turn to freeze.

The reflexes of a lifetime die hard. In the few moments while Britt was still surprised and hesitating, Lars saw an opening, and for one brief, glorious instant he was once again a warrior: a hundred kilos of muscle, steely nerves, and total dedication to the United Nations Peacekeeper Corps. As if in slow motion, he feinted with his left hand, lashed out with the smartpad in his right, batted the pistol aside while gathering his legs under him like mighty coil springs, and threw himself into a heroic headlong leap at the large red security alarm button on the other side of the interocitor console.

He never made it. Too many years of doughnuts, sugared coffee, and living in the low-G parts of Lunar domes had taken their toll on the master sergeant's body; he was now closer to one hundred fifty kilograms of slack muscle and adipose tissue, and his rebuilt titanium knees simply weren't up to the job. His outstretched fingers fell agonizing inches short, as he landed on the floor with an "oof" that knocked the wind out of him, and before he could recover, a heavy gun butt crashed down on the back of his skull. Then the waves of pain came rolling in like the breakers on the beach at Chenghai, and as his world faded out to a bloody red and black, it finally dawned on him.

The eight-letter word for "subvert."

Sabotage.

"Think he's dead?" One of the men nudged Lars with his toe.

"Think I care?" Britt Godfrey peeled off his holo-hood and shook out his short blond hair.

The third member of the spook team finished a look-and-peek around the corner, then rejoined Britt and the other two. "What went wrong? I thought you said he made his rounds at the top of the hour?"

"He was supposed to." Britt shrugged.

The third man wasted another glance at Lars. "And *we* were supposed to avoid confrontation. Major Nakagawa is gonna be pissed if you killed him."

Britt sniffed. "Nakagawa can bite me bloomin' bum. He never had to work for this clown." He let out a bitter little laugh and kicked the unconscious man, then turned to the fourth member of the team, who was hunched over the open control panel. "Any luck with that cracker yet, Roberts?"

Ken Roberts shook his head slightly, but kept his attention focused on a small black box haywired into the panel. "Uh-uh. We're in, but I'm still trying to get through to Dalton. I'm getting a busy signal from his computer."

"Oh, God," muttered the second commando, shaking his hooded head. "The kid probably got bored waiting and started playing games or something."

Britt's eyes narrowed. "You're bloody kiddin' me, right,

Willits?" He glared menacingly at Roberts. "You said we could rely on 'im!"

Roberts grimaced. "I *said* we needed him for the remote hack. I never said he was dependable."

Willits giggled nervously under his hood. "And why shouldn't we trust a kid who thinks his family name is Starkiller, y'know? When he isn't calling himself Icesparrow or whatever."

"You mean Icehawk." Roberts shrugged. "So Dalt's a pathological gamer. That doesn't mean he's a complete flake. Maybe something's come up." For what seemed like the hundredth time, he punched a button on the device plugged into the control panel.

"Joe's Pool Hall. Who in the hall do you want?" a familiar voice squawked out of the device, and the four waiting men nearly jumped out of their skin. "That you, Ken?"

"Where the hell were you?" Britt snarled.

"Who's that?" Dalton asked.

"Ahh . . . never mind, Dalt." Roberts angrily waved Britt away from the panel. "You ready to rock?"

"Oh, yeah. Okay, I got your dataflow reading through. Looks like . . . Oh, this'll be easy. They're two revs behind on the OSS."

"OSS?" whispered Willits.

"Operating system security," Roberts replied. "That's good."

"Good, is it? Well, hurry it up, will you?" Britt cradled his pistol and looked around nervously. "How long is this gonna take?"

Roberts patted the black box and smiled reassuringly. "Shouldn't be long now."

Britt scowled and checked the load status of his pistol again. It was becoming a nervous tic. "I still don't see why you needed to involve this boyo. Why couldn't you just do it yourself?"

Roberts gave Britt an irritated stare. "Because we're not just hacking into some yo-yo's private pornopix collection;

we're up against a very serious security system here. I could handle the local stuff, like the access codes for the doors, with just the cracker, but to take over the launch control system you need more juice than that little thing's got. So we needed someone to operate from remote, and we needed somebody good enough to make it work, like Dalton."

"Oh." Britt wrinkled his brow and looked perplexed for a moment, then shrugged and edged up to the nearest corner and took a quick peek around it.

The fourth commando was kneeling next to Lars, dabbing at a trickle of red from the fallen man's ear. "Look, he's bleeding."

"Let 'im bleed," Britt snapped over his shoulder. "Stinking One Worlder. He'd just as soon turn you in to the Stasi as look at you."

"Stasi?" The kneeling man looked up.

"Von Braun slang," one of the others volunteered. "UN Special Aerospace Security. UNISAS. You know, the guys who make the arrests that never show up on the news, never come to trial, and way too often lead to fatal airlock 'accidents'?"

"Oh," the kneeling man said. "In Volodya we call them the Loyalty Cops."

Britt edged into the conversation. "Well, they're going to be calling *us* cryomeat unless we—"

"Open sesame!" Dalton's voice sang out of the device. "Damn, I'm good! Coming your way, Ken."

"Got it!" Roberts replied happily as he rapidly punched at the keypad. "Okay, I'm through the encryption, and . . ." He paused to quickly stroke a few more keys, bit his lip nervously, then push one more. "And we're in! System control is *ours!* Thanks, Dalt. Nice work."

"No problem, Ken. Don't do anything I wouldn't do. Over and out."

"Brilliant." Britt made sure his handgun was on safe, then tucked it into his waistband and pulled out a comm link. "Badger?" he said, thumbing a button. "The fox is in the henhouse. Repeat: the fox is in the bleedin' henhouse."

The man kneeling next to Lars looked up. "Henhouse?"

Office of the Governor, Port Aldrin
24 October 2069
21:47 GMT

Pieter von Hayek sat in his black chrome office chair like a convict in an execution chamber awaiting a call from the governor. *Except that I am the governor,* he reminded himself, *and this was all my idea.* He'd long since given up trying to project an aura of confidence to the dozen or so other people crowded into the small spartan office and was now simply hoping that his sweat wouldn't soak through the armpits of his best gray pinstripe suit.

This is what I promised I'd do, if elected, he reminded himself. He took off his bifocals, massaged the bridge of his long, aquiline nose, then put his glasses back on and picked up the photo in the ebony frame on his desk. It was a holo of his long-dead wife, Erika, still young and beautiful forever on film, cradling their son, Josef. *We committed to this day more than twenty years ago, my love. All my adult life I've worked toward this.* He set the picture down carefully.

So why do I want to scream out now, "Wait!"?

Somewhere in the room a personal comm unit chirped. Von Hayek glanced up; Patrick Adams, the governor's shadowy right hand, fished a phonewire out of his coat pocket and pressed it to his left ear. "Yes?" Adams listened, then nodded once, folded up the phonewire, and put it back in his pocket. He turned to the governor.

For a millisecond he smiled.

"Ladies? Gentlemen?" Adams strode across the room and took up his station at von Hayek's side. Like flowers tracking the sun, all faces in the room turned toward him. "It is my pleasure to announce that our people have taken operational control of all six cargo launchers. General Consensus reports no casualties, no violence, and no alarms." Adams stepped away from von Hayek, then turned to face him and bowed. "Governor? We await your orders."

Though his stomach was churning, von Hayek pasted a confident smile on his face. *No turning back now.* "My fellow governors," he began, addressing the dozen other men and women in the room. "I have tried many times to prepare words for this occasion. We owe our posterity some grand statement that will ring down through the ages; some careful explanation of how we have exhausted all diplomatic channels, grown weary of endless fruitless negotiations and how it is that now, only after all else has failed, we at last resort to the threat of violence in our quest for freedom.

"I have tried to find those stirring words, and I have failed. So let me just say this: the die is cast. As of this moment, we in this room are no longer the democratically elected but completely powerless governors of the UN's lunar possessions. We are now the Governing Council of the Free State Selena."

He picked up the comm unit from his desk. "So let's ring up New York and tell them the good news, shall we?"

PATRICK ADAMS

As with many of the pivotal characters in the 2069 Lunar Revolution, Patrick Adams is something of an enigma. First off, "Patrick Adams" was clearly his nom de guerre, as no record of the man exists before his abrupt appearance in 2067 as Pieter von Hayek's right-hand man. To this day, the story of Patrick Adams's true origin — and his ultimate fate — remains a mystery.

As for his exact role in the von Hayek administration, that also is the subject of considerable debate. His title was chief of staff, although it appears his actual duties went well beyond that. Depending on the occasion, he seems to have functioned as von Hayek's intelligence director, military adviser, public relations manager, or even nanny, as the situation demanded.

It is believed that Adams was an American, before he emigrated to the Moon. Beyond that, almost nothing is known about his personal life. Presumably he had one, although that may be an unjustified assumption.

— Chaim Noguchi, *A History of the Lunar Revolution*

CHAPTER 3

Antonio Ramón Aguila, undersecretary for lunar affairs, United Nations Committee on Lunar Development, sat behind his broad executive desk, in theory reading a highly technical report on thorium production, but in fact, daydreaming.

Look at this office, he thought, as his dark eyes traced patterns in the grain of the Bavarian walnut panels that lined the walls. *My father raised eleven children in a squalid shack no larger than this room. No electricity, no water, no sewer except the roadside ditch. Papa's world was made of corrugated tin and cast-off plastic, and his floor was hard-packed naked dirt. If he'd ever stumbled across a piece of expensive polished wood like this, he'd have burned it to keep his children warm.* A small, bitter smile played at the corners of Aguila's expressive lips as his gaze came to rest on the matched pair of French Provençal chairs in the corner. *We could have fed the whole barrio for a year on what my predecessor paid for those two chairs.*

Aguila looked away from the chairs and let his gaze

wander on, across twenty years' worth of accumulated symbols of his own success and power. Old collegiate athletic trophies, the brass furnished to a pleasant glow. A bookcase filled with century-old printed books, from back in the days when information was stored in toxic ink on murdered rain forests. A dozen or so quite authentic, and probably now quite illegal, primitive cultural artifacts, collected during his many fact-finding trips around the globe. Two carefully selected and gently understated pastel sketches, originals signed by Edgar Degas.

And below them, on the wall, in a simple black frame, his summa cum laude doctorate from Harvard Law School.

Not bad for a niño *who spent the first five years of his life scavenging for scraps in the garbage dumps of Santiago,* Aguila thought. *Not bad at* all *for an orphan of a civil war who learned to read in a UN refugee camp. And I'm not even forty yet.*

The thick red leather of his armchair creaked slightly as Aguila leaned back and allowed himself a moment of smugness. *So ask me again, you imbecile norte americanos: do I* really *believe the United Nations can make a difference?*

More than I believe in God, Aguila decided. *The church gave us priests and missionaries to save our souls, but the UN gave us food to save our* lives.

And with that thought Aguila sighed, leaned forward, and made one more attempt to read the report on thorium production. Like all technical writing, it was arcane at best, incomprehensibly dense at worst, and throughout written in a dry and academic style that simply begged the mind to wander. Aguila's mind soon did.

He was saved by the chirp of the office intercom. Aguila blanked the report window, put on his best serious business expression, and tapped a corner of the desktop. A video window flashed open on the dark simulated wood, and his personal assistant's face popped into view.

"Yes, Allegria?"

"Sir?" Allegria Saldana was just the way Aguila liked his women: intelligent, beautiful, competent, and subservient. "Pieter von Hayek is holding on line six."

Aguila frowned. "For me? That's odd."

"No, sir. He wanted Lord Haversham, but the secretary seems to have left the building for the day."

"Ah." Aguila nodded and let out a small sigh. "Lucky Haversham. Any idea what sort of bee is in von Hayek's bonnet this time?"

"No, sir. He insists on speaking to either Lord Haversham or you."

A thought struck Aguila and made him shudder. "He's not seeing little green men again, is he?"

"As I recall, they were large orange monsters, but no, sir, if he's seeing them again, he hasn't mentioned it."

Aguila sighed again, deeply this time, then took a deep breath and composed his features. "Very well, let's humor him. Put him through." Allegria blinked out, and three seconds later the patrician face of Pieter von Hayek popped into view.

"Governor," Aguila said, feigning a warm smile. "This is an unexpected pleasure. What can I do—"

"I expect you're babbling some meaningless niceties," von Hayek said. "The light-speed lag is going to make this— Ah, yes, there's your response now. As I was saying, the light-speed lag is going to make this difficult enough, so what you can do for me, young man, is be quiet and listen." Von Hayek looked down at something below the scan area of the video pickup, and the sound of rustling paper came through.

Aguila nodded politely, but said nothing.

"Good. Now"—the video pickup cut to a wide-angle shot, to reveal the cluster of people standing behind von Hayek—"as you can see, I have most of the other colonial governors here with me. We have taken a vote, and against the advice of some of our more bloody-minded colleagues, we have decided that it is only fair to give you and the CLD some advance warning."

"Warning?" Aguila blurted out, forgetting that he was not supposed to speak. "What—"

"In approximately fifteen minutes we will be broadcasting our formal Declaration of Independence. This is not a negotiating ploy, nor is it a declaration of war, but rest assured—"

"Wait!" Aguila waved a hand to catch von Hayek's attention. "Wait! Governor!"

"—that we have taken precautions to secure our . . . Ah, yes, there's your reaction now. I told you; please don't interrupt, young man. We will not negotiate with you. We are through negotiating with the CLD. We will discuss this matter only before the full General Assembly, *after* our representative has been recognized and seated. Do you understand this?" Von Hayek paused.

Aguila considered his answer. "Pieter," he said gently, as he pulled a calm and fatherly expression onto his face, "this can't work, you know. Your labor strike last year failed and only made things worse for you. I can't imagine the trade sanctions have improved your quality of life any. How can—"

Von Hayek interrupted, speaking slowly and enunciating carefully. "We control the automatic cargo launchers," he said. "Check with your SAS spies. I'm sure they can verify that what I've just said is true."

There was a long, long pause. Aguila kept his face carefully neutral. "Are the launchers still operating?" he said at last. The three-second light-speed lag crawled by like a snail.

"For now," von Hayek answered. "Whether they continue to do so depends on you."

Aguila stared blankly at the video image, and said nothing.

"Good," von Hayek said brightly. "Now if you will bear with me just a minute longer, I will present our list of demands." He paused to adjust his bifocals, then lifted a long sheet of paper and began reading.

"Point one: immediate recognition of the independence and sovereignity of the Free State Selena, to be composed of the former colonial possessions that have signed this declaration.

"Point two: immediate recognition and seating of our chosen representative in the United Nations General Assembly, with all voting rights and privileges customarily pertaining thereto.

"Point three: immediate removal of all United Nations Special Aerospace Security personnel stationed on Luna, both uniformed and undercover.

"Point four: immediate arrest and prosecution of Colonial Administrator Kinthavong, for bribery, corruption, abuse of authority, violation of the civil rights of lunar citizens . . ."

Still keeping his face carefully neutral, Aguila muted the microphone on his end of the conversation, then punched in the code for the second comm line. Another video window popped up next to the first, and Allegria's face flashed into view. "Sir?"

Aguila smiled so that he could speak without visibly moving his lips. "Allegria? 'ake a ten-second loop of 'e nodding and looking thoughtful. Cut it in to Hayek, and cut 'e out."

She tapped a few keys on her end. "Ready." Aguila closed his mouth, and focused on von Hayek's speech again.

"Point nine: immediate removal of all United Nations military personnel presently stationed on Luna, including the so-called scientific research teams operating in and around Copernicus Crater.

"Point ten: immediate . . ."

"Got it!" Allegria said. "Adjusting synchronization and . . . okay." Von Hayek's face and relentless voice blanked out. "Our favorite political gadfly is now talking to a digital loop. Will there be anything else?"

Aguila stroked his chin, as much to hide his worried scowl as to help his thinking. "Find Lord Haversham," he said at last. "Put Jurgen on it. Now. Then find out if any other members of the Committee on Lunar Development are still in the building."

He paused, this time furrowing his brow and not caring if his worry showed. "Wait. First, get me Mobutu in the Office of World Telecommunications. Then put in an urgent call to General Buchovsky at Peacekeeper HQ."

Allegria blinked. "It's that bad?"

"Yes, it's that bad. Then track down Kinthavong— No, never mind. I already know all his excuses by heart. But schedule a press conference for one hour from now, then do everything else I said."

Allegria nodded. "And then order in dinner, right? It's going to be another long evening?"

Aguila took a moment to look at the video image of his seemingly psychic assistant, and spared her a smile. "Yes, Allegria, I'm afraid it is. Those imbecile Loonies have finally done it."

Office of the Governor, Port Aldrin
24 October 2069
22:08 GMT

Pieter von Hayek was confused and angry. "What do you mean, the satellite's gone off-line?"

Patrick Adams swore and slammed a fist on the desktop comm unit. "I mean exactly that: the L-5 repeater has just gone off-line. We've lost UNET and all the primary comm channels." His phonewire chirped; he fished it out of his jacket pocket, pressed it to his left ear, and listened, frowning. "Secondaries also. We're locked out of all the geosynch nodes." He folded up the wire and put it back in his pocket.

Von Hayek was still struggling to understand. He shook his head. "What about the commercial networks?"

"They piggyback off the UNET. They're all gone too."

Von Hayek sagged back into his chair, took off his bifocals, and tapped the right earpiece against his lower teeth. "I don't understand. What can this mean?"

"It means," Adams said, "that it was a dumb idea to tip off the CLD. They've had the Office of World TeleComm pull the plug on us. Blacked out all Earth-Moon communications. Totally."

"You're joking! You mean there's *no* way we can get a signal through to Earth?"

"Well"—Adams shrugged and scratched his head—"there are the direct laser channels. I expect Kinthavong is burning his up right now. But at this time of day the ones *we* control can only hit North America, and only a few amateurs will be on to receive."

"That's a start," von Hayek said hopefully. "What about conventional radio?"

Adams shook his head. "We don't have a transmitter powerful enough to punch through all the local traffic down there. We could probably build one in two or three weeks. Maybe use the Rheinhold radioscope."

Von Hayek put his glasses back on and leaned forward to rest his elbows on his desk. "This is ludicrous. There are a half-billion satellite dishes down there, and you're saying we can't get through to *any* of them?"

Adams had run out of exasperated reactions. "Not without going through the satellite nodes. Those dishes are all aimed at geosynch points over the equator, and the angles of incidence are all wrong for us. But even if they weren't, the inverse square law comes into play. We're about twelve times farther out than a geosynch satellite, so we'd have to put out"—he paused, obviously trying to do the math in his head—"well, a *hell* of a lot of power just to override the satellite signal." Adams stopped speaking and waited for a cue from von Hayek.

None came.

"So," Adams said, "what do we do now, boss?"

Von Hayek took his elbows off the desk, sat up straight, and assumed a noble bearing. "We issue the declaration anyway, to our own people, if no one else. Whether or not Earth chooses to listen does not alter the fact that as of this day we *are* free."

Von Hayek took a deep breath, allowed a confident smile to spread across his face, and stood up. "Come along!" He started for the door to the council chamber.

Adams fell in one step behind him. "Go get 'em, tiger!"

Port Aldrin, Luna Block J64, Apartment 23
24 October 2069
22:14 GMT

The dinner was good, but Dalton had to admit that the dessert was better. He opened his eyes and looked over at Dara. He'd always liked her profile: from the side, her nose made a little ski jump that he liked to run his finger down. He lightly traced a finger from bridge to tip, and she twitched her nose like a bunny rabbit.

"Hmmm?" she murmured, sleepily.

"Honey? Mind if I, you know, call up DeShayne, and maybe play some more Black Flame?"

"Mmm-mm," she answered.

"Cool! Thanks." He rolled onto his back and summoned the flatscreen. It popped out from the headboard and lowered itself in front of his face as stereo speakers extruded from its sides. "Login UNET," he said when it was in place.

Instead of the usual SSW gateway, though, a simple line of text appeared: "ERROR 404: NO SUCH LINK EXISTS."

"Huh? That's weird." He licked his lips, cleared his throat, and tried again, a little louder. "Login UNET."

"ERROR 404: NO SUCH LINK EXISTS."

Dalton got a hand free of the covers and slapped the side of the screen. In the known history of the universe, thumping on a remote terminal had never fixed a network server problem, but it made him feel better. "Login UNET!"

"ERROR 404: NO SUCH LINK EXISTS."

"Okay, this is getting nowhere." Dalton tried to shake his head, but the position of the screen made that difficult. "Maybe there's bad sunspot activity or something." He thought it over some more and decided to try a different approach. "All right, login LunaWeb." A moment later the familiar background shot of the Tranquillity Base monument appeared, and then the screen filled up with icons. A pulsing red mailbox in the upper left corner got his attention. His fingers found the pointer controls on the sides of the flatscreen, and he picked and clicked on the mailbox.

There were three chimes—the cue for an urgent broadcast message—and then the soft voice of the Port Aldrin Central Computer was purring through the speakers. "Due to circumstances beyond our control, all links to UNET, the Solar Wide Web, and all other non-Lunar networks are temporarily out of service. We apologize for the inconvenience. Have a nice day."

Dalton frowned at his screen, which had returned to the expectant mailbox. It blinked at him irritatingly, teasing him with the promise of messages waiting right before his eyes, but as inaccessible as Pluto. As he glared at the screen, another chime sounded and a window opened up in the lower left corner to reveal an unfamiliar face.

"Dalton Star . . . Starkiller, is it?"

Dalton couldn't see the man's eyes; he was looking down from the vidcam, obviously reading from a piece of paper. The man looked up. "Is that you?"

"That's me," Dalton replied.

"Excellent. Listen, I've been told you're some kind of computer specialist. A hacker. Good at breaking into things."

"Maybe," Dalton said suspiciously, wondering if the authorities were on to his recent activities. "Who are you?"

"Patrick Adams. I'm the director of, ah, Special Information Services."

"I've never heard of you."

"No, I suppose you haven't. Just a minute." The man appeared to reach down, then displayed an official-looking badge. "I'm a special aide to the governor. See?"

Alarmed, Dalton began to stammer. "Um, yeah, well, look . . . last night, it really wasn't any big deal—"

"You don't understand," Adams cut in. "I *want* you to hack into something. UNET is down, and the governor wants to see if we can get it back up. Got it?"

"Sure . . . sure, I got it." Dalton leaned forward eagerly. "So I'll bet you want me to try cracking one of the UNET servers."

"Exactly. Preferably one of the satellite-based ones. If you can just get us past their security, our technicians can restore our access. I'm told you'll need one of our priority access codes to even get the comm center to answer, so I'm sending one to your machine now. I'm told you might be familiar with a Brigitte Becker in NetOps?"

"You mean Brooklyn? Sure."

"Good. Contact her if you manage to get access into UNET. Otherwise, well, don't worry about it."

"Got it." Dalton bit his lip. "Director Adams, can I ask you one thing?"

"You can ask."

"Okay, then. Why?"

Adams smiled enigmatically. "You'll find out soon enough. Good luck, Starkiller." He closed the connection.

A few hours later, Dalton was tired, irritable, dispirited, and feeling more than a little outclassed. He'd tried every trick in his fairly substantial bag of tricks, and not one of them had worked. Not one!

He glared at the screen, trying to force open the server with the sheer force of his will, but like everything else he'd tried, the effort was to no avail.

"Locksmith? No. Morfkey? No," he muttered to himself. "One point six? No, if one-eight didn't do it, one-six wouldn't either. If I'd paid the upgrade I could've tried one-nine-five, but that probably wouldn't have gone either."

He drummed his fingers on the top of his head. "Okay, but at least we know the I.D. isn't a standard Mastho alphanumeric pattern; otherwise the Locksmith deepscan would've at least registered a hit."

Dalton rubbed at his itching eyes. Mmmm, that felt good! Suddenly his eyes snapped open. They were reddened and dry from hours of staring at the flatscreen, but there was a manic fire in them.

"They can't be that out-of-date, can they? On a UNET server? But maybe no one ever tries to hack these things. That would explain why all the new stuff isn't working."

He tapped the pointer and called up an old routine he'd written while still a college boy back on Earth.

"Let's see how you deal with the Nibbler, Mr. Net Security Expert!"

Dalton feverishly stroked the keypad and set the strategy for his final assault. Before pressing the last key, he closed his eyes and prayed to the etheric electronic gods.

Triumphantly, he sat back and waited expectantly as his pet algorithm attacked the digital defenses of the UNET server. There was a long pause, and then a small light glowed green and a short message appeared: "NICE TRY, MONKEY BOY. ACCESS DENIED."

Fabulous, he thought. *Just what I needed. A NetSec administrator with an attitude.*

Tired, irritable, dispirited, outclassed, and now insulted, Dalton gave up. It was almost too much of an effort to call up Brigitte Becker's access from his address book.

"LunaNet Ops. Becker here," the second shift NetOps manager answered. "Make it quick."

"Say no go, Brooklyn. I came, I saw, and they kicked my ass."

"Dalton? Is that you?" Becker leaned in closer to the video pickup and squinted. "Do you have your face pressed right up against the screen?"

"Something like that." Dalton grabbed the edges of the flatscreen and pushed it back a few inches. "Say, what's going on with UNET? This guy Adams had me trying to hack an orbital server, but the security was too amped."

Becker was still squinting at the video pickup. "Nice hair. Did you just wake up or what?"

"Yeah. Now about UNET—"

"I got it, I got it. You didn't get in. That's okay. Nobody could. It doesn't matter now. Quick, log to RealNews One. They're going to play it again!"

Dalton was bewildered, but agreed. "Okay." He selected and clicked on the icon for the local video news channel, then looked back at Becker's window. "So are you going to tell me what's going on?"

"Dalton," Becker said, smiling, "who did you vote for in the last election?"

He shrugged. "Von Hayek and the Independence Party, of course, just like everyone else. Not that it did any good."

Becker nodded. "Well, you just watch News One, and I think maybe you'll like what you see. Becker out." Her window blanked and shrank. Dalton turned his attention to the news channel and bumped the volume up a notch.

The view showed a room—some governmenty-looking thing, he thought. A line of people sat across the back of the room in front of a gray curtain and behind a lectern. He zoomed in and recognized faces: Veerhoven from Rheinhold Colony, Kozhevnikov from Volodya, Montclair from Von Braun . . .

Okay, another Council of Governors meeting. So what? They were just going to do a lot of talking and pass some more resolutions that would immediately be vetoed by the CLD. BFD.

A flurry of polite applause came through the audio channel and got Dalton's attention. A moment later Pieter von Hayek stepped into view and took up his position behind the lectern. The applause peaked; von Hayek acknowledged it and gestured for quiet. The clapping slowly tapered away.

Von Hayek shuffled some notes on the lectern, fiddled with his bifocals as always, then looked straight at the video pickup and smiled in the way that always made Dalton feel as if the governor was smiling directly at him, personally. That was the strange thing about von Hayek, Dalton thought. He'd met the governor in person once and mistaken him for the nerdy econ prof he used to be before he emigrated to the Moon and got into politics. But put von Hayek behind a lectern and in front of a TV camera and let him start talking, and all of a sudden he turned into someone the masses were willing to follow to the very ends of the Earth. Or farther.

"Ladies and gentleman," von Hayek said softly, "my fellow citizens. The council and I labored long and hard to find exactly the right words for this moment. We consulted many historical documents"—Von Hayek paused to wrestle visibly with a catch in his throat—"and in the end we decided that there is no finer way to say it than this." He paused again, this time to bite his lower lip and wipe with a finger at a lone tear that had escaped from under his left bifocal lens.

"'We hold these truths to be self-evident,'" von Hayek began reading from his notes in a voice that was barely more than a choked whisper, and all the more powerful and captivating because of its softness. "'That all men and women are created equal, that they are endowed by their Creator with certain unalienable Rights, that among these are Life, Liberty and the pursuit of Happiness.'" Von Hayek appeared to find strength as the words flowed, and his voice grew louder, and he stood up straighter.

"'That to secure these rights, Governments are instituted among men, deriving their just powers from the consent of the governed.'" Von Hayek clearly abandoned his notes now, as well as all pretense of emotional restraint, and was working from memory. "'That whenever any form of government becomes destructive of these ends, it is the Right of the People to alter or abolish it, and to institute *new* Government, laying its foundation on such principles and organizing its powers in such form as to them shall seem most likely to protect the rights of the people and to ensure their safety and happiness!'"

Dara rolled over about then, and nudged Dalton firmly. "Hon*ey*," she murmured, "I don't mind if you play, but turn it down. I'm trying to sleep."

Dalton nudged her right back. "I think you'd better wake up and see this." He pushed the flatscreen out to arm's length and turned the volume up to full.

"'But when a long train of abuses and usurpations, pursuing invariably the same Object, evinces a design to reduce them under absolute Despotism, it is their right, it is their duty, to throw off such Government, and to provide new guards for their future security.'"

Dara was wide awake now. "Omigod," she whispered. "Is this for real?"

Dalton nodded. "I think so. But I think von Hayek is quoting from something, and it sounds sort of familiar."

Dara rolled over and gave Dalton the widest-eyed stare he'd ever seen. "It should. That's the Declaration of Independence."

ANTONIO AGUILA

Historians continue to debate the question: what motivated
Antonio Aguila? Some point to his wretched childhood in Chile
and say he was a textbook example of Freudian overcompen-
sation, striving all his life to make up for the deprivations and
horrors of his earliest years. Others point to his privileged
upbringing after he was adopted out of a refugee camp and
brought to the United States. They say he was a supremely
ambitious and cynical man who made every move with one eye
on the goal of someday reaching the secretary-general's
office.

A third school of thought is perhaps the most disturbing. It
holds that Aguila was that most dangerous of men, a true
believer in the United Nations and its goal of a peaceful,
unified world. According to this theory, Aguila was so blinded
by the rightness of his vision that he completely failed to
realize he'd become what he professed to hate most: an
imperialist of the first order, willing to do or say anything in his
pursuit of a higher good.

— Chaim Noguchi, *A History of the Lunar Revolution*

CHAPTER 4

Antonio Aguila stood in the wings, surreptitiously watching the crowd of reporters who were chatting and jostling for space in the packed briefing room.

"You look thoughtful," Allegria said. "Care to share?"

"Poodles," Aguila said.

Allegria only looked puzzled.

"I was thinking of poodles," he clarified. "Or perhaps Lhasas—you know, lapdogs. Leave them alone and they spend all their time nipping at each other's heels and sniffing each other's tails. But step into the room and hold high a morsel and you have their undivided and obedient attention." He turned to Allegria, smiled tightly, and nodded slightly in the direction of the reporters. "What do you think? Shall I make them sit up on their hind legs and beg?"

Allegria was saved from answering by Jurgen Flanders, who burst through the back door just then. "Señor Aguila! I can't find Lord Haversham anywhere!"

Aguila waited a cold, silent interval, calculated to convey

just what he thought of Jurgen's entrance. On the whole, Aguila found his newly assigned assistant to be too blond, too Euro, and too excitable; but he was also proving to be too energetic to simply get rid of.

The seconds ticked by. Just when he sensed Jurgen was about to speak again, Aguila answered. "Did you try his apartment?"

"Yes, and—"

"And all of his favorite restaurants?"

"Yes, and—"

"Then when you have eliminated the obvious, Jurgen, what is left?"

The younger man simply looked at Aguila with his blank, blue-eyed Nordic baby face.

"Jurgen," Aguila said, not unkindly, "I want you to check every bathhouse and steam room between here and Times Square."

Those pale blue eyes went wide. "But—"

"Now, Jurgen. Go. Scoot." Aguila waved the young man on his way, then turned back to Allegria. "Well, it's time. Shall we?"

Allegria nodded quickly and, trailing a respectful three paces behind, followed Aguila out onto the dais.

Sit! Aguila thought, as he surveyed the packed room. *Roll over!* Then the moment of shuddering terror struck him, as it always did, when twenty or more red-eyed TV cameras flared on like laser gunsights and the room erupted in a blinding sea of still-camera flash units, just like the artillery bombardment of Talcahuano. And for scant microseconds he was a shuddering five-year-old again, hiding in a stinking wet sewage culvert, suffocating under the weight of his dead older brother, and begging God for the flash and thunder of the bombs to stop, only when it did stop, it wasn't God, but a smiling man with a gentle voice and a sky-blue uniform . . .

The moment of terror passed, as always. Aguila made it to the lectern and tapped the central microphone a few times, more to get the reporters' attention than to test if it was working.

The mob sat down. They grew quiet. Fighting the image of mouths hanging open with little pink tongues lolling out through rows of sharp white teeth, Aguila glanced at his notes and began to speak: "This afternoon at approximately five-thirteen New York time, a small terrorist splinter group calling itself the People's Eristic Nucleus for International Stasis temporarily disrupted all communications between Earth and the Lunar Colonies."

There was shocked silence for a second, then an eruption of questions. Aguila waved the reporters down, and when they were all sitting again, resumed.

"I have spoken with Director Mobutu in the UNCOMM, the Office of World Telecommunications. He assures me that we have recovered complete control of all satellites and data channels. However, there is some evidence that the terrorists may have planted viruses, logic bombs, or other hostile software in the lunar end of the telecommunications system. Therefore, the Committee on Lunar Development has reluctantly taken the painful step of ordering all commercial and private channels shut down until such time as our UNET engineers can verify the safety and integrity of the system."

This time, the shocked silence stretched on much longer.

"Again, we realize that this action is quite inconvenient and may even seem alarming, and it is only with the greatest reluctance that we have taken it. But with the memory of the North Korean reactor virus so fresh in our memory"— this drew a shocked gasp from the reporters, which was exactly the reaction Aguila was looking for—"we on the CLD felt it was much safer to err on the side of excessive caution."

The buzz in the room turned into a positive and supportive murmur. Aguila, starting to feel confident about the spin he was putting on this story, went for the clincher.

"Two points need to be stressed. The first is that this was the action of a small group of deeply disturbed people; in no way does it reflect the feelings of the majority of the Lunar Colonists. The Council of Lunar Governors remains fully committed to the peaceful resolution of our few minor political differences and in fact is providing invaluable assistance to UNISAS personnel in the identification and apprehension of the parties responsible for this act."

Looking out into the room, Aguila saw a few heads beginning to nod, then more. Inwardly he snickered at the way the *norte-americano* reporters prided themselves on their "objectivity," but outwardly he kept his face stern and confident.

"The second point is that at no time was there any threat to the hydroponic food factories or the automatic cargo launching sites. These facilities are now and will remain safely in United Nations hands, and they will continue to operate at full capacity. The rumors of impending food shortages are just that—wild rumors with absolutely no basis in fact. This is exactly the sort of hysteria the terrorists were hoping to generate by their actions, and anyone who repeats these rumors is playing into the terrorists' hands."

Aguila finished reading his statement and paused to survey the sea of bobbing heads, at last confident that he had the reporters in his pocket. He smiled. "Now, are there any questions?"

"Señor Aguila!" a woman in the front row with thick blond hair called out. "Is it true that the SAS has already identified the alleged terrorists?"

Aguila shook his head demurely. "I am not at liberty to comment on that. I can, however, repeat that the Council of Lunar Governors is cooperating fully with us, and we expect to begin making arrests shortly."

A man in a blue suit with plastic hair replaced the blond woman. "Señor Aguila, does the Office of World TeleComm have an estimate of how soon full UNET access will be restored?"

Aguila shook his head again. "All I can say there is that we have the fullest confidence that UNCOMM will spare no effort to make sure the system is safe and virus-free. If that means an outage of several days, well, it is regrettable but necessary."

Six more hands shot up. "Señor Aguila!" Allegria tapped him on the shoulder and gave him his exit cue. Aguila leaned forward and smiled.

"I'm sorry. I would very much like to provide you with more details, but that is all we can say at the present time. The Committee on Lunar Development will issue press releases as soon as more information becomes available. Good day." Aguila smiled again, nodded, and stepped away from the lectern. Fighting the urge to flee the barrage of flash units and shouted questions, he strolled crisply off the dais, followed by Allegria.

The moment they got offstage, he turned to her. "Well? How do you think it went?"

Allegria nodded, a glint of admiration in her dark brown eyes. "Perfectly. If I hadn't known better, I'd have believed it myself." She found an isolated corner, pulled Aguila aside, and dipped a hand into her blazer pocket. "In the meantime they've found General Buchovsky. He's waiting on the scrambled line." She pulled out a phone and passed it to Aguila.

Aguila punched in the verification code for the scrambler, put the phone to his ear, and was greeted by a stream of guttural and profane Russian. He endured the outburst, then smiled. "And a pleasant good morning to you too, Fyodr. What time is it there? Three A.M.? Four?" He held the phone away from his ear as another torrent of obscenities poured forth.

"Da," Aguila said when the well ran dry. "I understand what an inconvenience this is, and I'm certain she is beautiful. But, General, we have an urgent situation developing. *Da,* on Luna." This time the general's response was far more subdued.

"Nyet," Aguila said, shaking his head. "We're still trying to pull together a quorum, but it may not get to a vote tonight."

The general muttered a protest.

"Nyet, nyet, I would never try to bypass the Security Council, Fyodr, you know that. But I also know how much you hate getting blindsided by these political things."

The general's brain was apparently up to full speed now, for his next speech was a series of short, pointed questions.

Aguila checked his watch. "Within eighteen hours, I expect. And you know the Security Council. Once they make a decision, they will expect you to act on it yesterday." Aguila nodded. *"Da,* no problem. You're welcome. *Do svidaniya."* Aguila folded up the phone and handed it back to Allegria. She looked at him, an unspoken question in her deep brown eyes.

"Buchovsky is with us," Aguila answered. "The rest of the committee is with us. Now all we have to do is find that wretched Haversham."

Office of the Governor, Port Aldrin
24 October 2069
23:58 GMT

Patrick Adams knocked gently, then went in without waiting for a response. "Governor, it's almost midnight. They aren't going to answer."

Pieter von Hayek sat in his black chrome chair, fingers tented, chin on his chest, bifocals on the desk before him, staring blankly into space. He neither moved nor spoke.

Adams decided to try humor. "C'mon, gov. It's the UN. They're constitutionally incapable of making decisions. It's seven in the evening, New York time, and they're probably still out trolling the bars and brothels, trying to round up enough diplomats to make one functional brain." He forced out a dry chuckle.

No response from von Hayek.

Adams grew worried. The governor's cardiac problems had always been a badly concealed secret, and now von Hayek seemed unusually pale and drawn. Adams took a step forward and reached for von Hayek's left wrist.

Von Hayek testily snatched it away. "I'm fine, thank you." He glared at Adams for a moment; then his gaze softened, and he sighed. "Sorry I snapped. I just . . . I don't understand this." He bit his lower lip and shook his head in frustration. "Threats, bargaining, acceptance, rejection: I expected Kinthavong or the CLD to do or say *something* by now. But this silent waiting—"

"Is maddening. I know." Adams arched an eyebrow, cocked his head, and caught the governor's eye. "Did you ever consider that maybe it's deliberate? That they *want* you to sweat?"

Von Hayek shrugged. "Why? That would require a strategy, which implies some degree of cogent thought, which we know is impossible for them. Besides, that would only escalate the tension and make it harder to negotiate. They'd almost be *daring* us to shut down the food factories."

"Exactly." Adams stared coolly at von Hayek, watching the idea seep in. Not for the first time, Adams was slightly surprised at how von Hayek could be so brilliant in some areas of politics and such a babe in the woods in others. *Well,* thought Adams, *after all, he* does *prefer chess to poker.*

Von Hayek sighed, then sat up and blinked rapidly, as if suddenly realizing where he was. "I've got to get out of this office," he said as he reached for his bifocals and put them on. "But I couldn't possibly sleep now. Any suggestions, Patrick?"

Adams smiled and helped von Hayek out of his chair. "Well, gov, there's one hell of an Independence Day party going on down in Broadway Gallery, and about ten thousand citizens want to buy you a drink. Let's start there."

Von Hayek started for the door, then paused briefly as a frown crossed his face. "You sure this'll be okay?"

"Relax. Yuji Nakagawa is on watch with your boy, Josef. If the CLD tries anything stupid, which they won't, Yuji and Josef will let me know." Adams patted the jacket pocket that contained his phonewire and smiled.

Von Hayek nodded. "After you, then, Mr. Adams."

Adams shook his head. "No, sir. After you, Mr. President." Von Hayek went out, and Adams shut off the office lights and followed him.

"You know, Patrick, I don't like that title. Let's think up a new one. How about 'first councillor'?"

"Tomorrow, sir. There'll be plenty of time for that tomorrow."

Fort Bragg, North Carolina
24 October 2069
10:22 P.M. EST

Captain Eileen Mahoney was conducting the post-op review, and unlike Captain Mahoney, it was not pretty. "Okay, kids, let's take it from the top one more time. What was the point of UrbPac Six?"

Lieutenant Malcolm Jamal looked around at the five other dispirited junior officers in the room, then grudgingly raised his hand.

Mahoney nodded at him. "Jamal?"

"Sir," Jamal said, in a flat voice. "Urban Pacification Exercise Six was a domestic urban guerrilla containment scenario, sir. Our objective was to eliminate armed resistance and secure tactical control of four square blocks of a city. Sir."

Captain Mahoney nodded again. "Very good. Now would you care to explain to me why an entire company of the 82nd Airborne could not take that area from a bunch of *civilians?*"

"Bunny!" Lieutenant Sara Parker objected. "That's not

44

fair! The opposition was played by Charlie Company. Real civilians would never fight like that!"

Captain Mahoney, who was known in Bravo Company as Devil Bunny, or Bunny for short, turned and glared at Parker until she blushed to the roots of her fake blond hair and sat down again.

"You're right, Parker," Bunny said. "Real civilians would castrate our wounded and drag the bodies through the streets. Of course, *you* wouldn't stay alive long enough to see that."

Parker winced. "Sir? She was just a child. How was I supposed to—"

"Parker," Bunny said, shaking her head, "for your information, that *child* who shot you in the back was Colonel Mehta's ten-year-old daughter, and she really *can* handle a pistol like that." Bunny took a deep breath, and turned to the group at large. As one, the lieutenants braced for impact.

"Look, people, everything the opposition did today was based on documented cases from military history! Never underestimate civilian guerrillas who are fighting for their homes and the lives of their families. They may be badly undergunned and real short in the TO&E department, but they have got determination by the ton and a *murderous* capacity to improvise!"

Bunny stopped shouting, caught her breath, and smiled at Lieutenant Jamal. "So, Malcolm, what did *you* think of Charlie Company's improvisations?"

Jamal slouched back in his chair, tapped a finger on his smartpad, and considered his answer. "I think the judges screwed us, sir. If that'd been real gasoline, I'd have lost one squad, tops. No way I'd have lost the whole platoon."

Bunny shrugged. "I don't know. They caught you out in the open, on the external fire escape. A five-gallon bucket of gasoline dropped from the roof makes a hell of a fuel-air bomb, you know?" She shrugged again. "But, okay, even if the judges did overrate it . . ."

Jamal nodded and frowned. "I know, sir. What the hell was my whole platoon doing on the fire escape in the first place? I screwed up. But Second Platoon was taking fire from the upper-story windows on the front of the building, and I figured my guys could go in the back way, surprise the enemy, and take the place by storm. Big mistake."

Bunny nodded. "A mistake that cost you twenty KIAs today. What did you learn?"

Jamal sighed. "To stick by the book, sir. Advance by squad; leapfrog by fire teams. Take the high ground first, then clear from the top down. All the stuff that's easy to remember when you're not flying on hype."

Bunny smiled in a satisfied sort of way. "Right. Which is why you have to stay cool, no matter what. And always watch out for the lone nut on the roof." She turned back to the group as a whole, sorted through faces, and selected a fresh victim. "Lieutenant Singh!"

Singh looked up from his smartpad, his dark eyes went wide, and he leaped to his feet and saluted crisply. An instant later the rest of the lieutenants followed suit, and an instant after that Bunny realized they were not looking at her. She spun around.

"Colonel Houston!" Bunny snapped to and cracked off a salute. "Sir!"

The tall senior officer stepped through the open doorway and returned the salute. "As you were," he said to the lieutenants. They shifted to at-ease. Houston turned to Bunny. "How's the debriefing going, Captain Mahoney?"

Bunny nodded and tried her best to stand at ease, but she never felt comfortable around the colonel. There was always a sense of danger about the man, as if he were a venomous snake with a hidden agenda. Not to mention how he rarely, if ever, gave her any respect. "It goes well, sir," she replied. "We're making progress."

"Good." Houston checked his watch, then looked back at the captain. "Can you have it zipped in ten minutes?"

"Of course, sir. May I ask why?"

"There's a briefing in General Jackson's office at twenty-three hundred hours, and I want you there." He took a step closer to her; she fought the urge to shrink back. "The UN and the Russkies are up to something."

He licked his lips and smiled. "Something *big.*"

CHAPTER 5

General Buchovsky wrapped up his briefing. "And that is how it stands. Our intelligence suggests that sixteen major colonies have joined in this revolt—far too many for the CLD and their Special Aerospace Security to handle alone. They will have to turn to the Security Council for help, and the council will have to turn to a member nation with sufficient low-G trained troops and major spacelift capability."

President Saratov examined her nails and pondered the news. "A Russian military presence on the moon," she said at last. "We have not had such a thing since—"

"The Djakarta Conference in 2054," Foreign Minister Chapeyev interjected.

Saratov looked at Buchovsky. "And you say the old gunships are still intact?"

"According to our sources, yes. They are being kept under peace bond at depots in Sinus Roris and Lacus Mortis."

Saratov nodded slowly. "Our former countrymen at Volodya would be happy to see us, don't you think?"

48

Buchovsky smiled broadly. "They would welcome us with bread and salt, Madam President."

Slowly Saratov's thin lips spread into a tight smile. She turned to Foreign Minister Chapeyev. "It is one-thirty in the morning in New York. I suggest we wake up Ambassador Ligachev."

Port Aldrin, Luna
Block J64, Apartment 23
25 October 2069
06:30 GMT

An alarm clock was blaring on the Forbidden Gates of Hell. The mighty Icehawk raised his hands to his head and tried to squeeze his throbbing brains back into his fractured skull.

Dara flopped across his chest and turned off the alarm. "Good God, is it morning already?" She blinked, rubbed her eyes, and squinted at the clock again. "Damn, it is." Rolling off of Dalton, she climbed out of bed and began collecting her underwear, which was strewn all over the bedroom floor.

Dalton tried to sit up, but the mad spinning of the walls made him flop down again. *Gravity generator must be acting up again,* he thought. *Better call Dome Maintenance and complain.*

By and by he noticed Dara had gotten dressed and was standing in front of the mirror combing her hair in short, angry jerks. He rolled onto his side. "Hey." She either didn't hear or was ignoring him. Dalton licked his parched lips. "Hey! Where you going?"

"Today may be the dawn of a new era," she said, not taking her eyes off the mirror, "and you may have the mother of all hangovers." She finished with her hair and slapped the comb down on the dresser. "But some of us have to work today, and it would have been nice to have breakfast with you!" Dara spun around, blasted Dalton with a full charge of repressed anger, and stalked out of the bedroom.

"Wait, honey!" Dalton tried to roll out of bed, but the local gravity was still unstable. "What's . . . What did I—" He heard the front door hum open and hiss shut. "Dara?"

No answer.

Dalton flopped back onto his bed and closed his eyes. "God," he said, "if I live to be a million, I will never understand women." He rolled over and buried his face in the pillow. It was still warm and fragrant with the scent of her perfume.

Dalton smiled and went back to sleep.

About two hours later the frantic chirping of the comm system brought him back to a semblance of life. Dalton rolled over, pulled the flatscreen down from the headboard, and tapped the icon to acknowledge the call. "Yeah?"

"Dalton?" The face that popped into view was that of a thin, bookish-looking middle-aged black man with a neatly shaved head and round steel-rimmed spectacles: Terrell Davis, the first-shift NetOps manager. Dalton's boss.

Dalton's bloodshot eyes snapped wide open. "Uh, good morning Mr. Davis! I, uh—"

Terrell took a good look at Dalton through the viewscreen, then shook his head and laughed. "Never mind, kid, I understand. Another bad case of Independence Day flu. I'll put you down as working at home this morning, but do you think you might be able to get your butt in here by noon? Half the staff is out today."

Dalton nodded vigorously. The sloshing of his brain inside his skull hurt. "Yeah, sure. Noon. No problem."

Terrell nodded. "Good. Later, then. Bye."

Terrell's window blanked and shrank, and Dalton pushed the flatscreen up and out of the way. He wasted a few minutes wondering where he'd left his underwear the night before, then said to hell with it and staggered into the shower. The hot water came on with a welcome hiss; he pushed his face into the needles of stinging water and slowly began to feel somewhat more lifelike. Then for a moment he fished up a memory of his life back on Earth, where showers had serious pressure and the water wasn't so tightly rationed.

"Three-minute warning," the Port Aldrin Central Computer said. "You have three minutes of hot water remaining."

Dalton found his tube of soap gel and got busy.

Office of the Governor, Port Aldrin
25 October 2069
09:08 GMT

Patrick Adams wandered into the office with a double synthecaf in one hand and his electric shaver in the other, and almost dropped them both when he found Pieter von Hayek already there and hard at work. "Uh, g'morning, gov. Any news?"

Von Hayek looked up from the report on his desk, pushed his bifocals back up over the bridge of his nose, and shook his head. "No. Not so much as a squeak out of New York."

Adams took a sip of his hot coffee, then shrugged. "Well, it is four in the morning down there. What did you expect?"

"Honestly? Nothing, from the official channels. But it's noon in Moscow, five P.M. in Beijing, and seven P.M. in Melbourne, and I really expected someone to try opening an alternate comm link."

Adams nodded thoughtfully. "What about our local UNuchs?"

"Kinthavong continues to claim he's cut off; he's lying, of course. Copernicus and Eddington Colonies are still talking to us, but only just barely. A bunch of Kinthavong's goons tried to break up an Independence Day party in Kepler last night, but word is, it turned into a riot and our citizens beat the living tar out of them." Von Hayek smiled enigmatically and tapped a finger on the report on his desk.

"Uh-oh," Adams said. "I know that look. You're having an idea, aren't you? Out with it."

The governor leaned back in his black chrome chair and fixed Adams with the look that once again gave Adams the feeling of glimpsing infinitely complex wheels within wheels, all turning with great precision to achieve some almost unfathomable end. "You know how we've been talking about ways to motivate citizens to join the Lunar Defense Force? Just to make our threat of armed resistance look a little more credible?"

Adams looked at the report on von Hayek's desk, then back into the governor's eyes. "Unprovoked attack, wasn't it? A lot of serious injuries to innocent bystanders? UNISAS goons opened fire on an unarmed crowd and left, say, three dead?"

Von Hayek clucked his tongue. "We never lie to the people, Patrick. That's what gives us the moral high ground."

Adams nodded and took a quick gulp of his coffee. "Right. All the same, it wouldn't hurt if the rumor mill began to churn at full speed, would it?"

The governor let out a barely perceptible nod.

Adams turned and headed for the door.

"Oh," the governor called out, "and, Patrick?"

Adams stopped in the doorway and turned around. "Yes?"

"Let's have my heartfelt appeal for moderation standing by, just in case things get out of hand."

UN Headquarters, New York
25 October 2069
8:07 A.M. EST

Antonio Ramón Aguila sat quietly in his office, fingers tented, assessing the situation. So far, all was going as well as could be expected. The world news media had swallowed the "terrorists" cover story without so much as batting an eyelash, and they were now repeating and enhancing the story with predictable enthusiasm.

Outside of the UN, only a few North American amateurs had managed to pick up the Lunar Declaration of Independence, but SAS techs had successfully planted enough strategic leaks on the Web to preemptively destroy the credibility of any samizdat that might result. Very late in the evening Aguila had even managed to pull together an ad hoc meeting of the CLD and had gotten sufficient votes to take the issue to the Security Council. The council was to convene at nine o'clock this morning, and Aguila would go in waving his latest bit of news: overnight polls showing that 72 percent of the population favored immediate and decisive military action against the "terrorists"—as if anyone on the Security Council cared what the masses thought.

Now all that was left was to find Lord Edward Haversham and make sure he didn't say anything embarrassing in public.

How much longer? Aguila wondered, not for the first time. *Surely the secretary-general must see that I am the real power in the CLD and that Haversham is merely a useless dotard. Must I continue to play the loyal lackey until Haversham dies?*

Aguila relished that thought a moment, imagining himself at Haversham's state funeral, nobly rising above his personal grief to accept the post of United Nations secretary for Lunar affairs and chairman of the CLD. A tight smile found its way onto his face.

The office intercom chirped. Aguila's smile vanished, he tapped the acknowledge touchpad, and Allegria's face popped into view. "Sir? We've found Lord Haversham."

"Face-down in the East River?" Aguila said hopefully.

"No, sir. He's just come into the building. Apparently he decided to try a new restaurant last night, then take in a play, but he forgot to take his comm pad or tell anyone where he was going."

How convenient, thought Aguila. *And in the meantime the CLD is very nearly paralyzed for sixteen hours because the chairman is missing in inaction. Are you really that much of a fool, Edward?*

"Sir?" Allegria prompted.

"Has anyone briefed him on the current situation?"

"Jurgen tried, in the elevator on the way up. He says Haversham didn't seem terribly interested."

Aguila nodded. "As I expected. Very well. See if you can book me for a meeting with him as soon as possible."

"I already have, sir. It's at eight-fifteen in Haversham's office."

Aguila checked his real-time clock. "Splendid. Then you have time to fetch me a fresh cup of coffee."

Allegria leaned in close to the video pickup, fixed Aguila with her serious dark brown eyes, and dropped her voice to a breathy whisper. "Antonio darling," she said softly, "I would do anything for you—lie, cheat, steal, commit perjury, even kill . . . but, Antonio, I do not fetch coffee."

"We hold these truths to be self-evident, that all men are created equal, that they are endowed by their Creator with certain unalienable rights—"

Lord Edward Haversham, chairman emeritus of the United Nations Committee on Lunar Development, looked up at Aguila and frowned. "Turn that down, would you? It's ruining my concentration." Aguila thumbed the remote control for the wall-mounted flatscreen, and Haversham went back to addressing the ball.

Tick! The putt rolled across twelve feet of lush Persian carpet, only to dink off the lip of the bone china teacup. "Bloody Iranian carpet," Haversham muttered. "I asked for Malaysian—*they* understand golf—but nooo . . ."

"Ahem." Aguila cleared his throat, took a small step forward, and focused the full force of his gaze on Haversham.

"Ah, yes, Antonio old boy. Tell me, what is it exactly that's got your knickers in a twist this time?" Haversham strolled across the carpet, recovered the ball, but left the teacup where it lay.

Aguila nodded at the flatscreen and thumbed the volume up.

"We colonists came to the Moon because we were promised a chance to build a better life for ourselves and our children. Now we find that we are little more than indentured servants in the coldest and most remote gulag the Earth has ever known. . . ."

Haversham pursed his lips distastefully and turned to Aguila. "You had UNCOMM jam that, I expect."

Aguila nodded. "Of course. There was some leakage, but we have planted a counter-story, and most people will believe the declaration is a hoax."

"Hmm." Haversham paused to watch the recorded program a few seconds longer, then muted the sound. "You know, I must admit I am impressed. Old Pieter certainly does come off better on video than he does in real life, what say?"

"Some people have that gift, sir."

"Indeed." Haversham nodded slowly, then reached some kind of conclusion. "Well, then, I suppose the question of the day is, how should we respond? Is that why you're here?"

Aguila allowed himself a thin smile. "Your insight astounds me, sir."

"Lord," Haversham corrected. "Hereditary title. I was never knighted, you know." He dropped the golf ball on the carpet and began lining up for another putt.

Aguila blinked in puzzlement until he recognized Haversham's non sequitur for what it was and realized the old fool had gone off-track again. "We couldn't find you last night," Aguila said slowly and clearly. "So I convened an ad hoc meeting of the CLD. We've already reached a conclusion."

Haversham hunched over the ball and considered Aguila from the corner of his eye. "My, my, getting ambitious, aren't we?"

Aguila refused to be sidetracked again. "Our vote was eleven to one to take this matter to the Security Council, with a recommendation that responsibility for the situation be turned over to the Committee on World Peace."

Haversham stood up with a start, frowned, and shook his head sharply. "No! I disagree completely! Bad idea, that."

"Sir? We've already voted."

For the first time, Haversham looked alarmed. "You said it was eleven to one. Who was the one?"

"Akuii-Bua. She agreed with us but felt we shouldn't vote until we found you. Sir, the meeting is set for nine o'clock this morning." Aguila pulled back the sleeve of his Savile Row suit jacket and checked his watch. "That is in a little over half an hour. Wouldn't you like to review the report I'm going to present?"

Haversham took a long pause, staring straight at Aguila with unabashed anger, and all trace of age or weakness vanished from his pale gray eyes. "Why? For years you've been seeking an excuse to kick out the civilian government and institute direct rule. Isn't that what you're going to recommend now?"

Aguila fell silent. Once again Haversham had managed to surprise him with a moment of startling lucidity.

"Antonio," Haversham went on, changing to a gentler voice, "those are our *children* up there. If you'd done any serious reading of history at all, you'd have realized this moment was inevitable." Haversham paused. "True," he added, apparently to himself, "it's happening twenty years earlier than I expected, but . . ." His voice tapered off.

Aguila jumped into the gap. "Sir, I—"

"No," Haversham interrupted, *"you* listen. The problem here is that the original colonies were built by Americans and Russians, and we've spent the last thirty years packing the place full of hotheads, malcontents, and refugees! When we founded the CLD two decades ago I told them the thing to do was clear the whole lot out and replace them with nice docile Canadians, or maybe Belgians. But we didn't, and now we've got *this* mess!"

"Sir—"

"Now, Antonio, we have one chance left. If we play this right, we can co-opt the revolution and lay the foundation for an interplanetary commonwealth that will bind the worlds together long after you and I are dust and forgotten! But if you go charging in now with a gang of jackbooted thugs . . ."

Haversham sighed, and his face sagged. The outburst clearly had taken a lot out of him. He looked at Aguila, a childlike hurt showing in his eyes. "There really was only *one* vote against this madness?"

Aguila kept his face impassive. "You may present a dissenting opinion, if you like." Without a backward glance, he turned and strode out of Haversham's office.

THE UNITED NATIONS REACTS

The United Nations' response to the Lunar Declaration of Independence was, of course, entirely predictable. First, they imposed a news blackout to ensure that all parties were operating with insufficient information. Next, Undersecretary Aguila held a press conference in which he flatly denied that there was any trouble at all. Following this, the Committee on Lunar Development (UNCLD) met in secret session and boldly voted to fob the problem off on the Security Council.

The Security Council emergency session took place the next morning, on 25 October, under conditions of strictest secrecy. At this meeting the United States of North America (USNA), eager to regain control of those colonial possessions it had given up in the 2054 Djakarta Conference, presented a detailed plan which called for using the Americans' vaunted Rapid Deployment Force to restore order in the rebelling colonies and which, not incidentally, put the Americans in sole charge.

This plan was of course immediately vetoed by the other permanent members of the Security Council, only to be followed by the Russian Kosmospetznaz plan, which differed in some particulars, but sprang from much the same motivation and achieved much the same effect, in that it nearly precipitated a fistfight between the ambassadors from France, China, and the New German Unity (NDE).

There were other moments of high drama and poignancy in this session as well: Field Marshal Bernard Leighton-Smythe, supreme commander of the Peacekeeper Corps, threatening to knock the Québecois and West Samoan ambassadors' heads together if they did not behave; Dr. Indira Singh, head of the UN Food and Agriculture Office (UNIFAO), admitting that without lunar food production, the Earth would face mass starvation in just slightly over eight weeks; elderly Lord Edward Haversham, founder and chairman emeritus of the CLD, arguing eloquently, if futilely, that there was still time to pursue a diplomatic solution. Even now one wonders if the history of the past century might have been vastly different, had the members of the Security Council spared a moment to listen to Lord Haversham — or, for that matter, to each other.

Instead, in the end it was Shi Cheng Wu, chairman of the Committee on World Peace (UNCWP), who won the day with his proposal. Operation Restore Justice called for the creation and deployment of a multinational peacekeeping team called ATFOR, the All-Terran Antiterrorism Force. Combining elements of the Russian Navy and the American Special Forces as well as the Danish, Ivory Coast, Papua New Guinean, and Palestinian armies, ATFOR was a compromise solution that — to view it in the most charitable possible light — pleased no one.

It has been said that a camel is a horse designed by a committee. If so, then ATFOR was created to be a cranky and lame camel with a foul disposition and severe flea problems.

— Chaim Noguchi, *A History of the Lunar Revolution*

CHAPTER 6

Office of the Governor, Port Aldrin
25 October 2069
17:31 GMT

The comm unit on von Hayek's desk chirped. Like a pouncing cat, he was on it. "Yes?"

"Governor?" The voice was that of Patrick Adams, calling from his own office. "General Consensus reports something odd. UNET just came back on-line all by itself for point-oh-two-five seconds. Then it blacked out again."

"Did anything get through?"

"That's the strangest part. It looks like just an ordinary blip packet—junk mail, personal e-mail, UNET system messages, that sort of stuff. There's only one thing with a UN origin tag on it, and it's meaningless. Gibberish."

Von Hayek grabbed the comm unit with both hands and with white knuckles. "What is it?"

"A background report on thorium production. But it's almost unintelligible, and the data tables don't checksum."

Von Hayek sucked in his breath sharply. "Route that report to me. Immediately!"

There was a pause, possibly while Adams shrugged.

"Okay." Moments later the report file popped up on von Hayek's desktop.

Von Hayek wasted a minute reading the first page, just to see if Adams was going to find an excuse to barge in and interrupt him. In that time he learned that Patrick was right: the report *was* dense, incomprehensible, loaded with arcane information, and written in a dry and academic style virtually guaranteed to make the mind wander. Von Hayek's mind nearly did.

But his desktop timer pinged; the minute had passed without interruption. Von Hayek took one more glance to make sure his office door was closed and locked, then moved the report file into his desktop compression processor and applied his decryption key.

Seconds later the real meaning hidden in the gibberish appeared in a pop-up window: "Security Council has chosen military option. Expect drop-in guests within 96 hours. No more info at this time. Regrets, Beacon."

Port Aldrin, Luna
Hrbek Memorial Gym
25 October 2069
20:00 GMT.

"Hey, Starkiller! What are you doing here?" Dalton looked up with a start and glanced around the gym until he spotted a striking blond woman a full head taller than everyone around her.

"Svetlana!" Dalton broke away from the group he was with and wormed his way through the crowd, trying to get closer to her. Svetlana Kosov was a friend, sort of. He'd partnered with her on Treasures of Tarmin a year or so back and had gotten halfway through level 23 before he realized that Ivan the Not Bad was actually a woman. Since then he'd made a point of playing Deadly Disks with her at least once a month, time permitting.

Dalton broke through the last knot of people and got close

enough to speak without shouting. "So, Kosov. You're joining the militia?"

"Thinking about it," she said. "Figure they need medics as well as fighters. What's your excuse?"

Dalton tried to find something cocky and brave to say, but settled for something closer to the truth. "I've got friends over in Kepler. When I heard about that massacre last night—"

"Massacre?" Kosov's bright blue eyes went wide. "I heard the UNI-thugs broke some skulls and legs, but I didn't hear about anything about a massacre."

Dalton shrugged indifferently but secretly treasured his sense of being privy to inside information. "Oh, yeah, it's all over the chat nodes. Some SAS officers opened fire on a crowd. Governor's office is trying to hush it up so there won't be a riot, but I heard they killed three people."

"You heard wrong." Some black-haired guy Dalton didn't know pushed himself into the conversation. "I got a friend whose wife works in the same dome as the Kepler emergency room, and she says it was five dead, seven wounded."

Another person joined in the conversation then, a skinny teenager with more freckles than bare face. "You folks talking about that mess in Korolev yesterday? The one where the blues shot up that corridor party?"

The black-haired guy shook his head. "No. This was Kepler, late last night."

Freckle Face's jaw dropped. "Kepler too? God, the dirt-bags are killing us left and right! We gotta defend ourselves!"

Svetlana seized this opportunity to step back into the conversation. "Well, that's why we're all here, boys. To show those UN bastards they can't kick us around."

"Damn right," the black-haired guy affirmed.

"Hey," Freckle Face wondered aloud, "you think they got enough guns for all of us?" He craned his neck and looked around the gym. "I mean, there's gotta be, oh, forty or fifty people in here tonight."

Svetlana stood on tiptoe, towering over Freckle Face, and surveyed the crowd. "Thirty-eight, actually." She settled back to her normal posture. "And what? You think they're just going to pass out guns like party favors?"

Freckle Face shrugged. "Well, sure. I mean, we gotta be ready in case the CLD tries a sneak attack, right?"

Svetlana pursed her red lips. "Do you really think that's likely?"

Freckle Face looked nonplussed.

The black-haired guy pushed in again. "Look, kid," he said to Freckle Face, "the Earth is 384,000 kilometers away. No way they can launch a major sneak attack: we'll see their translunar injection burn, and that'll give us three days' advance warning, at least. The point of our being here tonight is to show Kinthavong and his blue dogs we mean business. Once the UN sees that, they'll back down and start negotiating."

"You really think so?" Freckle Face looked disappointed.

Dalton clapped a hand on the kid's shoulder. "Aw, don't let those two bring you down. I'm sure we'll get plenty of chance to suit up and play soldier." He smiled and offered Freckle Face a handshake. "Starkiller's the name. Dalton Starkiller."

The kid's face lit up, which made his freckles look like sunspots on Betelgeuse. *"The* Dalton Starkiller? *Icehawk?"* He seized Dalton's hand and shook it vigorously. "You're the guy who holds the all-dome record for Space Hawk!"

Dalton nodded, trying to smile demurely but ending up smug. "Yep. That's me."

"Jeff Mahoney!" the kid said, still shaking Dalton's hand. "But you can call me Stormrider! And I've got to tell you it is an honor to meet you, sir! I downloaded a macro of your play on the last Nightstalker match, and it was, well . . . beautiful!"

"Thank you," Dalton said as he started wondering how he was going to get his hand back.

"Starkiller?" the black-haired guy whispered to Svetlana. "What the hell kind of name is Starkiller?"

"I heard he changed it when he immigrated," Svetlana whispered back. "It used to be Totschlägenstern."

"I mean," Mahoney prattled on, "the way you smoked that hormagaunt on level 15. Stellar!"

"Nothing to it," Dalton said, finally prying himself out of the handshake and feeling more than a bit embarrassed. Actually, in that match he'd switched to the plasma sword because he was running low on rockets and hadn't expect to find anything worse than a coldwraith down that corridor. When the hormagaunt jumped out, he'd had no time to switch weapons; and while everyone else assumed the fight was an incredible display of skill and bravado, Dalton knew in his heart that if he'd even suspected there was a hormagaunt in the shadows, he'd have hosed the corridor down with homing fusion grenades and then tried a different corridor.

"I can't believe this," young Mahoney continued babbling. "We got Icehawk on our side! Icehawk and Stormrider, fighting shoulder to shoulder! Those dirtbags don't know what they're in for!"

Dalton looked to Svetlana, who only smiled and rolled her eyes.

A commotion broke out by one of the doors to the gym, which finally got Mahoney's attention and shut him up. People began jostling for position and craning their necks; Dalton found an opening in the crowd, grabbed Svetlana's hand, and tried to work his way to the front.

"Attention!" a new voice bellowed from somewhere over by the door. The buzz of conversation died away, and Svetlana stopped moving, dragging Dalton to a halt.

"Okay, people," the new voice continued, "let's start by forming a line so's everyone can see! Y'all can form a line, can'tcha?"

This time Svetlana started moving first. Dalton tagged along, and after a minute or so of shuffling around, the group in the gym had formed a rough facsimile of a straight line. The black-haired guy had somehow managed to end up standing on Svetlana's right, and young Mahoney was standing off to Dalton's left.

Two men stood at one end of the gym, facing the line.

Both wore the new white-with-gold-trim uniform of the Lunar Defense Force. The tall one was a lean, sunburned, and rawboned Anglo, with a droopy brown mustache and, of all things, a white cowboy hat, while the short one was thin, muscular, dour-faced and unmistakably pure Japanese. The two men exchanged glances; then the tall one put his hands on his hips and took a deep breath.

"Howdy!" he shouted, in a voice that made young Mahoney jump. "Ah'm Major Lloyd Thompson, formerly of the short-lived Republic of Texas, as if y'all couldn't guess! My partner here," he extended a hand toward the other man, "is Major Yuji Nakagawa, formerly of His Majesty's equally short-lived New Imperial Japanese Navy!

"We are here tonight because we are professional soldiers and officers in the Lunar Defense Force! *You* are here for a much better reason: because you are citizen volunteers, willing to bear arms in the defense of your homes and families!"

Without realizing it, Dalton stood up a little straighter and puffed his chest up a little.

"Now," Thompson said, sweeping his gaze up and down the line, "who here is responsible for organizing this cozy little get-together?"

Hesitantly, almost shyly, Dalton's boss, Terrell Davis, stepped forward, along with another middle-aged man. "I guess we are. I mean, Bob here is the one who knew someone in the LDF, and I—"

Thompson strode forward and seized Terrell's hand. "That's *exactly* the kind of initiative we need in the LDF Militia!" Thompson dug a hand into his shirt pocket and came up with two pairs of simple gold bars. "Congratulations, Lieutenants!" He handed one set of bars to Terrell and the other to Bob, then stepped back and saluted proudly. After some confusion, Terrell and Bob returned the salute, sloppily.

"Easiest promotion you ever got, innit?" Thompson said with a smile. "The bars go on your collar, like this." He tilted his head back to display the gold oak leaves on his own uniform collar. Terrell and Bob stepped back into line and started futzing with their insignia, while Thompson pivoted and strode back to front and center, next to Nakagawa.

"Now!" Thompson resumed, in his parade-field bellow, "we don't have the time to turn y'all into professional soldiers, and frankly, I don't believe that's what y'all really want." This got a collective laugh from the group, which died away quickly when everyone saw that Major Nakagawa was scowling. "So what we're gonna cover in this meetin', and in the next few days, is real basic military organization. That, and we're gonna get y'all checked out on the powered battle suit, which is the *real* uniform of the LDF!"

Thompson looked down at his clothing and made a little hand gesture to direct attention to himself. "This thing here is just our formal monkey suit, y'know? For parades and banquets and all that crap. If y'all really want one, you're gonna hafta enlist in the Regulars."

Something in the word "enlist" made Dalton shudder inwardly. He noticed that young Mahoney was nodding and smiling, though.

"However," Thompson shouted, "tonight we are gonna begin with some basic training in the ab-so-lutely fundamental fightin' infantry skill. Major Nakagawa?" The other LDF officer turned his back to the line, and when he turned around again, he was holding a briefcase-sized brushed aluminum case in his hands. He popped the latches and, using both hands, held the case wide open to display its contents.

It held four pistols.

Thompson grabbed one and held it aloft. "This," Thompson bellowed, "is the Heckler and Koch LP-seven Mark Five. Standard military police–issue laser pistol. This little sucker here is the basic combat weapon of the LDF."

"Wow," young Mahoney gasped. And Dalton had to admit that for a gun, the Mark Five *was* pretty sexy. Without thinking, he took a small step forward.

So did everyone else, except Svetlana.

"Don't crowd," Major Thompson said. "We only got four

pistols here tonight, but rest assured, when the time comes we'll have enough for everybody. Tonight we're just gonna concentrate on gettin' y'all checked out on basic operations and safety, and maybe if you're real good we'll let y'all do a little target practice."

"Cool," Dalton and young Mahoney moaned together.

GENERAL JACKSON, ON THE LDF

The LDF? Don't make me laugh. It's a Potemkin army, with delusions of grandeur! Peace Corps Intel estimates they have 250 soldiers, tops, and most of them are either disgruntled veterans or cashiered junior officers from third-rate Fourth World armies. Their organizational structure looks like the damn Bolivian navy — all admirals, no deckhands. Their arsenal: well, let's just say we know there are fewer than fifty serviceable weapons in private hands on the moon, and I think that speaks for itself. As for this "General Consensus" of theirs — clearly a nom de guerre, and a particularly idiotic one at that — his speech patterns show he's obviously ex-American, and the USNA Army can account for *all* of its former officers above the rank of captain!

In short, the LDF is a contemptible little band of street thugs and losers led by a fraud and armed with nothing more lethal than hot air. I predict they will melt away at the first sight of official United Nations Peacekeepers. They'll scurry away to hide in dark nooks and crannies just like the cockroaches they are!

So to answer to your question: how do I feel about sending the 82nd Airborne up against the LDF? Why not ask me how I'd feel about going up against the South Central Crips?''

In fairness to General Jackson, it should be pointed out that he made these remarks in October 2069, some eight months before the beginning of the Crips' 2070 Summer in Hell campaign. To this day, despite all American and United Nations claims to the contrary, the South Central Crips (SCC) still control all territory south of Beverly Hills and west of Interstate 5.

— Chaim Noguchi, *A History of the Lunar Revolution*

CHAPTER 7

Patrick Adams knocked lightly on the doorframe, then went in. "Governor, it's one o'clock in the morning. You need your sleep."

Von Hayek didn't look up. "I can't sleep. Every time I close my eyes I see blue-uniformed storm troopers marching through this city."

Adams tried a smile; the effort was wasted. "C'mon, gov, your secret intelligence source must be wrong. If the UN really was sending in the Peacekeepers, they'd have to be launching right now to make the window. I've got twelve autotelescopes locked in on Earth, and not one of them has logged any major spaceflight activity."

Von Hayek toyed with his bifocals. "Maybe there's a hole in your surveillance. Maybe the Peacekeepers have a stealth launch technique that we don't know about."

Adams shrugged. "Maybe. Or maybe they think this is important enough to risk the high-G forty-hour transit, but I don't suppose that's likely. You've seen General Consensus's analysis. If the Security Council votes to send in

Peacekeepers, it'll take them a week, minimum, to organize the force and transport it here. Anything less than that and the boys in blue will arrive either too space-sick or too underequipped to fight."

Von Hayek finally looked up at Adams. His eyes were bloodshot and red-rimmed from lack of sleep. "Or perhaps General Consensus has miscalculated. Are you sure the militia recruitment meetings were conspicuous enough?"

Adams let out a little snort. "Gov, they couldn't have been more conspicuous if we'd mailed each SAS informant a handwritten invitation. The Security Council *must* know we've got more than two thousand volunteers in the colonial militia."

"How many of those can we rely on?"

Adams considered his answer. "Most of them, I'd say. Pieter, you always underestimate how popular this revolution is. Not only have we got more militia members than we can arm, but we've also picked up three hundred eager new recruits for the regular LDF."

Von Hayek nodded slowly. "Good. Now, about weapons: you're sure the UN knows that we're armed?"

"If they don't, Kinthavong is either stone blind or asleep at the switch. We're keeping the heavy stuff under wraps for now, but your boy, Josef, has had LDF officers swaggering all over the place, each of them packing two laser pistols. All the SAS had to do was count."

A sobering thought apparently occurred to von Hayek then. His eyes slowly widened, and he took off his bifocals and bit lightly on an earpiece. "Patrick?" he said softly, as he took the earpiece out of his mouth. "What if no one's paying attention to Kinthavong anymore?"

Adams felt a deep, cold chill settle into his spine. "Then the UN just might believe a small strike force could succeed," Adams answered in a hollow voice, as he started to worry through the implications. "The troops they'd send would be lightly armed; with minimal support staff. Battalion strength, tops. *That* they could transport in one jump. They wouldn't have enough people to occupy and hold all thirteen colonies, but if they hit just a few strategic targets . . ." His voice tapered off.

Von Hayek put his glasses back on and fixed Adams with a steady stare. *"Which* targets?"

Adams stroked his chin, subconsciously noting that he needed to shave. "Well, General Consensus has always assumed they'd start by reinforcing Lacus Mortis and Sinus Roris. But if they're planning to use a blitzkrieg strategy, they'll either try to grab some of the cargo launchers or else . . ." Again his voice tapered off, and he looked straight at von Hayek.

"Or else what, Patrick?"

"They'll try a surgical strike to decapitate the government." Adams gulped and licked his lips. "They'll be hunting for *you,* sir."

Von Hayek nodded. "Yes. I thought as much." He pursed his lips and scowled slightly. "Well, I knew the job was dangerous when I took it." He turned in his chair, picked up the ebony-framed holo of his long-dead wife, and seemed to communicate with it. Adams fought the urge to intrude and peek at the picture.

The moment passed. Von Hayek set the picture down and turned to Adams. "Okay, Patrick, here's what I want. First off, are any of the other governors still here in Aldrin?"

"Trelstad and Veerhoven are. Kozhevnikov too, I think."

"Well, get hold of them and tell them to go home. No point giving the UN an eggs-in-one-basket target. In fact, since Trelstad is my second, I'd be happier if she went to Farside for a few days."

"Got it. I'll pass that along. Next?"

"Patrick, at all costs, we must protect our civilians. How do our evacuation plans look?"

Adams nodded. "Actually, since most of our reactors were built by the Russians, we've got really *good* evacuation plans."

"Wonderful. We might want to consider a few emergency drills. Let me think about that." Von Hayek looked down at his desktop, seeming to search for the notes that weren't there, then back to Adams. "Next: how's the MANTA project coming along?"

Reflexively, Adams looked around to make sure no one else was within earshot. "The engineers have hit a new snag. We're still at least two weeks away from beta test. Maybe more."

Von Hayek balled up a skinny fist and thumped his desktop, making the various video windows and icons jump like dried beans. "Damn. We really could use MANTA right about now."

Adams reddened slightly under the implied rebuke. "I know, sir. My people are giving it their best."

"I'm sure they are, Patrick." Von Hayek looked down again and casually blanked a few comm windows even though they appeared to be inactive. "Now," he continued, in a voice barely above a whisper, "what about our friends on Farside? Any chance of pulling a fresh rabbit out of that hat?"

Adams shook his head. "Not on ninety-six hours' notice, sir."

Von Hayek frowned. "I thought not. But I figured it was worth asking."

"Of course, sir."

"Very well." Von Hayek rolled his chair back from the desk, reached over to the left bin drawer, and tapped in a code on the lock keypad. "Okay, here's the big one. If the Peacekeepers *do* hit us, and if they hit us hard, our only hope is to make this so expensive for them that they decide to go back to the negotiating table." The lock clicked; the drawer slid open.

"Patrick?" the governor said, as he reached into the drawer and extracted a dull black plastic case. "I want all the cargo launchers rigged for demolition."

Adams arched an eyebrow. "Risky strategy, sir. We won't know where the Peacekeepers are going to hit until they get here. There won't be much time to evacuate civilians."

"There isn't much time *now*. I'm giving you forty-eight hours." Von Hayek laid the plastic case on his desktop, and pressed a thumb to the lock. A bar of green light swept over his finger, and the lock opened.

Adams was still dumbstruck. "Pete . . . Governor . . . Sir? Forty-eight hours? But—"

"Then you'd better get going on it, hadn't you?"

Adams blinked again, then turned and started for the door.

"Wait. Patrick?"

Adams turned around to see that von Hayek had lifted open the top of the case. There were two small chrome pistols inside.

Pieter von Hayek smiled in a way that reminded Adams of Pieter's son, Josef, and for that reason made Adam's skin crawl. "Josef sent these over," Pieter said as he lifted out a pistol and offered it to Adams. "He thought we might need them."

Adams considered the pistol, then looked in the first councillor's eyes. They stared at each other for a long moment; then Adams accepted it. "Thank you, sir. But I have to tell you, I hope to God I never have to use it."

Von Hayek picked up the other pistol, and tested its heft. "Frankly, Patrick, so do I."

THE DECEPTIVE CALM
BEFORE THE STORM

The days immediately following an apparently successful revolution are always a heady time. In this, the new citizens of the Free State Selena were no different from the Muscovites of 1917, the Czechoslovaks of 1968, the Berliners of 1989, or the Tiananmen Square survivors of 2012. Within hours of Governor von Hayek's Declaration of Independence the people were thronging the malls and galleries of their domed cities, cheering for parades, celebrating wildly, and generally congratulating themselves on their stunning good sense and good fortune. This general air of surreal excitement resulted not only in a notable surge in the birthrate come July 2070 but also in a brief, intensely enthusiastic, and occasionally quite promising flowering in the creative arts.

For example, the Volodyan poet-playwright Dmitri Khy is said to have listened to the declaration, turned off his media center, then sat down before his computer and in forty-eight hours, nonstop, composed a brilliant new work, savagely satirizing the United Nations Committee on Lunar Development in general and Lord Edward Haversham in particular. Such was the tenor of the moment that he was able to collect a group of prominent actors, secure satellite access time, and present a live reading of the rough draft a mere three days later, on the morning of October 28. Those lucky enough to catch the performance said the new play was both viciously intelligent and profoundly funny and that the finished version would no doubt have been the capstone on Dmitri Khy's long and distinguished literary career.

It is indeed a tragedy that no one thought to record the broadcast, and that Khy put off sending a backup copy of the script to his agent in Port Aldrin. For on the morning of October 28, of course, Dmitri Khy, along with so many others, had less than twelve hours left to live.

— Chaim Noguchi, *A History of the Lunar Revolution*

CHAPTER 8

It'd been a really nice dinner. Then Dara had spoiled it by mentioning the M-word again.

"Honey," Dalton said, shaking his head, "we've been through this a hundred times. I am not going to quit the militia."

"But, darling," Dara pleaded, as she tried to take his hand. Dalton pulled back. "You saw the announcement on RealNews One this afternoon. The UN caved. Secretary Kinthavong has agreed to all our demands and handed over the government to von Hayek. All he wants now is a fair trial and safe passage to Copernicus."

Dalton snorted. "Right. And suddenly we're supposed to trust that little gangster?"

"Why not? It's over. We won."

Dalton fidgeted with his juice box, then put it down without taking a sip. "That's what Kinthavong says. But I won't believe it"—he pointed upward in the universal Lunar shorthand for Earth—"until they reopen UNET and I hear them saying it. In a regular newscast. To their own people."

Dara looked at Dalton, with the expression that always gave him the feeling she was sizing him up, like something delicious she was considering whether or not to pick. "Now you're starting to sound paranoid, like your friend Ken Roberts. I don't want him." She leaned forward across the table and caught Dalton's right hand in both of hers. "I want *you*. At home, in bed, where you belong." Her smile slid into a salacious grin, and she winked. "You should be happy that I miss you when you stay out late."

Dalton sighed and extracted his hand from her grip. "The militia meetings are important. To me and to the colony."

Dara snickered. "Oh, spare me. You just get off on clanking around in that armored battlesuit!" Dalton's eyebrows went up in surprise, and Dara snickered again. "You talk in your sleep," she explained.

That got a snort of annoyance out of Dalton. "Dara—"

Whatever he was about to say next was lost forever in the first blast of the alarm siren. Dalton cringed at the piercing wail, and it took him a few seconds more to realize that every other siren and alarm within earshot was also blaring. The nearest ones sounded as if they were right in his ears.

Dara was already on her feet. "That sounds like . . . *airlock rupture!*" She grabbed Dalton's hand. "Come on! This way!" Shoving the table aside, she dragged Dalton out of his chair. "We've got to find a survival shelter!"

Dalton dug in his heels and pulled back. "*No!* There's a militia emergency suit locker right—"

As abruptly as they'd started, the klaxons stopped. Dalton stopped too, with Dara piling up next to him, all his attention suddenly focused on the eerie silence.

"False alarm?" Dara whispered hopefully.

"Shh." Dalton bit his lip, closed his eyes, and after a moment he heard it: the flat, synthetic voice of the Port Aldrin Central Computer, muttering through every intercom speaker and comm panel in the domed city.

"*Code seven. Code seven. Code seven . . .*"

Dara's pale face blanched a sickly white. "Oh, sweet Jesus," she murmured, "it can't be. This must be a drill."

Dalton shuddered, then grabbed her hand. "*Come on!*" This time when he tugged, there was no resistance, and a moment later they were both racing down the corridor. Already Dalton could feel his ears popping as the air pressure dropped. They rounded a corner and nearly collided with a crowd of thirty or so fellow dome dwellers, all wrestling with white emergency vacuum suits.

The crowd had a strangely calming effect on Dalton. Though quite clearly frightened, everyone was observing lifeboat-drill discipline, queueing up in orderly rows to accept the packages that three white-suited emergency workers were doling out from the locker, and then stepping off to the side to put them on.

A fourth figure—a tall man in a white battlesuit with a gold-mirrored visor and a gold oak leaf on the helmet— wandered around the fringes of the group, making sure the anxious crowd stayed calm. "Stay cool, y'all. Just stay cool, y'hear?" His amplified voice crackled out of a comm unit on his chest. One frantic woman tried to elbow past him. "Hang on there, ma'am. We'll have a suit for y'all real soon."

"But my little girl—" the woman protested.

"We'll have one for her too, ma'am. Don't fret. We got kiddie suits here too; everything's gonna be fine. Just remember, get yours on first, then help your daughter into hers." He gently nudged the woman back into line. A few moments later one of the emergency workers handed her a small suit with a helmet attached, and she breathed an audible sigh of relief. The man in the battlesuit patted her on the back, then looked up and saw Dalton.

"Militiaman Starkiller? Your platoon is 'sposed to muster in Sector Three-B."

Dalton took a step closer and tried to peer through the reflective visor. "Major Thompson? I thought your voice sounded familiar. I was having dinner—"

Thompson stood up a fraction of an inch taller. "That's Major Thompson, *sir,* Militiaman!"

Immediately Dalton snapped to attention and managed a sloppy salute.

"All right, enough of that crud," Thompson said as he turned around and pulled a small laser pistol out of a nearby locker. "Here, take this."

Dalton carefully took the laser pistol and looked it over with an appraising eye: Heckler & Koch LP-7 Mark Two, an older model with a little holster wear around the muzzle and trigger guard but otherwise in good condition.

"It ain't much, but it's all I can spare," Major Thompson said. He passed Dalton two power cells for the pistol. "We got heavier stuff cached in Sector Five, but your platoon is assigned to Sector Three-B. Grab something better when y'all get the chance." Major Thompson turned to the white-suited emergency workers and raised his voice to his trademark bellow. "Hey, we got us a militiaman here! Are there any more of them armored suits?" Someone passed over a bulky white package.

"Thanks." Dalton took the suit and juggled it, the pistol, and the power cells for a few moments, then handed the gun to Dara and started tearing open the suit package. "Uh, Major Thompson? Sir? Any idea what the hell's going on?"

Before Thompson could respond, the alarm sirens let out another blast, the intercom system buzzed to life, and a tense human voice replaced the drone of the Central Computer.

"This is not a drill! Repeat, this is *not* a drill! Port Aldrin is under attack by UN Peacekeepers. All LDF and militia personnel report to duty stations immediately. All civilians report to the nearest evacuation point! Again, this is not a drill. Armed and hostile UN troops have penetrated Sectors Four-A, Six-A, and Nine-C." There was a pause. "Avoid those areas. All LDF and militia personnel, report in *now!"*

The voice cut out, and a moment later the synthetic voice of the Central Computer resumed its chanting: *"Code seven. Code seven. Code seven . . ."*

Major Thompson turned to Dalton. "That about answer your question? Now y'all know as much as I do."

Dalton shook his head. "But I thought we were supposed

to get advance warning. I thought there was supposed to be no way an Earth ship could approach—"

The major shrugged. "Obviously we thought wrong. I expect we'll sort this out later, if'n we get the chance. But right now your job is to join your unit and get your butt in action. Is that clear?"

"Yes, sir!" Thompson went back to crowd control, and Dalton turned his full attention to donning the armored battlesuit. He stepped into the leggings, slid the heavy white one-piece garment easily up over his slender torso, and sealed the tabs at his throat. He unsnapped the leash that tethered the helmet to the suit's waist and lifted it up to place it over his head. But before he could pull it down, a slender hand grabbed his shoulder.

"Dalton, please. Be careful." He turned around to face Dara, who was already wearing her vacuum suit—the civilian model, with no ballistic plating and the headgear tilted back from the shoulders. Tears welled up in her brown eyes as she leaned forward and gave him a long, anxious kiss. "You don't have to do this to impress me," she whispered. "We can still catch the evacuation shuttle."

Dalton took a long look at her pretty, tear-streaked face, then pulled back. "No. I'm in the militia." He gave her what he hoped was a confident grin, then pulled his helmet on, activated the suit's comm circuit, and linked to Dara's channel. She pulled her helmet on.

"Don't worry," Dalton said, once they were linked. "The UN troops are just dirtsuckers, used to pushing peasants around in one-G. They'll be too busy recovering from grav sickness to give us any kind of real fight." He took the laser pistol from her, pushed the spare power cell into his belt pouch, and slapped the other cell into the pistol's loading well. With a satisfying whine, the pistol hummed to life and the status indicators flashed green.

"Besides," he said, brandishing the pistol, "as soon as they see these, they'll turn tail and start crying for their negotiators." He checked the pistol to make sure it was on safe, then holstered it and tried to take one more good look at Dara. The mirror plating on their visors made that impossible, but something in the set of her shoulders suggested she wasn't buying his bravado.

Come to think of it, neither was he. *I shouldn't have eaten that krillsteak,* he thought. *Great thing about these mirror shades, though—if I puke now, she'll never know.*

Whatever Dara was thinking, she chose to keep it to herself. "Just be careful," she repeated. "Come back in one piece."

"Don't worry, babe." He nodded, clumsy in the suit, and gently touched her faceplate. "I will." The more he thought about it, the more Dalton realized he intended to be *very* careful, especially as this seemed to be shaking out to be the real thing. Real Peacekeepers, with real guns.

Major Thompson interrupted. "Okay, Starkiller, enough with the tender good-byes already. Now shag your butt over to Sector Three-B and join your unit." The major paused. When he spoke again, his voice was gentler. "And good luck to you both, okay?"

"Sir!" Dalton saluted. After Thompson had turned his back, Dalton snuck in one last quick squeeze with Dara, then slapped the large square button that activated the battlesuit's augmentations and started off toward Sector 3. At first his legs pumped slowly and clumsily as the internal engines whined up to speed; then he settled into a rapid stride as the suit cycled up to full power.

"Cool," he said aloud, to himself. "I wonder—"

"Radio silence?" Major Thompson suggested from hundreds of meters behind him. Dalton punched off the comm system, and went back to checking out the suit.

During his militia unit's first practice in augmented battlesuits, Dalton had marveled at how the thing enhanced his every movement, providing him with greater speed and power despite the suit's extra weight. Now, after three days of training, Dalton was feeling experienced enough to be jaded. This particular suit wasn't anywhere near state of the art—none of the militiamen's were—but it was only about twelve years old, and definitely in better shape than some he'd seen.

Satisfied, Dalton stopped checking out the suit and settled into a steady pace as he ran down the corridors accompanied only by the sound of his own breathing and the clank of his metal-soled boots on the plazmetal flooring. *Just focus on running,* a little voice in the back of his head said. *Don't think about what's waiting at the other end.*

In Sector 4C he raced passed a knot of civilians fleeing the other way. Most of them were already in their white emergency vacuum suits, but around one corner he found a helmetless young woman sitting on the floor, shaking with silent sobs, an unsuited infant cradled in her arms. The baby wasn't moving, he noticed, and crimson blood was bubbling from the child's nose and ears.

Don't think about it. Just move. Dalton clenched his jaw tighter and picked up his speed.

Sector 3 came into view. Ahead he saw green lights flashing against the dark gray walls, like heat lightning in a July midnight sky. He slowed to a walk, drew his pistol, and psyched himself up to be ready for anything.

Anything except the blast of hot green hellfire that tore a chunk from the wall inches above his head.

"Help!" he shrieked as he dived to the floor and blindly fired a wild shot. Four answering beams lanced out in response, exploding against the wall above him and sending molten metal and plastic raining down. He rolled frantically to his right, desperately seeking cover, but there was none to be found.

Slowly, microsecond by microsecond, the first shock of panic yielded to white-hot anger. *Those goddam dirtbags are trying to kill me!*

At that point his militia training finally started to kick in, and as four blue-suited UN soldiers moved into view and raised their weapons, he seemed to hear Lloyd Thompson's voice in his mind: *Lay the front sight on the center of mass, Private. Don't fret about how many targets there are. Just concentrate on one and keep shooting till he's down. Now squeeze that trigger slow, like you're strokin' your girlfriend—* A bright red beam lanced out toward the lead Peacekeeper's head and sent him flying backwards, but Dalton felt disappointed, because he'd seen the blue flash of an energy shield around the soldier and knew the dirtsucker hadn't even been hurt. *Never mind that. Y'all are either showing off or shooting high. Forget head shots; just correct your sight picture and keep on firing.*

Prone in a battlesuit was a difficult position to shoot from. Dalton rose to one knee, but before he could squeeze off another shot, three bolts of energy slammed into his chest shield, smashing him to the floor like a swatted bug. For a few last fractions of a second his eyes were dazzled by the brilliant blue flares and spatters of madly clashing energy fields enveloping him. Then something wet and red exploded inside his head, and everything went black.

Second Battalion Forward HQ
USN *Schwarzkopf,* CVN (S) -93
28 October 2069
22:30 GMT

General J. T. "Ripper" Jackson considered himself a hard case. In thirty years of peacekeeping duty he'd seen peasants hacked to death with machetes, mass graves from the Idaho ethnic cleansing, and his own troops accidentally blown to bits by "friendly fire."

For three hours now he'd been in the *Schwarzkopf's* comm center, monitoring the action on the lunar surface without so much as a flicker of emotion, but this latest report from Delta Company made his neck hair prickle and his blood run cold. "This," he growled, thumping a ramrod-straight index finger on the comm tech sergeant's sternum, "is classified and does not leave this room. If so much as a *whisper* of this report leaks out, I will have your stripes, your ears, and any other part of you I happen to think of. Is that clear?"

The sergeant gulped nervously. "Yes, sir!"

"Good." Jackson turned to the officer who'd brought the report. "Now, Major Xiong, I trust your shuttle is fueled and standing by?"

The little navy popinjay saluted proudly. "Yes, sir!"

"Great. Then let's haul our butts down there and see if we can't sort out this . . . this—" Jackson gestured in frustration, and desperately wished for a cigar to chomp through.

"Sir?" the comm sergeant asked timidly. "If Field Marshal Leighton-Smythe calls, what do I tell him?"

Jackson scowled. "Tell him I'm, uh, checking out firsthand an unsubstantiated report of, er, rebel atrocities. Got it?"

The sergeant looked puzzled and lifted the disk carrying the Delta Company CO's report. "But, sir, this—"

"Dammit, man!" Jackson barked. "Do I have to tell you *everything?* Erase it!"

"Yes, sir!" The sergeant saluted crisply.

Jackson wheeled and, followed by Xiong, headed for the shuttle dock.

Twenty minutes later, Lieutenant Xiong dropped a battlesuited Jackson and his adjutant, Pierce, just outside the Volodya south airlock. They found a squad of Delta Company troopers waiting there to meet them. Some nameless lieutenant in blue armor stepped forward and saluted. "General Jackson, sir!"

Jackson didn't bother to return the salute. "Where the hell is Colonel Bowen?" he growled.

"Just inside the airlock, sir! We've been having a little trouble with snipers outside the dome."

"Snipers?" Jackson snorted. "Then what the blue blazes am *I* doing out here?" Suddenly aware that the one gold star on his helmet might look like a target, Jackson broke into a quick shuffling run across the regolith toward the open airlock door. The corporal barked a command, and the troopers fell in around Jackson and formed a human shield.

They made the airlock without incident. Colonel Bowen, also in battlesuit, was waiting just inside the inner door with another squad of troopers. "General Jackson," he said, offering a salute, then a handshake. "Thanks for coming down so quickly."

"Don't thank me yet," Jackson growled, ignoring Bowen's outstretched hand. "The way I see it, right now *you* are the sorry s.o.b. responsible for this four-star exercise in cluster coitus."

"Sir!" Bowen said, perhaps a bit too quickly. "It was an intelligence screwup! My men were only following orders!"

"Colonel Bowen," Jackson said, as he leaned back and sized up the man. "Have you ever witnessed a war crimes trial? That's the first thing the defendant says when he opens his defense, and it's the last thing he says before he drops through the gallows."

It was hard to tell through the gold-plated helmet visor, but Bowen seemed a bit shaken by that thought.

Jackson gave the colonel another appraising look, then glanced around the corridor. "So, Bowen, are you planning to restore internal environment anytime soon? My suit telltales say it's near vacuum in here."

"The— The—" Bowen swallowed so hard, the sound was audible through the battlesuit comm system. "The rebels have sabotaged the Central Computer. Life support is completely out. I've got engineers trying to hotwire around the damage, but—"

"Yeah," Jackson grumbled, "I know engineers. It'll take three days to do it and all the parts are on back order. Okay, then, let's have a look at the real reason why I'm here."

Bowen hesitated. "Are you sure? It's . . . pretty ghastly."

"Colonel," Jackson said, "I have been with the Peacekeepers for fully thirty years, since back when there was still such a thing as the United States Marine Corps. I have seen action in Asia, Africa, and Europe and in Central, North, and South America, including the Idaho Christian War, and I seriously doubt that anything you can show me will shock this particular tough old bird."

Bowen turned around and glanced up the corridor. "Well, okay then . . ."

Fifteen minutes later Jackson was sitting on the hard floor, struggling not to throw up inside his helmet. "Bowen!" he gasped. "For God's sake, man, what the hell happened?"

"Intelligence failure," the colonel said gently, a note of

deep pain in his voice. "We were following our orders. First Platoon was to make a dynamic entry over there." Bowen pointed at a gaping hole in the far wall. Through the hole, gray rock and naked stars were visible. "Intel said this was unoccupied warehouse space. We were very careful about that. The commando unit stealthed in, set charges, and at zero hour, blew the wall."

Jackson got his rampaging stomach under control, staggered to his feet, and stared at the heap of tiny corpses.

"The Volodyans must have been short of pressure suits," Bowen said softly. "They were using this as a staging area for civilian evacuation. As near as we can tell, there were about sixty children in here, mostly infants and toddlers." Bowen's voice cracked, and something that could have been a sob filtered through the suit's comm system.

"Explosive decompression," Jackson said, his voice barely more than a hoarse whisper. "What a hell of a way for babies to die." The general shut his eyes tight, choked down his gorge, and spent a long moment shuddering.

Bowen's voice brought him out of it. "Sir? Now do you understand why we're having so much trouble pacifying Volodya? There's only a handful of rebels left alive, but they're fighting like devils. Can you blame them?"

The long dark trip through his private hell passed. General Jackson took a deep breath, stood up ramrod straight, and became once more the iron-willed soldier of the new world order. "Burn them," he growled.

Bowen didn't understand. "Sir?"

"That's an order, Bowen! The minute you get air restored, get some plasma guns in here and incinerate everything. Not one speck of organic matter is to remain. Is that clear?"

"Yes, sir . . . I mean, no, sir. I don't—"

"This. Never. Happened." Jackson enunciated each word like a gunshot. "Got that? Find the battlesuit vid records. Grab the remote probes. Erase everything. Then burn the erased cores. If it ever leaks out that our troops did something like this, the UN won't even bother with a war crimes trial. We'll be drawn and quartered on live TV!"

Bowen staggered back from the general's shouting, then nodded.

Any further discussion was cut off by the sudden arrival of Jackson's adjutant. "Sir!" He saluted crisply. "The Central Computer is partially reactivated!" Jackson and Bowen followed the adjutant out into the corridor. He led them to the nearest Central terminal.

"The engineers are puzzled, though," the adjutant added. "All they can get is this message." He punched a few keys and pulled up a line of text on the video display: "CHERNOBYL SEQUENCE ACTIVATED."

"Chernobyl?" Jackson whispered. "Holy Mother of—"

Instantly he slapped the oversize button on his chest that brought his suit shields up to full power, then punched his comm unit into broadband command frequency. "Space Command! I need an immediate dust-off, Volodya south airlock! All units, disengage and evacuate *now!*"

He felt the awesome rumble through his boots, an instant before the ceiling boiled away and the soldiers started screaming. Then a titanic shock wave lifted him off the floor and cast him lightly into the sky, as the top half of Colonel Bowen's battlesuit cartwheeled past, trailing a pink plume of vacuum-frozen blood. Jackson's suit shields went into overload then, surrounding him in a corruscating blue envelope of exploding energies, and he lived just long enough to see the first flare of the unholy light that would melt his eyeballs and flash-cook his brain.

UN Headquarters, New York
28 October 2069
6:10 P.M. EST

New York City squatted like a vast dark and sparkling beast, basking in the afterglow of a flaming orange and purple sunset. Lord Edward Haversham stood at the railing of the rooftop heliport, trench coat collar up against the chill evening air, watching the streetlights flicker on across the cityscape below and gazing at the thin crescent moon hanging low and bone-white in the western sky.

Aguila let the elevator door hiss shut, dismissed the sunset with a glance, and joined Haversham at the edge of the roof. "They told me I'd find you up here."

Slowly, without taking his eyes off the moon, Haversham nodded. "It's all over by now, isn't it?"

Aguila glanced at his watch. "Yes, if everything went according to plan."

Haversham considered that information for half a minute or more. "Any word yet on resistance?"

Aguila fished his personal data assistant out of his jacket pocket, thumbed a few pads, and shook his head. "No, no reports of any kind. But then, you know the Peace Enforcement Command."

Haversham laughed mirthlessly and shook his head. "Oh, I most certainly do. Leighton-Smythe could teach clams to keep their gobs shut. We'll see CNN interviewing the widows before we get any solid news out of him." Haversham buried his hands in his pockets, hunched deeper in his trench coat, and went back to staring at the moon and sighing.

Aguila waited patiently.

After another half minute or so, Haversham said quietly, "Antonio?"

"Yes, Edward?"

"Are you sure you're doing the right thing?"

Aguila blinked, not quite understanding. "How do you mean? The Security Council's decision was clear. No one will question the legality of sending in the Peacekeepers."

"Hmm." Haversham frowned, sniffed, then stood silent awhile longer. Slowly the sky faded to a darker starry purple, and the fidgeting whispers matured into the beginnings of a steady cool breeze. "It's not legality that concerns me," Haversham said at last. "Even Adolf Hitler started out with legalities."

"Adolf Hitler," Aguila pointed out, "was a monster."

"Was he?" Haversham's flat statement was such a mindboggling heresy that Aguila actually gasped in surprise.

"No, don't misunderstand me," Haversham corrected quickly. "Hitler clearly *became* an unspeakable monster.

But did he have to? What if just one trusted friend had said to him in 1933, 'Adolf, this is madness. It may be legal, but it's *wrong.'*"

"Then that theoretical friend would have been the first one into the ovens," Aguila pointed out. "Nothing would have changed. The economic forces that drive history would still have been there; the twentieth century would still have unfolded exactly as it did."

Haversham looked down, pursed his lips, and ground a shoe in the gravel rooftop. "I suppose you're right. Bloody damned history." He sighed again, then looked up at Aguila and favored him with a sad smile. "A man gets to be my age, he starts to realize that soon he'll be a *part* of history." Haversham nodded over his shoulder in the general direction of the setting moon. "So what do you think your role will be? Cornwallis or Rabin?"

Aguila arched an eyebrow. "Sir?"

"Colonies are like children, Antonio; sooner or later they must be set free. Will you be remembered as the heavy hand of the old order or the statesman who helped build a new world?"

Aguila considered his answer, then spoke. "I think," he said slowly, "that you worry far too much. That"—he raised his left arm and pointed at the lunar crescent hanging fat and low in the western sky—"is a pathetic little brush-fire being staged by a bunch of noisy brats. In a day or so the Peacekeepers will have fully restored order. Within a week von Hayek and his gang of criminals will be back here"—he pointed emphatically at the rooftop of the building they stood upon—"awaiting trial for vandalizing UN property. Within a month this will all be forgotten, like those stupid *norte americano* grass-fire revolts of the 2030s!"

Haversham stole a glance at the moon, then looked at Aguila. "You really think so?"

"Absolutely." Aguila nodded confidently. "My place in history, my friend, will be as the hero who kept the food factories—"

Aguila froze, his left arm still pointed in an eloquent gesture at the moon, his eyes wide, his mouth hanging open in mid-syllable. "Madre de Dios!" he finally managed to whisper.

Haversham turned in time to catch the last dying flare of a hellish star-bright point of light on the lunar surface. Then his jaw sagged, too, and his breath came in ragged gasps.

"Mare Nubium," Aguila choked out. "That . . . must be Volodya."

"That," Haversham said with a shudder, when he found his voice again, "was without question a nuclear explosion." Slowly, as if his head were on a swivel, he turned to look at Aguila. The undersecretary was reflexively making the sign of the cross. When he realized Haversham was looking at him, Aguila quickly dropped his hands to his sides.

"Antonio old boy?" Haversham asked politely. "I've never been too good at this phase business." He nodded at the moon. "What would you say that is?"

Aguila considered the thin crescent a moment. "It is a new moon."

"Indeed." Haversham nodded and then, without another word, spun on his heel and stalked off toward the elevator.

CHAPTER 9

Port Aldrin, Lunar Sector 3B
28 October 2069
23:40 GMT

"Hey, Starkiller. Can you hear me?"

Consciousness came slinking back to Dalton like a furtive and nervous animal. He shook his head, which started the little man with the sledgehammer pounding on his cerebellum again. He opened his eyes. The world was all blurry, as if his eyes were lenses that were out of focus. Maybe cracked, too, he thought as a wave of nausea made the ceiling lights spin in crazy circles.

"Buddy, it's okay. You're gonna make it."

Wonderful, Dalton thought. *All hail the conquering hero. My first firefight and I manage to get off two whole shots before I get creamed.* He blinked again, then looked around. "I'm alive," he said. He was really surprised to discover this.

"That you are," the other voice said. It sounded pinched, mechanical. After a moment's confusion, Dalton placed it as a male voice coming through a battlesuit speaker. "We found you lying here. Thought you were toast at first, but your suit telltales said you were still alive. So we flipped you over, gave you a wake-up hypo, and I volunteered to stay here and get you back to the first-aid station. Think you can walk?"

"I . . . don't know. Maybe." Dalton tried to sit up, but another wave of nausea knocked him back down again. "Gimme a minute." The spinning corridor slowed a little. "What happened?"

The owner of the other voice stepped into view. *White suit,* Dalton noted with relief. *Good guy.*

The soldier spread his hands; Dalton guessed he was grinning inside his helmet. "We hit 'em from behind. Came out of that grate over there; there's a tunnel behind it, see? We must have arrived just after they whacked you, because they were still arguing about whether to take you prisoner or melt your head."

Dalton shuddered. "I lucked out, huh?"

"You sure did. It was ballsy, man, *real* ballsy, trying to take on four Bluesuits by yourself. But you gotta remember: you aren't Icehawk anymore. This is the real world, and you only get one death in this game. No replays."

Dalton managed to work himself up to a sitting position, and he squinted suspiciously at his distorted reflection in the other man's helmet visor. "Do I know you?"

"Oh. Sorry." The soldier punched a few buttons on his chest unit, then unsealed a latch and tilted back his helmet. "Jeff Mahoney, remember? From the militia meeting?" His voice sounded completely different, much younger, now that it wasn't being filtered through the comm unit. The freckle-faced kid grinned and offered Dalton a white-gloved hand. Gingerly, Dalton took it.

"I didn't see you after the first meeting," Dalton said. "Thought you quit."

Young Mahoney gave Dalton's hand a quick shake, then shook his own head, and grinned again. "Nah. I decided to join the Regulars instead. I got to tell you, it is *so* cool; this uniform is like a chick magnet." His smile faded. "The LDF slaps that gaming crap out of you pretty fast, though. First thing they teach you is that the Moon needs living soldiers, not dead heroes. If I'd tried a stunt like yours and lived to tell about it, well . . ."

Dalton felt ready to try standing up. With young Mahoney's help, he staggered to his feet. "Stunt? What do you mean?"

Mahoney grinned again, then fished in his belt pouch and produced Dalton's pistol. "Setting your piece on low, to stretch your power cell? You were doing head shots again, weren't you?"

Dalton accepted the pistol from Mahoney and checked the power-level indicator. Sure enough, the thing was set on low. Training power level. He must have reset it unconsciously out of sheer stupid habit when he loaded it.

Dalton managed a sickly smile. "Bad form, huh?"

Mahoney laughed. "No, *great* form! Ten for ten on style, man! But, Icehawk, that sort of stuff'll get you killed!" He leaned back and gave Dalton an appraising look. "You ready to try walking?"

Dalton took a hesitant step; his legs seemed to be working. "Yeah. Let's get the hell out of here."

With young Mahoney's help, Dalton made it back to the shield generator room that was temporarily serving as a first-aid station. Svetlana Kosov was there, along with three or four other medicos, doing what she could to patch up the wounded. As Dalton and Mahoney staggered in, she looked up from treating a flash burn and seemed genuinely pleased to see them.

"Dalton! I heard you bought it!"

"Me too. Jeff here"—he nodded at Mahoney—"er, Private Mahoney, saved my neck. Literally." He smiled, grabbed the kid by the arm, and gave him a shake. "Buddy, when this is all over I owe you a beer."

Mahoney's face clouded over. "I'm only seventeen," he said.

Svetlana chimed in. "Doesn't matter. New rule: if you're old enough to join the LDF, you're old enough to drink beer." That seemed to cheer Mahoney up considerably. Kosov turned to her patient, a dark-skinned woman in an engineer's jumpsuit, and handed her a tube of something. "Second degree, but not deep," Kosov said to the engineer. "It'll hurt like the dickens for a few days, then peel and get better. When the pain gets too bad, smear some of this on it." The engineer took the tube, hopped off the table, and hobbled out of the room.

"Next," Kosov said. She pointed at Dalton. Mahoney helped Dalton over to the examining table, then helped Kosov remove the suit chestplate. "What happened?" Kosov asked Mahoney.

"I—" Dalton started.

"Shield overload," Mahoney answered. "Icehawk here tried to take on four Peacekeepers all by himself. Set 'em up nicely for the kill by my squad, but almost got himself greased in the process."

Svetlana tsk-tsked. "So they blew his shields and he got caught in the feedback. Okay, I'm seeing some neural scrambling and trivial first-degree burns here." She poked a spot on Dalton's back.

He jumped. "Ow!"

"But nothing serious," Kosov continued. "Good. Normally I'd prescribe painkillers, lots of rest, and some post-trauma counseling. But we're low on painkillers and fresh out of psychiatrists, so take two of these." She fished a plastic vial out of her lab coat pocket and dumped some small yellow pills into Dalton's palm.

Dalton eyed the pills. "What are they?"

"Antidepressants. I live on 'em. Take two now and you'll buzz around the ceiling for half an hour. And then, young Jedi, you will sleep."

Dalton considered the pills again, then palmed them. "Antidepressants? Why are *you* taking them?"

Kosov looked at Dalton, her icy blue eyes suddenly endless and unfathomable, then looked at Mahoney. "You didn't tell him?" Mahoney shook his head slightly.

"Tell me what?" Dalton demanded.

"This was just a diversionary tactic," Svetlana said. "The

real attack was out west. Imbrium. Rheinhold." Tears started to well up in those blue eyes. "And Volodya. Volodya is gone."

Dalton didn't understand. "Volodya's been captured?"

"No," Mahoney interjected softly, "it's gone. Blown away. The UN dropped a whole battalion there, we think, and there was some kind of massacre. And then someone blew the main reactor."

"Mama," Kosov whispered softly. "Jaja. Alexei." She sagged against the examining table and suddenly looked terribly lost and alone. "Dmitri." A few tears fell in fat, salty drops.

For a moment Dalton and young Mahoney stared at each other, both wanting to help Kosov, but having no idea how.

"Private Mahoney!" a new voice boomed out in an acid-etched Cockney accent. Mahoney jumped to attention and spun to face the door. The voice boomed again. "If you're done flirting with the birds and rips, lad, we've a bleedin' *war* going on!"

Dalton rolled over painfully and caught a glimpse of the new speaker: a short, angry-looking man with pale white skin, a shock of yellow hair, and a full set of sergeant's stripes. He was standing just outside the door. Dalton wasted a moment trying to remember whether militiamen were supposed to salute LDF sergeants, then thought, *Screw it.*

Mahoney was still frozen like a deer in headlights.

The sergeant spared a glance at Kosov and sniffed. "Nice bum. Now, private," he snapped at Mahoney, "your unit is presently in Sector Two-C, and you 'ave exactly five minutes to 'aul your worthless carcass over there before I—"

"On my way, Sergeant Godfrey!" Mahoney yelped.

"Too right!" The sergeant sniffed again, then vanished down the corridor. Dalton set up and flopped off the examining table. Young Mahoney seemed to start breathing again. Dalton went to Kosov first, but she waved him away and went back to crying, so he turned to Jeff.

"So, Mahoney," Dalton asked, "who's Sergeant Psycho?"

Mahoney sucked in his breath sharply and blanched dead-white. "Don't ever call him that," he whispered urgently. "He'll rip your lungs out." Mahoney edged up to the doorway, stole a peek down the corridor, then relaxed slightly.

Mahoney turned to Dalton. "That was Britt Godfrey, one of the LDF's finest. The first sergeant from hell. Meanest little s.o.b. you'll ever meet, and the toughest, too. Word is he immigrated up here to dodge a multiple murder rap."

Dalton collected the pieces of his uniform, tried but failed to make eye contact one more time with Kosov, then followed Mahoney out into the corridor. "And he's on *our* side?"

Mahoney shrugged. "Hey, beggars can't be choosers, y'know? Seriously, you stay on the sergeant's good side and he'll give you the shirt off his back. Great sense of humor, too." Mahoney took another nervous glance down the corridor. "But some of his best friends got killed today, and that'd piss anyone off."

Mahoney pointed back the other way. "Look, when Britt said I had five minutes to get over to Sector Two-C, he meant it. So I've gotta run now, but there's a militia crash room up that way, to the left. Can't miss it."

Dalton nodded. "Look, I don't know how to say this—"

Mahoney shrugged. "Then don't. See you later, Icehawk." He turned, punched his suit up to power, and took off running.

Dalton watched him disappear down the corridor, then turned and trudged in the direction Mahoney had indicated.

"I really hope so, Stormrider."

Dalton was completely unprepared for the round of cheers that greeted him when he shuffled into the militia room. "Dalt, man, we heard you bought it!" Terrell Davis lunged forward and grabbed Dalton in a big bear hug. There was an awkward moment or two while Dalton tried to sort out whether Davis was his boss, his friend, or his commanding officer; then the shakes and shudders hit, and Dalton felt himself starting to come unglued and fall apart.

"'S okay, man," Davis said softly. "'S okay." Davis gently steered him down to a battered brown sofa pushed against the far wall. The other militia members came swarming in to touch him gently and offer kind words: the black-haired guy, who he now knew was Peter Mercer, a research scientist; the short, tight-knit middle-aged redhead, Ginny Anson; the college kid from Kepler, Katsuhiro; the overweight ex-Israeli, Joel. Bob Connors, Elke Schwartz, Kandaya Singh, Krissi Donatelli . . .

Someone pushed a cup of hot chicken soup into Dalton's hands, and he tried a sip. Something seemed to be wrong with his eyes. They were all blurry and wet.

"It's okay," Davis said again. "It's all right to freak out when it's over, Dalt. Hell, when I got here, first thing I wanted was a clean pair of boxer shorts, you know?" Someone in the back of the group sniggered; the laugh had a nervous and hysterical edge to it. "It's not funny!" Davis protested. "It's really not funny!" Despite Davis's protests, more militia members joined in the snickering, and within moments the whole group was laughing together, eyes and noses running freely.

The laughing seemed to break something loose inside of Dalton. He howled till his ribs hurt, then wiped his face on his sleeve, got down a couple large gulps of the soup, and started to feel alive again. A smile found its way onto his face, and he looked around the room at his comrades, his friends, his brothers in arms.

Svetlana Kosov was wrong. Dalton didn't need pills; he needed this.

Five minutes later he was snoring like a chain saw.

Undisclosed Location, Luna
29 October 2069
01:30 GMT

For Immediate Release:

My fellow citizens,

Yesterday at 7:00 P.M. Lunar Time the combined forces of the United Nations Peace Enforcement Command launched a surprise attack on the Free State domes of Port Aldrin, Von Braun, Imbrium, Rheinhold, and Volodya. Thanks to the brilliant leadership of General Consensus and the skill and bravery of our heroic self-defense forces we were able to repel this invasion, with only slight casualties to our side and grave losses to the jackbooted thugs of oppression, but the enemy has succeeded in taking temporary control of the Free State colony at Von Braun.

Sadly, the news from Volodya is worse. Following an unprovoked massacre of innocent noncombatants, and overwhelmed by the sheer weight of numbers thrown against them, the brave defenders of Volodya in a spectacular final gesture of defiance chose to detonate the nuclear core of their dome just as the UN troops began their final assault. Our best intelligence indicates the entire UN Second Battalion was annihilated in the blast. This, combined with enemy casualties in other locations, means that more than 480 enemy soldiers have been killed by our valiant defense forces, while our own losses have been comparatively light.

Therefore, let us not dwell on our losses, but rather let our hearts swell with pride. We have bloodied the enemy's nose, and he now knows that we will fight to the death to defend our homes. Yes, the UN armies will return, stronger next time and backed by all the mighty forces of Earth. Yes, they have occupied one of our cities and made of our people prisoners and refugees. Yes, our struggle is not yet over.

But we can look to the past and know that we are not alone! The eighteenth-century American revolutionaries—colonists like us—fought and defeated the most powerful empire of their day. Now we face the combined might of an entire planet, but we will be victorious because our cause is just. We will fight on—for freedom and the Free State. Remember Volodya!

May God bless you all and grant you luck in the days ahead.

> Pieter von Hayek
> First Councillor, the Free State Selena

Patrick Adams looked up expectantly. "Well?"

Pieter von Hayek finished reading the rough draft and frowned. "I don't know. 'Jackbooted thugs of oppression'? Isn't that a little . . . well, extreme?"

"But they do wear jackboots."

"Find another phrase. And that stuff about massacres and refugees? We want our people to be resolute, not hiding under their beds and wetting their pants."

"Okay, I'll soft-pedal it. Anything else?"

Von Hayek scanned the text. "Yes. 'Our best intelligence.' That implies we've also got second-best intelligence and maybe even really rotten intelligence. Just say 'our intelligence.'"

"Gotcha. Any more?"

Von Hayek studied something in the text, then leaned back and stroked his chin thoughtfully. "The ending needs work. This is a press release, not a sermon. Some of our people interpret the First Right to mean freedom *from* religion. Try to make it a bit less spiritual and more secular, if you can."

"Right." Adams nodded. "But, as usual, try to do so without pissing off the Coalition."

"Exactly." Von Hayek nodded, then turned to the next item on his agenda. "Now tell me: what the hell really happened at Volodya? The Volodyans were supposed to blow up the cargo launcher, not the whole damn city."

Adams shook his head and frowned deeply. "We don't know. Maybe we never will. I had five of my best people in there; two of them were friends. There was some kind of massacre, then a hellacious fight. The regulars got wiped out, and the militia got their asses kicked back to the core. Last thing I got was a fragmentary message about Masada, whatever that means. Then"—he made a little explosion gesture with his hands—*"kaboom!"*

Von Hayek nodded. "I understand. Any immediate reaction out of Copernicus or Eddington?"

"No. And now those two are occupied and under martial law, so don't expect anything in the future."

Von Hayek nodded again. "Farside?"

Adams shrugged. "Gillen claims they knew about it before she did. Something seismic. But it didn't disturb them."

"Very well." Von Hayek stole another glance at his agenda. "What about Von Braun and Rheinhold?"

"Von Braun surrendered with only token resistance. Montclair somehow managed to get himself captured—surprise, surprise. At Rheinhold, the UN skipped the habitat domes and went straight for the radioscope. They got it, too."

Von Hayek pursed his lips. "So much for our hope of setting up a direct radio channel to Earth. In retrospect, I never should have trusted Montclair. Oh, well, no use crying over leaked air." He stole a glance at his agenda. "You say the team that hit Aldrin almost made it to my office?"

"That seems to have been their objective. There were feints and diversions all over, but the team members who blew the airlock and made a laserline for your office weren't regular Peacekeepers. They were Special Ops of some kind—Americans, judging by their dental work. We're guessing they were 82nd Airborne, Delta Company. Your son, Josef, finally bagged the last one about a hundred meters short of target. And, boy, is he proud of himself."

"Any damage to the government offices?"

"Lots. We can have it cleaned up by morning, though. You want me to include something in the press release about how you're in a place of safety and in no danger?"

"No!" Von Hayek shook his head vigorously. "Absolutely not! The people must believe we're sharing their risks. In fact, stop the cleanup now, and get RealNews One in there. I want to wave the bloody shirt for all it's worth."

"Right." Adams fished his personal comm pad out of his pocket and tapped in a note to himself. "Anything else?"

Von Hayek glanced down. "No, that's everything on my agenda. What about yours?"

Adams checked his pad. "Just two items. One is that a couple of the evac shuttles didn't make it. We've located some wreckage in Imbrium, but we're still trying to determine whether they were shot down or just collided."

"Okay, keep me posted on that. What's the other?"

Adams looked down at his comm pad, licked his lips nervously, then looked up. "Governor, are you sure this isn't the time to move against Lacus Mortis? That old arsenal is just waiting for us, and we could certainly use the gunships."

Von Hayek shook his head. "No. A raid like that would be too provocative. Right now the UN is sitting there licking its wounds, realizing it's gotten into a real fight, and wondering if it has the belly to go through with this. General Consensus says it doesn't: the UN always loses its courage when the boys in blue start to die, and right about now the delegates should be looking for an excuse to break this off and go back to diplomacy. We need to give them that excuse. The general's analysis is that if we sit tight, they'll back off, rattle their sabers a bit, threaten us with sanctions, and then quietly suggest peace negotiations. But if we do anything to make them lose face in the media, they'll be forced to attack again just to maintain their credibility."

Adams took a deep breath and blew out a sigh. "So we sit on our hands and wait." He looked up at von Hayek. "Are you sure that they know this is the plan?"

Militia Crash Room, Port Aldrin
29 October 2069
04:30 GMT

The Red Cross volunteer gently shook Dalton awake. "Mr. Starkiller? Er, Dalton Starkiller?"

Dalton brushed her hand away. "Not now, honey," he mumbled. "I'm asleep."

"Mr. Starkiller, sir? I'm afraid I've got some bad news."

Dalton managed to open one eye and look at her. "Who are you? Can it wait till morning?"

"Jodi Potteiger, Red Cross. I've had some trouble tracking you down. You weren't in the domestic partners registry."

"So?" Then the idea started to seep through, and Dalton's other eye popped open. "Dara?"

"There's been an accident. Well, not an accident, I guess. Her shuttle was shot down near Imbrium." Jodi bit her lower lip, then blurted it out. "There were no survivors." The young woman reached out, gently touched his arm, then stood up. "I'm sorry."

Dalton's ears heard, but his mind refused to accept the words. *No. There's been a mistake. In the morning I'll wake up in my own bed, and Dara will be right there beside me.*

But morning, when it finally came, didn't change a thing.

UN Headquarters, New York
29 October 2069
07:30 EST

The limo pulled up to the curb and two plainclothes SAS men bailed out, followed by Antonio Aguila.

The network reporters, circling like a school of feeding

sharks, caught the scent of fresh blood and swarmed forward to form a gauntlet of cameras and microphones all the way up the granite steps. Aguila flipped the collar of his camel's hair coat up, as much to hide his face as to ward off the chill October wind, and plunged in.

"Señor Aguila! Has the Committee on Lunar Development issued an official statement regarding last night's explosion?"

"No comment."

"Señor Aguila! Is it true that Volodya Colony's main reactor was the same design as the infamous Chernobyl Number Four?"

"No comment."

"Señor Aguila! What of the claims that the explosion was actually caused by a nuclear weapon?"

The undersecretary stopped dead and turned around. "Off the record?" The nearest reporters nodded innocently. "Speaking strictly off the record, I can tell you that it was *not* a nuclear weapon. The Volodyan main reactor was built twenty years ago by Ukrainian engineers who cut way too many corners. We've been telling them for years that the reactor was unsafe and they needed to shut it down. Now it looks as if we've had a serious leakage up there." Aguila turned his back on the journalists and made to leave.

A GNN reporter pushed in front of him. "Leakage? Professor Paul Cornell says that was a twenty-kiloton blast!"

Aguila stopped again and this time turned around with icy slowness, deliberately showing his back to the GNN reporter. "May I remind everyone that Professor Cornell also says we are in the midst of a dangerous global warming?" He flashed a smile, pulled his hand out of his pocket, and pointed at an imaginary spot floating through the air. "Hey, look! It's snowing!" The reporters on the steps tittered.

Aguila turned back to the woman from GNN. "It was leakage. Our sources say it was a cloud of hot radioactive gas expanding rapidly in the vacuum and one-sixth G. Professor Cornell should stick to lecturing children."

The woman from GNN looked as if she didn't buy that, but she didn't get a chance to say anything more before a bodyguard nudged her out of the way. Aguila started to move again.

The reporters surged forward. "Señor Aguila!"

He lifted his head and shouted, "No comment!"

The heavy brass doors clanged shut behind him with ponderous finality.

FIRST STRIKE: AFTERMATH

Following the stunning defeat of General Jackson and the All-Terran Antiterrorism Force Second Battalion at Volodya, the Security Council meeting on 29 October was nasty, brutish, and short.

General Jackson was summarily relieved of command — posthumously, as it turned out — and General Marcia Daniels was moved up to take his place. Field Marshal Leighton-Smythe continued to argue that the basic ATFOR strategy was sound and that the downing of two civilian transports, which the USN Tigershark's battle computers had accidentally identified as combat craft, was justified.

In the end, however, the Security Council voted to adopt a modified version of the second Russian plan. This new plan, devised by General Fyodr Buchovsky, could best be described as conservative. For the next few weeks ATFOR would concentrate on ferrying troops and materials to Luna and on reinforcing existing positions, particularly the garrisons at Lacus Mortis and Sinus Roris.

It is thought the Security Council secretly believed this slow buildup of overwhelming force would eventually bring the lunar revolutionaries to their senses — and to the negotiating table — preferably without any more nuclear explosions.

Again the elderly Lord Haversham entered the picture, to argue that the revolutionaries were no doubt as horrified by the events at Volodya as were the United Nations ruling councils and that lifting the electronic blockade and restoring free communications between Earth and Moon would be a good first step toward restoring peaceful relations. He succeeded in convincing the Security Council that the Volodya blast was clearly a kamakazi-like act of defense, but his proposal to open peace negotiations was argued down, for reasons that were not immediately clear, by Shi Cheng Wu of the Committee on World Peace and Antonio Aguila of Haversham's own Committee on Lunar Development. In the end, the Security Council voted 12–2, with North Korea abstaining, to implement the Russian plan.

Meanwhile, on Luna, the LDF and the Council of Governors quickly realized that the war was not going to be settled in one bold stroke, and so they began planning strategy for the long haul. In the moves of Pieter von Hayek one can see the hand of the master chess player at work, plotting action twenty moves out and relishing the prospect of a protracted but bloodless battle of maneuver.

Sadly, however, while Governor von Hayek was once a chess master, General Marcia Daniels was once the captain of the West Point fencing team. In her moves one can see the actions of the master swordswoman: while the Russian and American navies continued to ferry troops and supplies up from Earth, she ordered a series of small guerrilla raids to assess the LDF's readiness, probe the lunar defenses, and train the disparate United Nations forces in the ticklish business of working together. Sometimes these probes yielded unexpected bonuses as well. Consider, for example, the raid on Korolev. . . .

— Chaim Noguchi, *A History of the Lunar Revolution*

CHAPTER 10

Aboard Assault Shuttle LST(N)-14
7 November 2069
06:00 GMT

"No, you're wrong!" Faroukh Ibn-Yusef exclaimed to Walid ibn Walid. "The Prophet prohibited images of people because we are made in the image of Allah, who is infinite. Images can be reduced to binary, to numbers, thus placing a finite limitation on the infinite, which is blasphemy!"

"That's ridiculous, Faroukh. The very concept of digital information didn't exist until a hundred years ago. You're saying the Prophet foresaw the development of computers? Pfah!"

A third man, like the others wearing a blue UN battlesuit that concealed all but his head, spat onto the black plaz deck. "The Prophet prohibited nothing. He communicated the vision that was sent to him through the archangel, that is all. The law is of Allah!"

Faroukh smiled. "Hamal is right, Walid. Only in modern times are we able to understand the wisdom behind that particular law. But would you dare to argue that Allah did not understand the truth of binary, even in the Prophet's early days in the desert? And is not the nature of man's soul itself binary, forced to choose between good and evil?"

Captain Eileen "Devil Bunny" Mahoney, deciding that enough was enough, butted in. "Stow it, Sergeant." She shook her head in exasperation. Five minutes to insertion in a hot LZ, and her boys were debating the nature of God. Again.

Bunny was pissed. In her initial briefing on Operation Restore Justice, she'd been relieved to learn that she'd been assigned as cadre officer to a Palestinian unit. At least the Palestians could fight, she'd thought at the time, remembering the Intra-Arab War of the 2050s, and they never tried to eat the enemy dead, as the New Guineans sometimes did.

That was before she'd actually met her troops and discovered that she was stuck with a bunch of would-be Sufis. *And the ones who aren't mystics* want *to die in battle. That's an express ticket to paradise.*

Uh-oh. Faroukh was staring at her for daring to interrupt again. She tried to shrug it off. "Well, binary or ASCII, Faroukh, right now I'm sure Allah wants you to make sure your weapon is charged up and set on full." She tried a smile.

Oops. Wrong move. Faroukh turned to Walid, and the two of them began speaking heatedly in Arabic, their sparsely bearded chins working with great vigor, their dark eyes darting narrow glances toward her.

Enough of this, Bunny decided. *If I can't get them to like me, then they damn well better* respect *me.* She bounced to her feet. "Speak English, troop!"

Walid looked at her with casual disdain. "Ah, the woman of scarlet has made a sound."

Enough! It was bad enough that they had to argue incessantly over the Koran. It was bad enough that they'd spent the last five days arguing over whether the current sharif of Iran was in fact the seventh incarnation of the second Imam. But she'd be damned if she let Walid call her a hooker again!

Bunny charged forward, simultaneously slapping the oversize button that took her battlesuit up to full power and slamming her helmet down over her head. Before Walid could react, she'd grabbed him by the gap between his breastplate and abdominal webbing and lifted him high over her head. Walid kicked once, then relaxed, quickly realizing that even a large and angry man could not overwhelm a woman in a powered battlesuit.

"Get this, Private," Bunny spat out. "My name is Captain Mahoney. You will call me 'Captain' or 'sir.' If I hear you refer to me by any other name, or if I hear you imply even one more time that I am a woman of ill repute, I will rip your genitals off with my bare hands. Is that clear?"

Walid nodded slightly. "Yes."

"Yes what?"

"Yes, sir, Captain Mahoney, sir."

"Very good." For a moment Bunny considered dropping him, then decided against it. It was one thing to instill some healthy fear in the man, quite another to humiliate him, especially as he might soon be standing behind her, holding a loaded weapon.

Bunny gently lowered Walid to the deck of the shuttle. "As you can see," she said through the suit comm system, "my face is now properly covered, so I won't be tempting you to sin for at least the next six hours. Will this do?"

Walid nodded more emphatically. "Yes, sir."

She turned to face the other eleven men in her platoon. Two of them, Masrur and Hasan, had powered up and risen to their feet, but the rest remained seated and seemed amused. She was glad to note that Hamal, the quiet one, was nodding, apparently well pleased that her face was now covered. Some of the more fanatical men regarded Hamal as an Imam-in-training, and she hoped that if she could earn his approval, the others would follow.

"Look, I'm not trying to seduce any of you, believe me," she assured them. "And I'm not trying to lead you to Gehenna—just the opposite. Hamal, I don't care what you say, this is not jihad, and nobody's going straight to paradise. Asrad, don't touch those grenades unless I tell you to! This is just a recon mission; no suicide bombings this time.

"Men, you don't have to like me. But if you want to survive this mission you're going to have to take orders from me. The Loonies are going to be ready for us this time, and they're not going to give up easily."

"Hmph!" Walid snorted behind her. She spun around, ready to deck him, but there was no challenge in his eyes, and he raised both hands peacefully, even as he lifted his eyebrows at the quickness of her response. "You really think they'll be able to resist us?" he asked.

It was an honest question, and she saw him hide a smile as her upraised hand dropped to her side.

"Second Battalion thought their mission would be easy, and look what it got them. The Loonies know how to move in low-G if the dome's gravity goes down. We don't. There's no telling what kind of surprises they might have ready."

"But they are not fighters or soldiers," Walid argued.

Faroukh nodded, for once agreeing with Walid. "They are infidels and scientists, not warriors of Allah." A number of the others agreed noisily, until a soft voice silenced them.

"What is a weapon?" Hamal said. "Many things are weapons. It is true that these infidels are not warriors like us. So who knows what horrors they may have created with their stinking Iblis-spawned technology. We must be strong in the faith and pray for victory."

Faroukh sighed and nodded. *"Inshallah."*

Bunny shook her head, desperately hoping Hamal wasn't going to declare it time for daily prayers, as the transport rocked gently and the landing warnings began to sound.

"Thirty seconds!" the pilot's voice crackled through the comm system. "LZ is hot!"

Bunny darted to her seat and reached for the buckle above her shoulder. "Stations, men! Power up and strap in!" She nodded with relief as she saw the men follow her orders. On the far side of the pod, she saw Walid feeling about his hip. She surreptitiously checked her own holster, then relaxed as she felt the familiar grip of the laser pistol.

"Blue Team?" she said.

Masrur's voice crackled in her ear. "Check."

"Green Team?"

Hasan chimed in. "Check."

"Red Team check," she called out, verifying it herself. "This is it, men. You know the drill. When we touch down and the hatch pops, exit Red-Green-Blue. And if you see anyone who isn't wearing UN blue, terminate without prejudice."

"What does that mean?" Asrad asked.

"Kill them," she clarified.

"Oh."

Bunny paused for a moment, then decided to go for it. "Allahu Akhbar!"

Wincing as the overamplified cheers sounded in her helmet, Bunny grinned despite herself. Maybe leading a bunch of hyped-up Palestinians into battle on the Moon wasn't exactly the career path her mother would have chosen for her in Kansas, but what the heck? Sometimes you just had to go your own way.

Less than two hours later Bunny and the three surviving members of Red Team were circling an octagonal structure that stood in the center of a large chamber on the east side of the Korolev dome.

She held up a hand as she stopped, then gestured to Asrad indicating that he should cover them from the wide stairs to the north. He saluted quickly and obeyed, backing away from them with his pistol carefully leveled towards the far corner of the octagon.

Their initial encounter with the LDF had cost Bunny most of Green Team as well as Red Three, but the Palestinians were learning to respect the rebels' ability to hit them when they weren't expecting it. Bunny suspected that her platoon's communications were compromised—hence the tight radio silence—and although she didn't know how the rebels were intercepting their transmissions, or even if it was possible for them to, she was determined to look into the matter. But that would have to wait until later; in the meantime there were more pressing matters.

A section of the octagon was concave, exposing a small ledge, and Nasrullah pointed his pistol at it and drew Bunny's attention to it. She waved him forward, and he leaped easily onto the ledge and pressed a small button on the octagon wall as the others covered him.

The wall turned into a vertical door that split in half to reveal a weapons cache containing ACRs, the automated combat lasers that were standard equipment for UN shock troops. ACRs were more powerful than the little laser pistols Bunny and her platoon carried, but they drained their power cells faster, too.

Nasrullah picked up an ACR and offered it to Bunny, but she pointed the palm of her hand at the floor and gestured sideways, then took the rifle. Holstering her pistol, she popped out the ACR's power cell, clipped it to her belt, and tossed the rifle back into the storage room as she leaped off the ledge, away from the octagon.

The Palestinian spread his hands, and Bunny knew he was frowning inside his helmet, but she repeated her negative gesture until he raised a hand in acquiescence. Although the thought of using the heavier weapons was tantalizing, Bunny knew there had to be a reason why the rebels weren't using them. Maybe they'd been booby-trapped. And even if they weren't, their discharge signature was notably different from that of the laser pistol. All the other Peacekeeper units involved in this mission were armed with the little H&K laser pistols; using a rebel ACR might well bring a barrage of so-called friendly fire down upon her unit.

Still, the discovery of the cache disturbed her for more than one reason. Where were the Loonies getting their heavy weapons? she wondered. And why weren't they using them? All the rebels her squad had encountered so far were armed with H&K pistols. This weapons cache didn't make sense, and Bunny didn't like things that didn't make sense.

A synthetic voice crackled in her ear as the battle computer broke radio silence and disturbed her thoughts. "Red

Team, Sector Three alert! Blue Team from Fourth Platoon reports contact with multiple hostile units."

She was grateful for the warning, as a moment later a green laser bolt exploded bare meters in front of her. She sprinted around the octagon and threw herself flat on the floor, then fired a quick burst at the first white-clad Loonie she saw. There were several of them and they were in a bad position, caught in a giant chamber between her Reds and the Blue Team from Fourth Platoon.

The Blue Team had entered from the north and had taken a position one level above the ground floor, behind two massive gray columns. From there they were content to hold their ground, keeping the exposed Loonies pinned without much risk to themselves.

Cowards, Bunny thought as a bolt exploded against her shields and she staggered. The Blue Team was safely hidden away, but she and her Reds were caught at the open entrance to the giant chamber, where there was no protection to be found. Ali Sayed had fallen in the first exchange, leaving only Bunny and Nasrullah to hold their position and keep the rebels trapped in the room. Unfortunately, they had little choice except to keep moving and shooting, and hope that the rebels' shields gave out first.

She fired two more quick bursts and grinned with satisfaction as a blue glow exploded around a Loonie, knocking him backwards a good six feet. As he slammed against a wall, a Blue Team trooper stepped out from behind his pillar and fired three shots into the man's chest. The rebel slumped to the floor as his shields were overloaded by the laser, killing him instantly.

Die, sucker, Bunny thought as she rolled to her left and fired another burst. It missed, and she heard a crash as a blue-clad figure fell heavily to the floor beside her.

It was Nasrullah, and he wasn't moving. She swore and triggered the command frequency.

"Asrad, forget that door and get over here now! Masrur, get your boys and whatever's left of Green to East Sector Three as fast as you can. We got two rebel teams trapped, but I got three down, and it looks like the Loonies trying to break west."

"Roger, Red Leader."

She fired another double burst and another white figure fell to the floor. *Masrur, where are you?* It wasn't long, but the strike team leader's response seemed to take hours.

"I'll be over as soon as I can," Masrur shouted. "We've got our hands full at the moment!" His voice clicked out.

Oh, shit, Bunny thought, and then she didn't have time to think any more as the five remaining Loonies charged towards her position, lasers blazing. Two members of the concealed Blue Team slipped out again from behind their pillars and concentrated fire on the rearmost rebel, who dropped to the floor in a massive blue-green energy discharge. Bunny fired a double burst at the visor of the rebel in front, then snarled with satisfaction as he clapped both hands to his head and fell.

She rolled behind Nasrullah's body, narrowly avoiding the beams that bit at the spot she'd just vacated. The three remaining rebels were only ten feet in front of her now, and she knew she'd be lucky if she managed to take even one of them down.

Where the hell is Asrad? she wondered, even as she fired a long burst that spun one of the rebels around and into a wall. He started to push off from the wall, but Asrad, coming at a run from around the corner, fired two quick shots, and the rebel collapsed, shields flaring. The other rebels returned fire, and Asrad dived behind a pile of wreckage, barely avoiding the laser beams that struck just above his head.

Everything seemed to move in slow motion as she frantically tried to swing the pistol across her body and bring it to bear on the last two rebels. But she could see she was going to be too late as they charged toward her, each with a laser leveled at her midsection.

Mahoney screamed as the green bolts smashed into her shields, sending her flying into a corner of the octagon behind her. Too stunned by the impact to even try to roll sideways and reach for the weapon she'd dropped, she stared dully at the ceiling and waited for the next burst to finish her off.

But it never came. The two men in white sprinted past her and past the octagonal weapons cache, ignoring both ATFOR troopers as they ran toward a blue door to the west. Asrad squeezed off a few wild shots at their disappearing back, but they hit well wide of the mark.

Bunny almost sobbed with relief, then gathered herself together enough to call out to Masrur. "Two of them got past us, and I think they're going for the airlock in West Sector Three."

"Roger, Red Leader."

There was a long moment of silence, when all Bunny heard was the sound of her breathing, then she heard a deep voice with an American accent.

"Ix-nay those Loonies you missed, honey bunny. They're deader'n a doornail. South Sector's clear too, just in case you were curious. Hang tight and we'll be there in a second."

Bunny rolled her eyes as she reached for the pistol she'd dropped. *Colonel Houston,* she thought. *Of all the bastards to get bailed out by.*

She switched to Houston's direct frequency. "Don't worry about it, Colonel. Fourth Platoon Blue Team is here with us."

"Roger. We'll go west, then, and help mop up. Tell Blue Leader to meet us there."

"Yes, sir." Bunny lay back and closed her eyes. Her ribs hurt.

Asrad spoke up. "Are you okay, Captain?" She opened her eyes. He was standing over her, extending a hand.

"I'm fine. Soon as I get my shields juiced, I'll be fine." But she didn't feel fine as she stood up and looked around the destruction in the chamber. Nasrullah and Ali Sayed lay dead, not far from the white-armored bodies of the two Loonies she and Asrad had killed. Farther down the hall, Fourth Platoon was stripping dead rebels of their pistols and power packs.

Oh no! She could have kicked herself, as the thought that her Blue Team was still engaged on the west side of the dome made its way through her foggy brain. "Masrur, report. We've got things under control here. Do you need help?"

To her endless relief, Masrur answered immediately. "Negative, Captain. We're still trying to dig a few last rebels out of their hole. There's four of them holed up behind some heavy machinery."

"Take your time, then, Masrur. I don't want any more casualties. No direct assault."

"Roger. After we got split up during the ambush, we hooked up with the First. They've got a few grenades, but we're going to see if we can get those rebels to surrender before we have to use them."

Great, Bunny thought. *First I lose half my men, then somebody else has to save the other half. Just perfect.*

She switched to a private frequency and asked the question she was dreading. "How many did you lose, Masrur."

"None of mine. But Rasul was the only Green to make it. He's with us."

"Hasan didn't make it?"

"He went down first, I think. Never had a chance. Red lose anyone?"

"Yunis in the ambush, Nasrullah and Ali Sayed later. Asrad is with me."

"Inshallah," Masrur replied philosophically. He offered no criticism, and his tone was as polite as ever.

But Bunny had no doubt that the respect she'd won with such difficulty on the transport was gone. Combat was the only test that mattered, and it was a test she'd failed badly. Out of her twelve men, she'd managed to lose six. And even looking back on what had happened, she still couldn't figure out what had gone wrong or where she'd screwed up.

War in general left little room for mistakes, but lunar combat left none. In the Moon's hostile environment, a soldier wasn't likely to get wounded, since a punctured battlesuit meant rapid death. And though energy shields were designed to effectively protect against projectile weapons, lasers and other energy weapons quickly burned them away to nothing.

It was Hasan's death that bothered her the most. Although she would miss Faroukh's wit and ready laugh, the joker's razor-edged tongue had also caused many disruptions. But Hasan, the reflective NCO of Green Team, had always been a reliable and steady element in Squad Two. Now he was dead, and with him his solid support. At least it had been quick.

Where did the Loonies get the lasers? Bunny wondered. *HQ told us they'd only have bullet-guns, or homemade beamers in the worst case. But H&Ks?*

"Captain?" Masrur was still waiting for his orders.

"Oh . . . sorry, Masrur. Stay with First Platoon for now. Asrad and I will join up with Fourth, then meet you near the Sector Three airlock when things are wrapped up here. You might want to tell Captain Mathews to save the grenades. Colonel Houston has an LG-Four team that can blast the rebels out if they won't come out on their own."

"Roger, Captain. See you soon."

Inside her helmet, Bunny shook her head as Asrad handed her three energy packs. There was a snick as she plugged two of them into place, and a brief bluish glow as the shield power returned to full. She attached the third to her belt, then popped a new power cell into her pistol.

I'm still missing something, she thought. *The Loonies have weapons cached all over the place, but it's almost like they don't know where everything is. There's something that doesn't make sense here, and I don't like it.*

New York City
7 November 2069
3:00 A.M. EST

The bedside comm unit chirped urgently. Jurgen Flanders rolled over, brushed his unruly blond hair back from his face, and fumbled around until he found his glasses. Groping for the light switch, he found his alarm clock instead. "Three A.M.? Who in God's name would be calling me at—" The comm unit chirped again.

He thumbed the acknowledge button. "Yes, Señor Aguila?"

"Jurgen, I have got a job for you. The ATFOR units are continuing to turn up caches of weapons. *Military* weapons."

Jurgen blinked and rubbed his face with his free hand. "Yeah. So?"

"So how did the Lunar colonists *do* it? Where did these weapons come from? How did the rebels manage to acquire battlesuits nearly as good as our own?"

Jurgen yawned. "Beats me. How?"

"That is what I want you to find out. We have the ship's manifest for every transport that has gone to the Moon in the last twenty years. I need you to search those records and find out how the weapons were smuggled in. And I need a complete report no later than eight o'clock."

"Eight A.M.? But that's"—Jurgen paused to do the subtraction—"five hours!"

"Right. So you'd better get busy." Aguila rang off.

Jurgen waited until the call was safely disconnected, then sat up in bed, switched on the bedside light, and looked straight at the comm panel. "I quit," he said, his voice loud and clear. Then he noticed the caller I.D. readout, rubbed his eyes, and took a closer look.

"He called from the *office?*" Jurgen said in quiet wonder.

THE GRIMALDI GAMBIT

As the stalemate ground on into its third week, two things became painfully evident to von Hayek and the Council of Lunar Governors. The first was that the United Nations was in no mood to negotiate and was in fact continuing to reinforce its position with fresh shipments of troops and matériel. True, there was a form of nonverbal communication going on, via the automatic cargo launchers. When the rebels tried shutting them down, General Daniels stepped up her raids; when the food shipments resumed, General Daniels backed off somewhat, but did not stop. More than once von Hayek, Adams, and the council toyed with the idea of demolishing the launchers, but in truth they all realized this would be a futile and suicidal tactic. The food shipments were the rebels' only real bargaining chip: if the launchers were wrecked, there would be nothing left to stop ATFOR from attacking in full force.

So the idea of another, somewhat more controlled Volodya remained a tantalizing phantasm, and the rebels concentrated on the second great problem. Despite the rapidly increasing competence of the LDF and the Lunar Militia, it was becoming painfully obvious that the lightly armed and armored lunar soldiers could not hope to stand against the newer and more powerful weapons that ATFOR was bringing to bear. True, the rebel labs were producing some astonishing new developments — the portable railgun, for example, and of course MANTA, the top-secret development that overshadowed all others — but the grim truth was that the rebels could not hope to survive, unless they could destroy or, better yet, appropriate the newly arrived United Nations weapons.

With this thought in mind, von Hayek reconsidered the MANTA project. It was by this time showing tremendous promise and had become stable and replicable in the lab, although it had yet to work under field conditions. Thus, in desperation, was conceived the high-stakes gamble known as the Grimaldi Raid.

— Chaim Noguchi, *A History of the Lunar Revolution*

CHAPTER 11

Port Aldrin, Luna
Block J64, Apartment 23
14 November 2069
09:30 GMT

Dalton lay alone in his bed, staring at the ceiling. It'd been two weeks now since Dara died. Two weeks of shuffling through life, getting out of bed when Terrell Davis made him do it, eating food when Svetlana Kosov stopped by and ordered it. He'd made it into work a few days, not that there was much to do. Hit a couple of militia training meetings, but just couldn't get into it. Shaved when he remembered to, brushed his teeth when they felt gritty. But otherwise he just lay in bed, staring at the pale gray ceiling.

In an abstract way he noticed that he was hungry. Svetlana hadn't stopped by in a day or two, now that he thought about it. She'd been getting increasingly wiggy from those antidepressants she was popping like candy; maybe she'd finally flipped out. If so, so what? Maybe she was lucky. Dara was dead, and nothing was ever going to change that.

Unconsciously Dalton dragged a hand up to his chest and dropped it on his sternum. Where was the hole? From the inside it felt like there should have been a hole the size of a basketball there. But instead, all Dalton felt was . . .

Nothing.

That was the scary part. It wasn't as if he and Dara had been head over heels in love. Sometimes he'd thought they were, but they weren't engaged or married or even officially going steady. They hadn't even been particularly good friends outside of the bedroom.

Still he missed her. But he didn't miss *her*. She would never again knock at the door, nag him about his laundry, or try to talk him into changing the way he cut his hair. . . .

The comm system chirped. Irritably he reached up and thumbed the acknowledge button. "What?"

"Icehawk? It's me, Jeff. How you doing?"

"Okay." Faintly Dalton felt the soft twitch of something in his jaw muscles that might have been an embryonic smile. Young Jeff Mahoney had apparently taken it upon himself to haul Dalton out of this funk. He'd been calling at least twice daily when he was off duty, trying to talk Dalton into playing some games, working overtime to drag him out of his shell. It was almost touching, the kid was so earnest. Dalton could see him in a few years, bringing old man Starkiller a deck of cards and some nuts for the squirrels, taking his wheelchair for a roll in the park.

"So," Mahoney said, "you feel up to playing Beamrider?"

Dalton thought it over. "What the hell. Sure. Give me a minute." He pulled the flatscreen down from its recess in the headboard, logged into LunaWeb, and jumped into the game.

"Pssht. Captain Icehawk, report!" Young Mahoney's voice sounded strangely distorted through the speakers. Probably some audio filtering algorithm in the game, Dalton thought.

He checked his heads-up display. Oh, blast, level 23 again. "Uh, FlightCom? I'm picking up a distress signal from the third moon." Dalton tried, he really *tried* to get into the spirit of the game.

"Uh, roger that, Captain," Mahoney answered. "We're getting something very strange here, too. I'm looking at a multiscan of the pulse frequencies, and we're getting thousands of hits. Three thousand one hundred thirty-six, to be exact, and they weren't there twenty minutes ago."

Dalton yawned. "Frequency seems to indicate you're picking up the drive signature from some kind of a starship, sir."

Mahoney seemed excited. "As incredible as it may seem, that's what the techs say, too! But the drive type is totally different from anything we've ever seen before. And there's three thousand of them . . . more!"

Dalton scratched his head. "Okay, uh, request permission to break my patrol and check it out, sir."

"Negative that, Captain. We're sending in a flight of heavy fighters. That scout of yours doesn't have the armor or shields to stand up to heavy weapons, and if this *is* an invasion fleet, they'll be armed for bear."

Dalton checked his heads-up display one more time, then decided, what the hell. "Screw it, Mahoney. I'm going in. Record this play, if you wanna."

"Captain Icehawk! You are violating—" Mahoney dropped out of character. "Dalt, you're gonna kill yourself!"

"That's the idea, Mahoney." Dalton powered up his weapons, diverted all reserves to his forward shields, and dived straight into the heart of the enemy fleet. He lasted almost thirty seconds before his screen flared white in the final explosion.

"Uh, Dalt?" Mahoney was back to normal voice now; a kid, nervous. "Are you okay?"

Dalton pushed the screen away from his face and thought about it a moment. "No, I'm not. I'm a mess."

"Uh-huh." Mahoney paused. "Well, do you think you could clean yourself up in the next half hour or so?"

"Why? You wanna have"—Dalton checked his real-time clock—"brunch?"

"No. But I want to stop by. It's important."

Dalton considered it and again decided, what the hell. "Sure. Whatever. Here, in half an hour?"

"Right. Bye." Mahoney rang off. Dalton got to his feet, shuffled to the bathroom, and looked at his face in the mirror. Then he found his tube of soap gel and a washcloth and got busy.

At ten hundred hours on the dot, Jeff Mahoney showed up, along with Sergeant Britt Godfrey. With some misgivings, Dalton let them in and ordered up coffee. Then he cleared enough space for the three of them to sit.

Britt took the cup Dalton offered him, downed a gulp, and nearly spat. "Ow! That's bloody 'ot!"

"Sorry," Dalton said. "There's a war going on, you know. Some of Central's peripheral systems are getting wonky."

"Right." Britt blew across the top of the cup to cool it some, then tried another sip. This time it seemed to be okay.

"So," Dalton said, breaking the silence, "I take it this isn't a social visit."

Britt looked at Mahoney, then back to Dalton, and nodded. "I'll get right to the point, what? I wouldn't be 'ere, except General Consensus ordered me and Private Mahoney 'ere put in a word for you. I've got a message for you, Starkiller." Britt put extra emphasis on the name, as if he had trouble getting it out. "It turns out we 'ave a friend in common, and this friend told me to tell you that Ken sent me."

Dalton's mind turned over with a clunk, and he actually started to smile. "You know Ken Roberts? I haven't seen him since we hacked this. . . . How is he?"

Britt frowned. "Dead, actually. Roberts bought it in the raid on Kepler last night."

Dalton's smile collapsed.

Britt went on. "Died in my arms, actually. One of the best friends I ever 'ad, and those blue bleedin' sods did for him. Took 'im a while to die too, worse luck."

Dalton felt as if he was going to throw up. "Why are you telling me this?"

"'Cause Corporal Roberts wasn't just me friend, 'e was me compspec—the platoon's computer specialist."

"I—I had no idea. I thought he was just a security—"

"Now, we've got ourselves a big mission lined up tonight. But we can't do it without a compspec, see? Bloody *big* mission. Might even change the tide of the war."

Dalton started to see where this was heading. "And you want me to volunteer to take Roberts's place?"

Britt shrugged. "It's your choice, boyo. You could stay 'ere, if you like, layin' about like a puddle of festerin', self-pityin' slime. Or—"

Dalton set down his coffee cup with a thump. "I don't need this. No way."

For the first time a flash of anger showed in Britt's blue eyes. "Fine! You want to ignore the last words of a dyin' man, that's your lookout! Roberts knew 'e was a goner, and what did 'e do? Whine? Cry? No, 'e spent 'is last moments tellin' me to find *you!* Told me you were the only one who could take 'is spot! But I guess 'e was wrong, eh?"

For the first time in two weeks, Dalton felt something. *Anger.* Building, bubbling, red-hot *anger.* "You bastard!"

"C'mon, Starkiller! Bleedin' ground'ogs killed your woman! Shot 'er right out of the sky! And all you can do is lay yourself low? A *man* would rip somebody's bloody *throat* out!"

Dalton bounced to his feet. "You filthy bastard! I—" Dalton's fists clenched uncontrollably into tight knots of hatred. "Maybe I will, Sergeant Psycho!" Dalton lunged forward; Mahoney intercepted him.

Britt sat back, smiled, lifted his cooling cup of coffee and took a sip. "There now," he said, gently, "that wasn't so 'ard, was it?"

Lunar Surface, Near Grimaldi
14 November 2069
20:13 GMT

Dalton cringed as the UN gunship made another silent pass overhead. It was difficult to see the ship against the endless background of space and even harder to judge distances in vacuum, but he could have sworn the ship was hovering barely a hundred meters over his head.

Suddenly a beam of red-gold light stabbed down toward the canyon in which the LDF commandos were concealed, and Dalton jumped. The lance of light bit into the regolith and carved a new crater, but the dust settled quickly in the vacuum. Another blast followed, and another, and Dalton tried to press himself even closer to the canyon walls.

A text message glowed in front of his eyes on his heads-up display: "Hold position. Move when clear."

Dalton fumbled with the keypad on the left forearm of his suit. This was something new that regular LDF had and the militia didn't. Non Verbal laser suit-to-suit communications: 150 word vocabulary line-of-sight transmission only, but it was almost impossible to intercept. Dalton tapped in his response to the message: "Roger. Enemy soon. Roger. Yes, Roger. Roger, stop."

Dalton swore. Despite the mirrored faceplates, he was sure he could see Britt laughing at him. *Okay, Sergeant Psycho, let's give you a new comm system and see how well you deal.* Almost too late he felt that weird shift in his inner ear that could only mean one thing: grav field. He ducked back into the shadows as the gunship made another pass.

Neck hair prickling, Dalton watched the silent, murderous thing. *Where's our intelligence?* he wondered. *We should have been warned.* These were old Russian gunships, he knew, from back in the early colonial days. They'd been stored under UN peace bond at Lacus Mortis for twenty years or more; everyone on Luna knew that. But now the CWP had gotten them working again. Another dangerous, and unexpected, development.

No more time to think about it. The message "Clear move now" appeared on his display. Dalton rose to his feet and followed the other commandos, moving in huge thirty-foot bounds up the side of the canyon and out onto the open lunar landscape. Although he knew better, he couldn't keep himself from looking up, half expecting the gunship to appear just overhead. Lacking the extreme fitness of the regular LDF commandos, he began to fall behind, and doubled his efforts in a desperate attempt to catch up. He could hear the whir of the servomechs as his legs pumped and he sailed ten feet over a broken sandy-gray boulder.

Wham! Dust scattered as he caught his foot on a protruding rock and smashed into the ground, stunned. It took him a moment to collect his wits and run through the reflexive check: no air leaks, no visor cracks, no problems with the suit systems. Then he looked around and realized he had no idea where Britt and the rest of the squad had gone. This was one of the older parts of the settled Moon, and he could see almost sixty years' accumulation of rover and boot tracks everywhere he looked.

But there, off to the right was a small rise that should afford a better view. He headed for it, hoping to run across some evidence the squad had passed that way. Heart pounding, he made it to the top.

He was utterly alone.

For a few seconds he wondered whether he should risk breaking radio silence. Then he remembered his suit radar, and flipped it on. There on his wrist display were eight blips, reading eight hundred meters south. Keeping one eye on the radar readout and the other on the terrain, he set off to rejoin the squad.

"Captain, I just picked up a radar transmit less than five klicks from here. Pretty small. Looks like a battlesuit unit."

The gunship captain grinned. "Great! Let's bag it."

"On our way. Hey, I'm getting a hit on a comm frequency, too."

The scanner operator put the audio on the speaker:

"Goddammit, Starkiller, turn that bleedin' radar off. You wanna get us all killed?"

The captain smiled. "Yes, offhand I'd say that's a rebel combat unit. Bearing?"

"Eighty-four. And I've got a target lock."

The gunner spoke up. "Permission to fire?"

The captain shook his head. "Negative. Let's find his friends first. Any luck?"

The scanner op swore. "He's heading for the base of that cliff! See that ledge sticking out of the canyon lip? There must be a cave under there. The scanners can't read through the rock."

The captain smacked an open palm with his fist. "Damn. I don't suppose we have any torps loaded."

"Negative, sir. Lasers only."

The captain sighed. "Well, I suppose if we can't dig them out, we'll have to bury them. Gunner, target that ledge and fire on my command."

"Damn! Captain, he made it under there!"

"Fire!"

The ground erupted around Dalton as he sprinted for the cover of the ledge, and then the whole moon seemed to come crashing down on him. The noise was ungodly, even conducted through his suit, and he screamed in horror as rocks and sand enveloped him, burying him alive.

Then he felt strong hands pulling him downward. A gold faceplate pressed against his own, and he stopped struggling as he heard a familiar hated voice.

"Bloody 'ell, Starkiller. Get yourself a grip."

"But we can't dig our way out of that!" He pointed at the collapsed debris above them.

"Don't need to. This is the tunnel we were 'eading for. We can make our way to Grimaldi underground from 'ere."

Britt let go of him, and Dalton fumbled blindly for the viewing mode controls. His visor flashed red as he hit the wrong button, then green as he found the right one, and after blinking a few times he was able to make out the details of the cavern they were standing in. It was a small rocky chamber with flimsy metal ladder bolted to the south wall next to a four-button control panel. The panel was blinking green, and he saw that the ladder descended past an open hatch cover.

The rest of the commandos had already clambered down the ladder, and Britt indicated Dalton should go next. He placed a tentative foot on the ladder and, relieved to find it was much sturdier than it looked, descended without daring to look into the eerie green depths of the mine below.

The young soldier rubbed at his eyes and fought the urge to yawn. Although the blue armor he wore bore the UN symbol, he didn't feel like a Peacekeeper, and he was less than happy about being stationed at Grimaldi.

More like a caretaker at a morgue, he thought. The white walls surrounding the massive computer panels behind him reminded him of the wind-worn tombstones in the cemetery behind his grandfather's house in Denmark. He had played there as a child, pretending there were ghosts lurking behind the headstones, vampires waiting to leap out and attack him as soon as he looked away.

He chuckled at the memory and, for old times' sake, opened his eyes wide and kept them open as long as he could. Just as they had done when he was a child, they soon became dry and uncomfortable, and he blinked several times to remove the sensation.

Motion caught his eye to the right, and he whirled, drawing and aiming his laser in one smooth motion. But it was just another laser probe, floating silently past the computer room on its programmed path. He sighed and returned the H&K to its holster, relieved and disappointed at the same time.

"Chee-eer-ree!" His jaw dropped as the probe screeched an alarm and darted forward, past a white column and out of view. Frowning, he slammed his helmet down over his head and drew his pistol again as he heard the probe firing its lasers down the staircase ahead of him.

He thumbed his radio on. "CenCom, I have probable

hostiles in Sector Two-B! CenCom, code yellow!" There was no reply. He slapped the transmitter on the right rear side of his helmet and tried again.

"CenCom, come in! CenCom, I've got a code yellow here!"

Still nothing. But the room flashed bright as three green beams shot upward from the stairs and blew the laser probe to pieces. Unnerved, the young Dane choked off a cry, then dropped to the floor and took cover behind a column. He edged toward the left side of the column and peered out, trying to see down the giant staircase. What he saw made his stomach drop, and for a weird instant he flashed back to the first time he'd seen an Omniscreen movie.

"CenCom, code red! Damn you, CenCom, this is a code red!"

Dalton and Britt hung back. Corporal Akkerman raced up the giant open staircase and made a twelve-meter leap to the top. "One thirty-six! I got dirts at one thirty-six!"

Britt's bellow made Dalton jump. "Where and how many? Count one, two, Akkerman. How many?"

"I see . . . one! That's one only, at Tango one kilo thirteen."

"Tango one kilo . . . thirteen. Okay, I got him, too. Stahl?"

The grenadier edged forward and popped off a shot.

For a brief moment Dalton thought the round grenade looked kind of pretty as it seemed to hang motionless and silver in the low-G environment. Then it detonated, and shards of plasteel and circuitry rained down.

"Scratch one Bluesuit!" Akkerman called out.

"A bing and a bang, ain't no big thang," Corporal Stahl said as he waggled the grenade launcher. "Another one bites the dust."

Akkerman finished his sweep, Jeff Mahoney took flank, and Colonel von Hayek gave the squad the silent hand signal to move out. For a moment Dalton hung back.

Psychos, he thought as he dashed to keep up. *I am surrounded by a band of raving psychotics.*

CHAPTER 12

Copernicus Colony, Luna
Number 4 Temporary Barracks
14 November 2069
20:45 GMT

"Turn out! Mount up! This ain't no drill!"

The braying voice fell silent a moment; then Bunny felt a metal-shod boot nudging her side. "You too, honey bunny!"

Bunny rolled over and shielded her eyes from the sudden glare. Between the raids at all hours, the time-zone shifts, and the way the two-week-long lunar day had screwed up her biorhythms, sleep had become a precious commodity, to be grabbed whenever possible and easily worth a man's life. Especially the life of a man who called her honey bunny. How the hell did Chuck Houston always manage to appear at the worst possible moments?

Houston nudged her again. "Come on, Mahoney!"

She got her eyes open. Houston was suited up in blue battle armor, so this was serious. "Damn, Colonel, what the hell do you want?"

"I want you and your squad suited up and ready to move out in ten minutes. Full suits, full power. Got that?"

"Yes, sir." Bunny managed a salute and sat up. Her voice

was scratchy, and her head throbbed from sleep deprivation. "Are we under attack, sir?"

"Not us. Grimaldi. A bunch of Loonie commandos made it in, and they're kicking butt on the garrison. We're going in by hopshuttle to fumigate the place."

"Gotcha. I'm on it, sir." Colonel Houston strode off, and Bunny started struggling into her armor.

Masrur was already on his feet and sliding into his battlesuit by the time Captain Mahoney made it down to the enlisted men's quarters. The locks slid into place with an audible click as his suit sealed, and he offered her a wry smile. "Grimaldi, is it? What's going on, sir?"

"Hold on. We don't have time to do this twice." She clapped her hands twice and let out a yell. It echoed in the small, unadorned room that had once been warehouse space. There were groans and muffled curses from the men, but she was pleased at how quickly they got out of their sleepsacks and into their battlesuits and fell in.

Incredible, thought Bunny. *Three weeks ago these guys were all Sufi mystics. But give them American cadre officers for a couple weeks, and they turn into GIs with scruffy beards.*

All except Walid, of course, who was still lying on his back with his eyes closed. She gave his bunk a kick. "Get your butt moving, Walid, or so help me I'll power up and kick your ass into orbit!"

He opened one eye and gazed at her dreamily. "Please tell me that I am dead and that you are one of the houris Allah provides for the faithful."

"Does this look like paradise to you? I don't *think* so. Now get up or I'll send you there myself."

"More likely the alternate destination," Masrur commented as he approached. "Walid, if you are not a lazy child of Iblis, then I do not know what you are."

Walid snorted. "Iblis? As far as I'm concerned, all of ATFOR can go to Iblis. I want to go home."

"Patience," Ali Ustad counseled Bunny as he joined the

group. Ali was a new replacement, and to Bunny's satisfaction he was already helmeted and powered up. A good omen, she decided.

"Uh, Captain Mahoney?" Ali added, in an aside to her. "Asrad was talking to Captain Knowlan. The Captain was worried about something—like, you know, Volodya."

Walid sat up straight in bed. "Volodya? You mean they could be dropping us in the middle of a goddam *nuke?* What kind of madness is this?" For a moment Bunny was pleased to see how fluently the Palestinians had learned to swear in English.

Masrur pushed forward. "Walid, shut up! No one said anything about the rebels trying to blow anything up."

"Yes, but who says they *aren't—"*

Enough, Bunny decided. "Quiet!" To her surprise, the men stopped arguing. "Look, we don't know anything yet. So let's get suited up and find out. Ali, come with me. Masrur, get your men out in the main hallway ASAFP. I don't know which airlock the hopshuttle will be at."

Masrur saluted and carried out his orders. Bunny, feeling nervous and exhausted, turned away from Walid and headed for the door. She caught up with Colonel Houston and a bunch of other American officers in the hallway.

"Colonel?" she heard Captain Knowlan ask. "Squad Four's ready. Shall I take them to the airlock, sir? And which one?"

"Yeah, do it now. Airlock Two. But don't let them nitro unless they really need it. We don't know what we're getting into yet, but indications are that it won't be a hot landing, so I want everybody calm and cool."

"Yes, sir." Knowlan turned on his heel and walked quickly toward his waiting men.

Bunny looked at the Colonel Houston's gold-visored faceplate as she brought her own helmet down over her head. "Colonel, I thought Grimaldi had a full garrison."

"No, skeleton only. And their CenCom went off-line twenty minutes ago. There haven't been any communications since."

"Damn." She slapped the power button and shivered as her suit's initial shield pulse zapped her with a static charge. "So we really don't know anything at all."

"Right. But a shipment of heavy weaponry was scheduled to land at Grimaldi yesterday, and that could be what the Loonies are after."

"That makes sense. But, sir, what if they're just out to blow up the dome, like at Volodya?"

The colonel shrugged. "Well in that case, Captain, we are well and truly screwed."

Fifteen minutes later the hopshuttle was beginning its final approach, and the silver-gray bubble that enclosed the Grimaldi Colony was growing visibly larger. Bunny felt her stomach tighten. *It's just nerves,* she told herself, *just nerves. Not fear.* But the knot inside grew tighter as the metallic dome expanded to fill her vision.

The pilot and his navgunner were both featureless behind their black-visored flight helmets, but she could sense that they were afraid, too. It was something in their posture, the tense awkwardness of their hands as they performed the familiar motions they must have performed a thousand times before.

"Any doubtfuls?" she leaned forward and called to the navgunner.

"Nothing," he assured her. "Hell, if their flight control system was active, you'd think we were dropping off the mail. Everything looks natural."

"Great," she said, relieved. But as she looked up at the screen displaying the external camera view, she saw the shuttle ahead of them stop its descent and level out, still twenty meters above the lunar surface. Not five seconds later she saw the first blue-clad figures drop from the belly of the wingless vehicle, falling slowly to the regolith below.

"What the *hell?*" Bunny swore angrily.

"Sorry, Captain. We've got orders straight from the wing CO for a bounce insert. We'd have done a high drop, except you aren't equipped for it."

"Damn!" She turned to her troops. "All right, men, it looks like the flyboys are in a hurry to get their butts out of here, so we're going to do a low drop. Blue-Green-Red is the order. Masrur, Shayek, you're responsible for getting your men on your feet and in the dome, got it? Okay, let's lose those straps, and whatever you do, don't lock your knees."

"The dust can be soft, but not so deep," Masrur added. "If you sink, don't panic, and remember we're radio silent. NVC only!"

"Sergeant, my touchpad isn't responding!" The voice of Mastora, one of the new men, held a note of panic as he frantically punched at his forearm.

Shayek, the NCO who had replaced Hasan as the Green Team leader, bent over to examine the touchpad, then raised his hands in dismay.

Masrur pointed to the man, and Rasul edged his way past two of the other Greens and ran his fingers over the lifeless black buttons. He grabbed the man's arm and, using both hands, whanged it loudly against the hard plaz side of the shuttle.

"Hey!" Shayek protested, but Mastora held up his arm triumphantly. The buttons on the touchpad were glowing a brilliant neon green. Rasul bowed deeply, and a couple of the troopers applauded.

Just in time, Bunny thought. Then the shuttle dropped suddenly and came to a halt as a panel slid back to reveal an opening in the floor.

"Go-go-*go!*" the navgunner shouted, and Bunny realized that the man was as scared as she was. If the nuclear core of the dome blew, everything inside the circle of the vast crater that enclosed Grimaldi would be vaporized. No doubt the pilots didn't plan to delay their departure for a second. Bunny couldn't blame them; she just wished she could stay on the vehicle and fly away with them.

I can't deal with this, she thought, and finally gave in to the impulse she'd been fighting since boarding the shuttle; she punched the command into her wristpad that sent a mild sedative coursing into her bloodstream. She immediately felt calmer, and it was with an almost tranquil air of detachment that she watched Shayek and the Green Team follow the last of Masrur's men out of the shuttle.

Who cares if the flyboys bug out? she thought. *We don't need them anyway.* Then it was her turn, and she cradled her pistol in both hands as she fell. Regulations called for keeping the weapon holstered during a low drop, but she was damned if she'd let it go. The ground came at her slowly, and the drugs in her system made the bluish gray surface appear to blur and swim. She didn't feel as if she was falling at all but rather floating gently to the surface, like a feather or a snowflake.

The impact brought her back to her senses with jarring jolt as she crumpled and rolled sideways. Then she was on her feet and moving in huge strides that took her into the airlock in only five bounds.

Colonel Houston was there, along with Squad One. She looked around and counted heads, relieved that the twelve members of her squad were all there.

Houston waved her over, and his voice spoke in her helmet. "No need for radio silence here. We've scanned the area and haven't picked up a thing yet. How was your flight?"

"A little rough on the landing, sir, but we're none the worse for wear."

"Good." He pressed a few buttons on his touchpad. "BatCom sent me a layout of this dome on the way over, and I just uploaded it to your suits. I want you to clear quadrant four, the area marked in blue. We don't have time for a thorough search, so go as quick as you can and let me know the minute you're done, because we're leaving quadrants one and three for last."

"Where's First Platoon going?"

"Straight for the core. I don't want to risk another Volodya. I'm taking this crew over to quadrant two; we'll secure the other main airlock, then make our way to the communications center."

"You want one of my teams?"

"No. The weapon crates from the recent shipment are probably in the warehouse, in your quad."

"Okay, I see them on the map. They're marked in green."

"Right. If the Loonies aren't going for the core, they're probably there, so you better be in full effect."

"Yes, sir. Good luck, sir."

Houston clapped her on the shoulder. "Just watch out for the second team this time. And think nice thoughts about First Platoon while you're at it."

"Yes, sir! I just wish we had a little pixie dust, sir." Bunny saluted and gestured to her men. "All right, Squad Two, call up your map and zoom to the blue area, quad four. We're on a fast search-and-destroy, but we also have to secure a weapons cargo in the warehouse area; that's green on the map. Red and Green Teams will enter the quadrant from the main hallway, and Blue will go around and move in from the south. Got it?" She clapped her hands. "Good. Let's do it!"

The air of confidence she was trying to project buoyed her up and banished her fears for a moment—until she heard Asrad over the comm link: "And if the core goes, may Allah receive our souls."

Dalton peered ahead into the murk at the tunnel's end, trying to see what luck, if any, Britt was having with the panel on the wall in front of him. The ventilation shaft was gray and dingy, and even with full light amplification it was somewhat difficult to make out details due to the monochromatic gray-and-white design of the walls.

He watched as Britt tried for the third time to slide a generic smartkey into a small slot on the panel, but as before, the lock's defenses easily defeated the key's descrambling virus and beeped out a warning. Since they'd already shut down the dome's communications center, they couldn't just tap into the Central Computer; instead, they had to work their way past the individual defenses of every door and elevator.

Thoughtfully tapping his gloved fingers on the soft gray insulation of the wall he was leaning on, Dalton extracted a device from his black utility belt and stepped forward.

"Maybe I can help," he suggested. Britt nodded and

stepped to the right, making room for Dalton in front of the panel.

Unlike Britt's smartkey, Dalton's norton had a thin cable sticking out of it, causing it to resemble a credit card with a rat's tail. He plugged the cable into a socket on his forearm, just above the touchpad, linking the norton to his suit's computer, then inserted the card into the lock slot. There was a brief pause, and a digital readout began appearing on his helmet's heads-up display.

The lock's antivirus was a standard one, hard if not impossible to bypass if you didn't recognize it or didn't have the proper tools, but it was no problem for Dalton. He murmured a few words into his speech link and clenched his fist in triumph as the v-hack identified him to the lock as a registered user. He pressed the button on the small panel next to the slot, and the lights on the panel switched from red to green just as a loud mechanical whine was heard. Somewhere nearby a door had been unlocked.

None of the commandos said anything, but Britt gave him a thumbs-up, and he could sense that the others were relieved that their intelligence was correct, and perhaps even somewhat impressed with him. Stahl's helmet angled toward him briefly in something that might have been a nod. Dalton began to understand that the commando team probably did need a computer specialist after all.

He removed the card from the slot and popped the cable out of his arm, then tucked the norton back into his belt. He started to fall into his place at the end of the line, but Akkerman, the Swiss commando from Volodya, stopped him with a hand on his shoulder. Akkerman tapped his own ACR, then pointed to Dalton, reminding him to draw his weapon. Dalton's newfound confidence began to dissipate again.

Dalton turned the corner and stopped in confusion. The narrow hallway ahead had four passageways leading off of it, two to the left and two to the right, and there was no sign of which way the others had gone. He turned and looked at Akkerman, but the Volodyan held two fingers up, then pointed to two different passageways, indicating that they should each examine one.

Not again, Dalton thought. Taking a deep breath to calm himself, he called up the mission map and examined it calmly. Okay, a right and right. No problem. He took the first passage to the right, turned right again at the next corner, and found himself face-to-face with a blue-armored UN trooper just stepping off the elevator.

"Yikes!" Dalton yelled, casting caution, radio silence, and his pistol aside as he quickly threw himself forward.

The UN trooper seemed just as surprised to see Dalton as Dalton was to see him, but he managed to get off a burst that bit into the wall just behind where Dalton's head had been a moment before. Dalton hit the floor hard, landing awkwardly on his left side a meter or two away from his weapon. He looked over at the pistol, then back up at where the trooper had been, but the Terran had moved too, wedging himself against the north wall and positioning himself for a finishing shot.

The shot never came, as Akkerman, coming around the corner, fired four shots in rapid succession that first blew the UN trooper back, then collapsed his shields. The blue-armored soldier fell to the floor, and one of the oxygen minitanks strapped to his belt came loose and rolled toward Dalton's face, finally coming to a stop with an audible clink on his visor.

Akkerman bent over to pick it up and gravely handed it to Dalton. "To the victors," he said.

"Behind you!" Dalton shouted.

Akkerman threw himself to one side just as a bronze laser probe floated in through the elevator shaft and opened fire. Two of the rounds smashed home and exploded in a blue-green arc, but Akkerman's shields held long enough to allow him to leap the other way and take cover around the corner. As the drone continued to fire at the commando, Dalton desperately crawled forward and reached out for the dead Terran's ACR.

Stretching his left arm as far as it would reach, he grasped the weapon and, rolling over on his back, fired the high-energy rifle at the probe over his head. The probe's paltry shields disintegrated immediately before the power of the ACR, and it exploded in a ball of flame, sending a violent shower of metallic shards slicing through the hallway and down upon Dalton as well.

His shields flared briefly but had no difficulty keeping the shrapnel from piercing his armor. Defending against metal projectiles was the sort of thing energy shields were originally designed for, and Dalton made a mental note always to remember to keep his batteries charged. Still lying flat on his back, he closed his eyes and murmured a brief prayer of thanksgiving.

"Good thinking, man!" he heard Akkerman say, and he opened his eyes to see the Volodyan standing over him. The commando holstered his pistol and extended a hand to help him to his feet. Dalton staggered as pain shot through his left knee, but it was just a momentary twinge, and after taking a few tentative steps, he found he was able to walk normally.

"Are you okay?"

"Yeah, I'm all right. I twisted my knee when I hit the deck."

Oh. Well, I think I know which way the others went."

"Great. We can't use our radar, right?"

"Right. That's how that gunship was able to hunt us down. We can't use our comm links, either. They're too easy to intercept. Line-of-sight tight beam laser like this is the only safe way to communicate."

Dalton grimaced, knowing that his ignorance and careless forgetfulness had almost gotten them all killed. "Don't worry, I won't forget again."

"No, you won't," Akkerman agreed. "But that doesn't matter now. Anyhow, follow me. I found a dead UN guard just around the corner while I was dodging that probe you killed. It's along our original route, so I'll bet our men came this way."

As they turned the next corner, though, they found that the corridor ended in a white plazbrick wall. Akkerman stopped abruptly, then slapped his leg in frustration.

"I should have known those maps were no good. But look: this is the hall, don't you think? Unless we got messed up again in that little rat's maze back there."

Dalton's eyes narrowed as he called the map up on his helmet display. This definitely seemed to be the correct path, and the dead guard surely indicated that the rest of the squad had been this way. He shut the map off and called up a 4x zoom filter on his visor.

Then he smiled. "We are going the right way, Akkerman. Look at this!"

There was a very thin gap between the top of the wall and the ceiling. Due to the white coloring of both and the dim lighting, the gap was hard to see, but it was there nonetheless. He tried to put his fingers in the crack and pry at it, but his armored gloves were too thick.

He turned to face his companion. "There's got to be some sort of triggering device around here somewhere. Take a look."

But after five minutes of fruitlessly prodding and pushing at every inch of the door as well as the nearby walls, they had to admit defeat.

Akkerman shrugged philosophically. "If we can't find our way to the warehouse and help secure it, we'll just have to try to tap into the Central Computer and shut the ion shield down. That's the prime objective anyway, and you don't need help for that. There's a ventilation system just back a bit the way we came. That panel you unlocked may or may not give us access to it, but we can at least have a look-see. Maybe we can find another way to get to the brain center."

"What do we do if we can't find another way there?"

"I don't know. Hide and hope, I guess. Or maybe we can get back to the shaft we came in through. But unless we find the way out on our own, taking down the shield is our only chance. With the shield up, there's no way our reinforcements can get in."

"Reinforcements?"

"Don't you worry about that. Just get the shield down, and everything will be okay. I promise. So let's check out that vent shaft, shall we?"

Dalton gave him a thumbs-up, but his thoughts were whirling like crazy. *High command told us reinforcements can't get here unless the ion shield is down,* he thought. *But that doesn't make sense, unless we have some sort of energy-based heavy artillery that the shield would negate. But shelling the dome can't be what we're after, because if they wanted us to destroy the dome, they'd just have us blow the reactor in the first place.*

He stared intently at the Volodyan's armored back as they retraced their path back to the elevator. Clearly, Akkerman knew something he didn't, but it was just as clear that the man had no intention of telling him. Well, that was okay. He had enough worries to concern himself with now without adding any more.

CHAPTER 13

Grimaldi Colony
14 November 2069
22:00 GMT

Colonel Josef von Hayek knew something was wrong even before the green laser flashed against his left shield. Squeezing off two bursts at his unseen assailant, he leaped off the platform he was standing on down to the plaz floor below.

A blue explosion engulfed him, and he was sent violently sprawling forward as his shields ablated the force of the lasers.

"Dammit, Stahl, get that launcher up here now!" he screamed as he rolled over, hoping desperately that the grenadier was within the short beam's radius.

Two laser drones appeared in front of him, dangerous and eerie as they rose silently, but they headed away from him, toward the rest of the squad. There was a blast and a flare of light, and a grenade arced past the probes to explode harmlessly on the far wall. One drone darted to Josef's right and began firing, while the other continued to rise slowly, as if locking on to a better firing angle. *Oh, no you don't*, thought Josef, as he centered his sights on the second drone.

Before he could squeeze the trigger, a heavy *chud-chud-chud* filled his speakers and he saw tracer rounds slicing through the probes as the chaingunner worked his rapid-fire weapon back and forth across the room. Both probes were enveloped in flame and dropped toward the floor, exploding as they fell.

Way to go, Britt. Josef pumped his fist and rose warily to his feet, his ACR pointed carefully in front of him. Moments later, Godfrey, Stahl, and Mahoney leaped down from the platform to join him. He waited a moment, then looked up at the platform, expecting Akkerman and Starkiller to leap down as well.

Puzzled, he stepped between Godfrey and Stahl as he switched his comm mode to short-beam array.

"Where's our net boy?"

"I don't know, Colonel," Britt replied. "I 'it the deck when those probes started shooting, and Stahl was behind me."

Stahl spoke up. "I was the last one through. I think I may have bumped an access panel while I was trying to bring this bitch into play." He patted the big bronze-and-red grenade launcher.

"Damn! Next time stick to your laser. Those little probes move faster than grenades do." Josef pointed at Britt. "Jump back up there and see if you can get the door open. We've got to find Starkiller. Without him we're in deep trouble."

"Akkerman is with him," Stahl pointed out, as the one-sixth-G gravity helped Britt make the three-meter leap with ease. "He can't get too lost." Colonel von Hayek said nothing, only waited with growing unease until Britt returned.

"Couldn't get the door open," Britt said. "It must have relocked when it closed. But you'd think Starkiller could do 'is rat-tail trick again, y'know?"

"Unless they got hit on that side."

Britt, for a change, was silent.

Colonel Josef von Hayek was lost in his own thoughts. *This whole raid is a botch. We should have scrubbed this mission after Roberts got killed. But General Consensus said we could pull it off, even with an amateur.*

"Colonel?" Britt asked. "Maybe I could give it another try?"

I wasn't willing to risk anyone else's life on this. There are only three men here who really know what this mission is about. But now our success hinges on MANTA, and MANTA won't work unless we get those shields down.

"Colonel?" Britt prompted again.

"No, we can't stay put any longer. Those probes are linked into a defense net, and the dirts will be sending troops down here to investigate, even if they didn't see us on the vid." He slapped a fresh power cell into his ACR and set his jaw. "We move."

"How?" Stahl pointed to a blue platform a meter or two higher than the one they'd come from. "Maybe if we climb back up on the other one we can jump across, but . . ."

"Colonel?" The commando Josef had sent out on scout returned. "I've found a hidden lift. It's a pop-up, under that floor grating there, see?"

Britt clapped the scout on the back. "Good work! That's our ticket." He turned to the others. "Now let's play a bit more carefully, lads. We're supposed to be pros, here."

Josef walked over to the grating. It looked like a typical nondescript metal grid. But upon closer examination, he saw a small button cleverly worked into its crosshatched pattern. He stepped onto the grate and pressed down hard on the button with his foot. With an explosive release of compressed air, the lift shot up five meters, carrying him up to the level of the blue platform.

Josef leaped over to the platform and, seeing no sign of enemy activity, waved the all-clear sign. After fifteen seconds, the lift lowered to the floor. The rest of the commandos boarded the lift and joined him on the platform, weapons held at the ready.

After holding up a hand and halting her squad, Bunny called up the vid broadcast by the drone just before it was destroyed. She mentally compared the glimpse of the room she'd seen with the green map of the dome displayed inside her helmet. Puzzled, she nearly gave up, but instead decided to contact the battle computer again.

What the hell, she thought. *We already broke silence when BatCom downloaded this to me. And this won't tell them anything they don't know, even if they can run an instant descram.*

"One Five Three Bravo One, you are logged in with level C access." The BatCom's voice software wasn't the monotone synthetic beloved by the old-science fiction vids, but it was recognizably inhuman nevertheless.

"BatCom," Mahoney said, "run me a compare on the vid clip you just sent with the blueprint of this dome, and ID the locale for me in red if you can find it. Give me probables of point nine and up."

"Roger, One Five Three Bravo One." There was a brief pause. "Search complete. There are three possible locations with probabilities higher than point nine. Transmission follows."

A soft *ping* sounded in her ears to let her know the transmission had ended, and she called up her map again. Three areas were glowing in red, but one location in particular caught her eye. It was near the warehouse where the recent shipment of plasma cannons had been stored.

"Got it!" she said to Asrad, who had taken the point ahead of her.

He turned around to let his tight-beam lens target her. "What's that, Captain?"

"I know where the rebels are. They just killed a couple of probes near the warehouse. They're approaching it from the southeast. If we hurry, we might be able to get there first."

"Let me see your map."

"Okay, but make it fast." Bunny turned her arm over and punched the transmit button on the keypad. The map with its highlighted regions appeared in front of the Asrad's face sooner than he expected, and he took an involuntary step back.

"See the red?"

"Yes, is that where the rebels are?"

"It's where they were three minutes ago. It should take them at least another five to get to the warehouse."

"Right. Praise Allah they're not heading for the reactor."

"Sure, but we can't let them break open those plasma guns before we get there." She pointed Asrad forward and waved to the rest of the squad. "Come on, boys, let's move!"

"Colonel, will you check these out?" Britt Godfrey ran an admiring hand over the bronze finish of one of the plasma cannons. He lifted the nozzle section in his hand; attached by a black cable to the minireactor built into a square backpack, it looked like a cross between a World War II flamethrower and a massive dowsing rod.

"Don't just stand there, Godfrey. Get the thing on and let's roll. We've only got fifteen minutes to get the shield down before the attack gets scrubbed." Feeling the time pressure build as the precious seconds ticked inexorably away, Josef von Hayek anxiously watched the entrances above them and to the west.

There was a sputtering, crackling noise behind him, and then the plasma cannon Stahl was holding sparked to life with a loud roar. It subsided to a distorted hiss as the commando dialed back the setting and wrestled the weapon under control. Between the two points of the fork there now was an electric blue arc, leaping dynamically in synch with the hisses and pops.

"Looks like they're on full bang, Colonel."

"Lovely. Now if we can only—"

He was interrupted by the *sssth-whoosh* of a gobbet of heated plasma being blasted out of a cannon. He started to turn around. "Britt, will you quit goofing around and—" Then he realized what was happening and jumped to his left, narrowly avoiding a blast of laser fire that burned a hole through the crate next to his head.

Britt didn't bother to reply as he ducked behind a large wooden crate and continued to fire at the blue-suited troopers who were taking up positions on a second story ledge on the north side of the warehouse.

"Colonel, where's the south exit?" Stahl shouted over the

furious roar of plasma fire. He was crouched low, scuttling along the south wall trying desperately to find the door.

Looking up, von Hayek saw another team of UN troopers storming in through the northwest entrance.

"There isn't one!" Josef screamed back. "We're trapped!"

Dalton nodded at Akkerman as he reached the far end of the hallway, and the Volodyan quickly caught up to him, then ran past him and around the corner as Dalton stepped out to cover him. In this leapfrogging manner, they'd successfully avoided probes and the occasional ATFOR patrols as they made their way back to the central ventilation system.

Using a long white half-wall as a springboard, they leaped up into a ventilation shaft that took them into the heart of the dome. The walls were soft and gray, insulated with a soft, dark webbing that made a recurring X design appear. It was a long and claustrophobic passage. Dalton and Akkerman turned right, then left, and leaped across a large pit to land in a narrow passageway heading north.

Akkerman stopped and turned around to face Dalton. "We're about to exit the vents, so keep your eyes open and be ready to shoot. There should be a security terminal that'll give you access to the Central Computer, but I expect it will be guarded."

Dalton nodded, and true to the Volodyan's word, they soon reached a place where the shaft overlooked a large room with dark gray pillars and computer panels on the walls. Dalton started to jump down, but Akkerman put a hand on his shoulder.

"I just flashed an IR scan. It showed two guards around the corner. I'm going to draw their fire. After I jump down, you count to ten, then jump down and move forward, but stay along the wall to your left. You should get a clear shot at the guards as they try to come at me. Got it?"

"Y-yeah . . . I got it."

The action went as Akkerman planned it: short and violent. Dalton walked up to the scattered, burned bones that were all that was left of the UN troopers and nudged one with his foot. He'd never even killed a mouse before, but somehow he'd expected it would be harder than this. Or at least that he'd feel something. *I swore I'd kill one of them for Dara, and I have. But I still feel . . . nothing.*

"Dalton, are you all right?" Akkerman laid a hand on Dalton's shoulder. "I expect you're feeling shocked now, but we have to move. Just keep it together, man. It's them or you."

"I understand," Dalton replied, marveling at how cold he felt. "Actually, I do understand."

Several minutes and two more dead guards later, Dalton found himself before the security terminal Akkerman had been hoping to find. The panels were huge, with numerous indicators and digital readouts, taking up more than eight meters of space and set four meters deep into the wall.

Akkerman looked at Dalton's norton skeptically. "I know you can open doors with that thing, but can you really break through their security with it? It seems awful—I don't know—simple."

Dalton smiled inside his helmet. "The trick isn't here." He tapped the norton. "It's in *here.*" He tapped his head. "Just keep my ass covered while I'm working on this, okay?"

From her vantage point on a high ledge, Bunny studied the cluttered warehouse. The rebel strike team, which seemed to consist of only four men, was pinned beneath her men and the two Charlie teams. One white-armored figure was down, but the plasma cannons gave the three remaining rebels nearly as much firepower as the three ATFOR teams could amass between them.

She cursed HQ for not providing them with grenades, which could easily have ended the standoff. But it had been typical of the UN—from some of the earliest peacekeeping missions in the Middle East almost a century before to last year's debacle on the Quebec-Canadian border—to place woefully underequipped troops directly in harm's way.

"BatCom, patch me through to Colonel Houston,

please," she requested. Now that the commandos were pinned, it didn't make much sense to worry about her comm link being intercepted.

"Roger, One Five Three Bravo One. Your link with unit One Five Three Alpha One is confirmed."

There was a short beep, and Houston's familiar voice came through her speakers. "What's going on, Mahoney?"

"Colonel, we've got three rebels caught in the warehouse here. I've got two teams from Third Platoon backing me up here and both exits covered, but they've got plasma cannons, so I don't dare risk a frontal assault."

"Right. Who you got from Charlie?"

"Two of Lieutenant Knowlan's squads. We've got big numbers here, but nothing better than lousy pistols. No grenades, no nothing. I need some backup here, preferably a couple launchers and maybe a chaingun or two."

"I'll see what I can get you. We've secured the core, but I don't want to pull anybody out of there until we're sure that's not the rebels' target. This could be a diversionary assault."

"Could be," she had to admit. "But I'll probably lose ten men trying to close with them from here. At least get me some heavier artillery."

"Okay, I'll get it to you as fast as I can. Can you hold tight for another fifteen minutes?"

"Don't see why not. We can't get at them, but if they try to break out, they'll lose their cover. Can you make it five?"

"Ten, and I'll have three missile drones activated and sent to you, plus a team from Alpha. Just hang tight and keep those Loonies under your thumb."

"Yes, sir. Mahoney out."

She closed the comm link and glared down at the giant crates blocking her line of fire. Out of the corner of her eye, she saw one of the men from Charlie rise up on one knee and fire a quick burst of three rounds before dropping back to his stomach. A purplish pink gobbet of heated plasma just barely missed melting his helmet as he sprawled.

Shaking her head, she went to broad band and yelled into

her mike. "All ATFOR units, cease firing immediately. Hold position and return fire only if they start coming our way. Otherwise make no move to attack. We've got reinforcements on the way, and I don't want anyone being stupid. Just hold your positions!"

Kneeling behind a giant crate, Britt turned to von Hayek. "All's quiet on the Western Front, mate."

"Too quiet," Stahl added. "What d'ya think they're up to?"

"Probably bringing up some heavier guns," Josef von Hayek observed. "They outnumber us, but if you've noticed, they've got nothing but H&K pistols. We've got us a little Mexican standoff here, and whoever's in charge on their side just realized it. They're going to keep us bottled up until they can reinforce."

"So what do we do, Colonel?"

"What else?" Von Hayek turned his wrist over and started punching his comm pad. "Scream for help."

"What's *that?*" Dalton asked as a string of yellow-orange text began streaming across the inside of his faceplate.

"S.O.S. The colonel's in trouble!" Akkerman was leaning against the southernmost computer panel, keeping watch while Dalton tried to work his way past the Grimaldi computer's security system. The norton had been slotted for more than ten minutes now, but Dalton still hadn't penetrated the sophisticated system.

Dalton watched the signal repeat. "Where are they?"

"They're warehouse," Akkerman said, "and it looks like they're trapped."

"So what can we do? It would take us at least fifteen minutes to get there from here, even if we had full access to the locks."

Akkerman snorted in frustration. "Don't worry about it. Just concentrate on getting that damn shield down."

"But—" Dalton didn't understand how shutting down the ion shield would help the rest of the squad. Once again he cursed Britt Godfrey for conning him into joining this mess. He'd thrown in out of anger, and there were too many things he hadn't asked about and Britt had never bothered to explain. Like how, exactly, they would get out of here.

Dalton returned his attention to the security system. He understood less about the mission than he had when it began, but he knew wasting time arguing with Akkerman wouldn't help him get the shield down.

The Grimaldi central security system was structured around the same AI as the door panel he'd cracked earlier, but its program was much more sophisticated. Simply gaining access to the computer itself wasn't the problem; that he'd already done by successfully masking himself with the identity and connection code of a cable maintenance tech. The hard part was convincing the system's netsec that his borrowed I.D. had the necessary authority to shut the shield down.

Of course, in vids, computer hackers always managed to grant themselves instant superuser status and obtain god-like control over the entire system. But in reality that was practically impossible, because there simply wasn't such thing as a super user anymore; netsec science had long ago evolved past the point where such access was provided to any one individual. Thus far Dalton had managed to bluff or otherwise worm his way into the "inven" node as well as "unet" and "lzone," but the nodes labeled "mil" and "admin" still hung before him like forbidden fruit, spelled in glowing red letters that indicated their inaccessibility.

Okay, at least I can see they're there. That's good. But let's try another angle. Who would have a good reason to have the shield downed? Dalton would have preferred to convince the system that he was a full-fledged admin, or better yet, a netsec tech, but sensitive positions like those usually required a retina scan or fingerprints. *An ATFOR patrol leader? No, because I'd have to change the patrol schedules to cover it, and "mil" is off limits. It shouldn't be someone stationed at the dome, anyhow, since if I can't get into "admin," a conflict could pop up and set a trigger off.*

He tapped a key on the touchpad and switched to voice mode, then back again, trying hard to come up with a solution. Meanwhile the norton's little virus kept chugging away, hurling thousands of possible I.D. and password combinations every second against the impenetrable walls of the "admin" node's security system.

CHAPTER 14

Fifteen thousand kilometers away from Grimaldi Colony, the technical director of the MANTA project was looking nervously at the digital time readout. Patrick Adams was just as worried as the scientist, but he refused to show it.

The technical director checked his watch, just in case it was more optimistic than the system clock. "Damn. Only five more minutes before we abort. What's taking Josef?"

Adams cleared his throat. "Who knows? And screw the schedule. We're going to give the boy as long as he needs." He took another sip of cold coffee. "We'll wait all night if we have to. Keep your people alert. Josef's window could appear at any moment, and it probably won't stay open long."

Bingo! Dalton stopped the norton's futile penetration routines and switched over to a manual terminal. He left the gates of "admin" behind and leaped over to "inven," where he quickly created a false shortage of chemicals essential to the oxygen recycling system. Then, in "lzone," he scheduled the arrival at the south cargo lock of a fictitious shuttle from

Sinus Roris carrying a load of weapons plus the urgently needed chemicals. The weapons would probably distract the attention of any roving security routines, while the little background subterfuge he'd constructed just might help the scenario hold up against a closer examination.

He waved Akkermann over. "I think I've got it, but the shield won't stay down for very long. I'll do what I can to prolong it, but we're probably looking at thirty seconds, a minute at the most. Will that do?"

Akkerman gave him a thumbs-up. "Plenty of time, as long as the folks at MANTA are still awake."

"MANTA?"

"Never mind." From Akkerman's body language, Dalton guessed he'd let something slip. "Congratulations, Starkiller. You've just received highest classified security clearance. Hope you know how to keep your lip zipped."

"I don't get it."

"You will. But for now get ready to move, because I'm about to give our position away to every combat drone and trooper in the dome. When will the shield drop?"

Dalton looked at his timer. "Two minutes, twenty seconds."

"Perfect!"

Josef von Hayek had to admit that while he'd been in some hairy situations before, this one pretty much took the cake and launched it out past Saturn. Another team of UN troopers entered from the second-story entrance to the west and were setting up what appeared to be an LM-411 mortar. Also another pair of flying drones had arrived, and these were bigger and equipped with missiles. The mortar was essentially a heavy and much less portable version of the pistol he wore holstered at his side, and while he had no doubt its power would suffice to blast through his shields, he was surprised that the Terrans were willing to sacrifice the plasma cannons still crated in the boxes that shielded the commandos.

Unless they want to take us alive. That was okay for the

others, he thought, and he would encourage Britt and Stahl to give themselves up. After two weeks of fighting, ATFOR still didn't have a single live POW to its credit, and the rumor was floating around the LDF that ATFOR had issued secret orders to summarily execute any captured "terrorists."

But the rumor was false, Josef knew. The truth was that lunar combat quickly sorted men into two groups—the quick and the dead—and left little opportunity for wounded prisoners. General Consensus held that this fact had to be working against the UN's public relations and that ATFOR would be eager to take prisoners.

So he wasn't worried about how his men would be treated. And he was also sure that he'd be treated like a prince, albeit a captured one. But he would also be a weapon for the UN to use against both his father and the cause. *Never!* He looked down at the thick silver tines of the plasma cannon and grinned ruefully. *Just stick your head in between them and pull: that'll melt her down real quick. A glorious death for the cause.*

He'd wait awhile, though. First he had to get the other two safely captured. If he ordered them to let the dirts know just who he was, they'd hold off on the mortar and missiles for a bit. He could demand a negotiating team and probably even a live camera. Then, just when billions of Terrans were watching the standoff in suspense, he'd do it.

Go out with a bang, baby, just like those Volodyans. Thinking of their cataclysmic gesture of defiance, he felt a tightness in his chest and a pressure behind his eyes. *I am lucky to have this opportunity to make such a dramatic statement before so many people.* After two thousand years, mankind still remembered Masada; in two thousand more, they would still remember Volodya. And perhaps—just maybe—him.

Unless, of course, they decide to blow us away with that damn thing, he thought ironically as he returned his attention to the fire team with the mortar up on the ledge. *Good thing Jeff and the others didn't get trapped here with us.*

Then he was startled by a familiar voice: "Colonel, are you there?"

"Akkerman! Where the hell are you? Is Starkiller still with—"

"Sir, get the disks ready *now!*"

"You mean MANTA—"

"Sir, you've got a thirty-second window starting in less than two minutes. Now get those goddam disks ready!" The link went dead, and von Hayek's mouth dropped open for only a second as he recovered from his astonishment and shrugged himself free of the plasma-gun harness.

"Stahl! Godfrey!" he shouted. "MANTA disks! Get them out now!" Free of the harness, he tore off his white backpack and hurriedly extracted a strange, luminescent blue square. It was no more than three inches thick, and as pliable as a sheet of rubber. Unlike rubber, however, it glowed with a pale blue light of its own.

"How much time do we have?" Stahl shouted. They were on regular frequencies now, not caring if their broadcasts were intercepted.

"None, so hurry up!" Von Hayek got his third and last disk laid out, then looked up at the ledge. "We've got to take that mortar out or they'll use it to cut us to shreds once they see what's going on!"

Bunny glared unhappily at the Danish major, who had taken over command of the situation once he'd arrived on the scene. She'd pressed for an immediate assault once the probes and mortar team arrived, but had been overruled by the major, who wanted to capture the trapped commandos.

Staring down from the ledge, she could see signs of movement behind the black crates. That made her uneasy; there was no way the rebels could get past a full squad of ATFOR troops plus the mortar team, laser drones, and garrison soldiers. But maybe escape was not their goal. *God, please don't let them have some kind of nuke down there!* A shiver ran down her spine, and she wondered if the Danish major would allow her to pull her men back.

"We have you surrounded." The major's amplified voice echoed throughout the vast chamber. "Lay down your arms and come forward with your hands on your heads. You will not be harmed. If you do not come out, you will be destroyed."

Good luck, Bunny thought as she waited expectantly for the defiant response she was sure would be forthcoming. None of the Loonies trapped at Imbrium had surrendered, instead forcing the Third Platoon to dig them out in a direct assault. Those rebels had died, of course, but not before killing a lieutenant and several squaddies.

But the expected volley never came, which only made Bunny all the more nervous. She looked over at the major and caught his attention by waving her hand.

"So now what?" Bunny asked him. "They're not coming out. I'm telling you, they're up to something down there. Take them out now!"

The major disagreed. "What would they be up to? Give them some time. They're not just going to come running out with their hands in the air."

"What if they've got a nuke?" Bunny conjectured. "Maybe they're wiring it up right now!"

"Maybe they are. Or maybe they've got a deadman's switch set to blow if we shoot them. Did you ever think about that?"

"No, but—"

"And do you really want to explain to Leighton-Smythe just why we had to destroy those crates? We need those cannons! And also, this is our first real chance to take some prisoners."

Dismayed, Bunny started to open her mouth, but before she managed to get any words out, there was a soft *whoosh* followed immediately by a loud explosion on the western ledge. Dropping to her stomach, she quickly looked down toward the crates but saw no flashes of white that would indicate activity among the commandos. Stunned and confused, she drew her laser and cautiously crawled back toward her squad.

* * *

"Is the shield down yet? Hurry, Starkiller. We've got to get out of here soon!"

Dalton waved him away irritably. "Hold on. I'm trying to concentrate!" He was now logged into the Grimaldi net as the pilot of the shuttle from Sinus Roris coming in on its final approach to the landing zone.

The trafficon requested his flight I.D. number, and one of the gremlins he was running returned it automatically. He mentally crossed his fingers, then breathed a sigh of relief when he saw the green light flashing its approval.

"Shuttle SR-A four, you are cleared for landing. Hold your current position until you hear the signal indicating the shield is clear." There was silence for a short moment that seemed like an eternity, and then the computer voice returned. "Five . . . four . . . three . . . two . . . one." There was a beep. Then: "You may begin your approach."

Yes! Dalton quickly hit his bugout key and abandoned the gremlin, leaving it to try to bluff the trafficon, which would grow confused and suspicious once its sensors reported that there was in fact no shuttle anywhere near Grimaldi. He was just about to log out for good when one of the gremlins he'd left futilely smashing itself against the security firewall unexpectedly returned.

"It's down!" one of the MANTA techs shouted. "The Grimaldi shield is down!" In the control room there was a loud cheer, though more than one throat sounded ragged with fatigue.

"Go, dammit!" Adams screamed at the waiting commandos. "Go, go, *go!*"

The commandos leaped forward and, one by one, disappeared in a blinding flash of blue light.

"Starkiller, we have to leave. *Now.* They'll be sending a patrol this way any minute!" There was a desperate edge to Akkerman's voice as he pleaded with Dalton, frequently casting a nervous eye down the corridor.

"Hang on. I've found something interesting."

"Oh, for God's sake, Dalton, we really don't have time for this."

"No, hang on. I just got access to the cameras attached to those floating probe things."

"Really?" In spite of himself, Akkerman was impressed. "Can you see anything?"

"Yeah, I think I can even control it, sort of."

"Control what?" Akkerman asked.

"The probe thing." Dalton reached over to the norton and flipped the mini-joystick up. "Holy cats!"

"What is it?"

"I think I just found Britt and two others. Damn, they're surrounded! Let's see if we can't do something about that."

There was another explosion, and Bunny felt her shields flare momentarily as a wave of heat passed over her. She rolled over on her back and saw that the mortar had been destroyed and the entire eastern ledge was engulfed in flame.

"It's the probes, it's the probes!" she heard Asrad shouting behind her.

She looked ahead of her and saw a missile probe slowly turning to face her. Three of its missiles were missing and had presumably been fired, but the sharp red tips of the remaining one pointed at her like a silent hunter's arrow aimed directly at her heart.

Her pistol was still in her hand, though, and she squeezed the trigger twice, firing two bursts that caught the little drone directly in the camera lens. It erupted into a small ball of fire and made a burning nosedive for the floor fifteen meters below. *Sweet Jesus, that was too close!* She turned to see her men advancing, firing at the two remaining probes and quickly destroying both.

"Let's get out of here!" Bunny gestured toward the door behind them. "That way!"

But when she reached the door, one man was already there, making a negative gesture with his hands. "It's locked! We can't—" A pink stream of hot plasma cut off his sentence as it burned through his shields and melted a hole in his chest.

Murad turned and fired two shots, but before he could get off a third, he was burned down as well.

Again she dropped to her stomach and, using her arms, spun herself around like a spider. Down below the ledge she could see white-clad troopers moving about and firing methodically. There seemed to be a lot of them, so she quickly started counting and came up with twenty. That was impossible, but there they were. Most of them were now armed with plasma cannons; she looked at the pistol in her hand and, shrugging helplessly, slid it into the holster at her hip. Where the hell had they come from? she wondered.

To the left, the last of the Third Platoon men fell to the Whitesuits, and she saw the Danish major stand up and put his hands on his head.

Well, when in Rome . . . Bunny stood up too, put her hands up, and indicated to her surviving men that they should do the same.

CHAPTER 15

Grimaldi
14 November 2069
22:00 GMT

Dalton whooped as the two missiles from the probe
slammed into the mortar. That would at least give the squad
a fighting chance, he thought. He turned the probe toward
the northern ledge and was disappointed when the vid
suddenly went black and kicked him out. He wondered if
he'd lost the link somehow or if somebody had taken it
down. Determined to help the commandos in any way he
could, he raced through the map and used his new security
access to lock all three entrances into the warehouse. He
figured that would even the odds a little if they couldn't
bring up any more artillery.

He noticed a yellow security alert suddenly start blinking
on the icon of a probe patrolling well to the south of the
warehouse. Curious, he switched his view over to the probe
and saw two white-armored LDF commandos, one leaping
to the side and firing wildly at the camera, the other
kneeling almost motionless before the blinking lights of a
computer panel. Something about the scene seemed
strangely familiar and he wrinkled his brow.

Then it hit him, literally, as a burst of blue light enshrouded him and his shields ablated before the force of a direct laser hit.

"Dammit, Dalton!" Akkerman screamed and fired another three-round burst at the hovering probe before it could fire again. All three beams struck home, and the probe exploded. "Get up! We gotta move now!"

Dalton struggled to his feet, leaning against the wall to help recover his balance. Realizing his norton had come unplugged from his forearm socket and was still jacked into the wall panel, he turned back—and saw UN troops coming toward them at a sprint from around the corner.

"Run, damn you. Run!" Akkerman was screaming at him, but Akkerman himself wasn't running. Instead, he was kneeling in a doorway and firing down the hall at the Bluesuits.

"No! We stick together," Dalton said.

"Wrong! I'm the soldier; you're the specialist! If only one of us gets out of here, it has to be you." Akkerman shifted his position slightly as the UN soldiers drew nearer. "Leave them to me. I'll catch up with you later, if I can."

Dalton turned and ran, his shoulders tense as he waited for the inevitable shot to hit him in the back. But it never came; aside from one errant beam that tore a chunk of plaz from the ceiling above him, nothing came near him. Akkerman must have succeeded in drawing their attention.

He sacrificed himself for me. Why? Having turned several corners, Dalton was now thoroughly lost, despite his map. Fighting a suicidal sense of desperation that urged him to walk back the way he had come, Dalton drew his pistol and continued to move on. *At least I took the shield down,* he thought. *I did whatever it was they brought me along to do. Was it enough to make a difference?*

"Can't anyone tell me what the hell is going on in there?" Chuck Houston gestured past the giant computers toward the north side of the control room, glaring at his beleaguered staff sergeant as he did so. They'd been receiving confusing and conflicting reports from several of the squad leaders who'd reported contact with the enemy, and even the occasional vid glimpse of white-armored commandos caught by roving laser probes hadn't answered any of his questions.

Where are they coming from? How many are there? Why are they equipped with such heavy battle armor? And where did they get it?

"They've gotta be mercs," he announced finally. "There's only fifty thousand people up here, for chrissake, and they're all scientists!"

This certainly wasn't like the battle at Tranquillity, where the Loonies had used mostly homemade weapons, or like the one at Imbrium, where they'd brought new model H&Ks to the party. And these Grimaldi invaders had better armor than his own platoon, which, combined with the plasma guns, let them easily overwhelm the outgunned ATFOR troopers.

"Have you been able to raise Captain Mahoney yet?" he asked for the fifth time, even though he knew the answer.

"No, sir," the comm tech replied patiently. "BatCom says her I.D. was green before she went off the net, but hasn't been able to connect with her since things went to hell in that warehouse. Captain DeVries thinks the Loonies might've dug a tunnel to the vents beneath the warehouse."

"Impossible! SpaceCom did a satscan."

"The Loonies' tunnel could've been shielded." Staff Sergeant Saunders had been listening.

"Two hundred klicks' worth? There isn't that much metal on the moon."

"Yeah, well those battlesuits shouldn't be here either."

Houston grimly watched the display before him. A squad of garrison troops supported by two probes, one of which was supplying the vid feed, had set up a defensive position not more than fifty meters outside of the command center.

The LDF troops rounding the corner didn't even bother to take cover; they simply let their heavy shields absorb the ineffective chemlaser fire, then returned a devastating barrage of plasma that forced the surviving Bluesuits to retreat.

The cam view dipped and weaved as the little probe tried

to avoid the molten streams, firing back its futile green bolts all the while, until it zigged when it should have zagged, and the view in the captain's display faded away to nothing.

"Colonel, BatCom's lost contact with Sergeant Fatwa. The rebels must be coming up from the south as well, sir."

The comm tech's voice was calm as usual, but Houston knew that he was starting to get worried. Their battle plan made no arrangements for a retreat, and the entire platoon knew quite well that there were no transports waiting for them outside the airlocks.

"Get me Major Xiong at SpaceCom. I want a hot link now!"

"Roger, Colonel." The comm tech ducked her head and spoke quickly and quietly as she rapidly punched buttons on her control panel. "You're in, sir."

"Ah, Colonel Houston, I see." The major's voice was distant, but polite. "What can I do for you? This is a matter of some urgency?"

"You could say that, Major. We need a dust-off, pronto. Looks like the zone'll be roasting in five, maybe less. We don't have time to wait for a shuttle from Imbrium. They've got heavy armor and plasguns, and our popguns can't stop them!"

"Heavy armor? Plasma guns? That can't be right!"

"I assure you it is, Major. Now, can you get us out of here?"

There was a long pause, and Houston held his breath. "This isn't, ah, another Volodya situation, is it?" the major said finally.

"No, sir, they don't need to blow this dome. They're kicking our butts right out of it."

"Very well," the major said, and Houston sighed with relief. "How many men do you have?"

Houston looked around him. Out of the platoon's twenty-five soldiers, only seven were left, including him. There were another five men from the Grimaldi garrison, plus three civilian ATFOR engineers.

"Fifteen in all, sir. We could probably cram ourselves into two gunships, maybe three."

"Okay. Hang on a second."

Houston waited anxiously, as the sounds of combat to the south grew louder. He waved to Sergeant Saunders. "We're going out the north airlock as soon as I give the word. Make sure the engineers and garrison boys are ready."

"Yes, sir."

"Colonel Houston?" Xiong asked.

"Right here, Major!"

"We've got two gunships on the way to you, ETA three minutes plus. I'll patch you through to them now. Good luck, Colonel."

"Thank you, sir." Chuck Houston had never meant those words more in his life.

"I hear somebody's looking for a lift?" The gunship pilot's voice was laconic, as if he flew into hot LZs every day just before breakfast. "This is Blue Dog One. What side you coming out on?"

"North side. There's fifteen of us all told. Do you have room?" Houston led his men out of the control center and into a long white corridor. Behind them, the Grimaldi engineers did their best to run with them, but in their unpowered vacuum suits, they couldn't keep pace with the others, who wore servomechanically enhanced battle-suits.

"Room enough," the pilot said. "Here's the drill. I'll hold and cover Dog Two while he picks up the first eight, then he'll lift and cover me while I get the rest. It'll be tight, but we can do it."

"Roger. See you there, Dog One."

Chuck Houston was sure he'd never seen anything so beautiful as the sight of the two gunships arcing over the horizon toward them. At a distance they looked like two small black objects flying out of the blue-white half-circle of the Earth, which was floating in the black sky far behind them. He fired a bright blue flare into the airless void, then returned the gray rod to his belt and looked back over his shoulder.

Staff Sergeant Saunders, who'd been bringing up the rear, was just coming out of the airlock. He waved her forward. "You were the last one out, right?"

"From our platoon, yeah. The garrison guys fell behind, but they should be here shortly."

"Right. The question is, how far behind them are the Loonies?"

"Good question, sir. Wish I knew."

"Yeah, me too. Goddammit, the engineers knew they had to keep up!"

He looked up toward the sky again and saw the first gunship start to descend. "All right, looks like they see us."

He pointed to the airlock. "Take up a defensive position facing the lock. Remember, some of our people will be coming out of there, so don't go shooting at the first thing that moves. And three of them are civs, so look first even if you see white."

The remnants of the Third Platoon scrambled to obey, ringing the closed lock and holding their lasers drawn as they assumed prone positions.

"Saunders, if those Loonies show their ugly faces, you call a mike-mike at the door."

"Roger, Colonel."

"Comm Tech, patch me in to the gunship that's flying cover."

"Yes, sir."

Houston waited and watched impatiently as the approaching gunship grew from a small speck high above them into a lethal dark gray arachnoid vehicle.

"Here you go," the comm tech said. "Dog One is on-line."

"Dog One, this is Colonel Houston. Do you read?"

"Roger, Colonel. Looks like your boys are expecting some heat. Romeo looking for a little lovin'?"

"He's on our tail all right. Want to set your sights on the door?"

168

"Nothing like a welcome mat measured in megajoules. We'll give him a ride he won't forget. And speaking of rides, looks like your taxi just showed up."

"Thanks, Dog One. Houston out."

Saunders already had the men up and running for the gunship, which was hovering barely two meters above the broken rock of the lunar sea. In the low gravity, Houston and his men covered the ten meters to the gunship in two bounds, then leaped up into the ship's belly. As soon as they were in, the ship began to rise and tilt away from the curved outline of the Grimaldi dome, but before the floor panel finished sliding over the opening, the airlock door of the dome began to open.

Houston was never sure whether the figures silhouetted in the light coming out of the lock were blue- or white-suited soldiers, because before they managed to step out onto the lunar surface, the covering gunship opened fire. The airlock disappeared in a hellish flash of yellow-green laserfire, destroying the lock and everything in it.

"Damn!" He swore, not realizing that his comm link wasn't off.

Saunders turned to look at him, and although her faceless helmet concealed all emotions, he knew there was a grim look hidden behind her silver visor. "They weren't ours, were they, Chuck?" she said on tight beam.

Finding it hard to swallow, he switched over to tight beam before replying. Hating himself, he nevertheless said what needed to be said. "No, of course not, Sergeant. Those were Whitesuits—rebels."

But as the gunship flew them to the safety of Imbrium, Chuck Houston knew he would hear reproachful voices in his dreams that night.

Dalton would never forget the sheer terror he'd experienced that day at Grimaldi. Without his squad members, his norton, and, after a surprise encounter with a fast-retreating UN garrison patrol, his pistol, he was un-equipped to do anything but run through the corridors of the dome, hiding whenever he heard movement nearby and hoping for a miracle.

The collision with the two-man patrol notwithstanding, it was the drones that were the worst. The patrols you could hear coming, if not their comm chatter, then the sharp clanking of their hard plaz boots on the equally hard plaz floors. Twice he'd rounded a corner and found himself at eye level with a silently floating probe; fortunately, both times he'd been behind it and managed to retreat before its sensors detected him.

The utility drill he'd found lying on the floor of an abandoned workshop was a comfort, but nothing more. He hoped it would somehow prove useful in close combat with the roving Bluesuits, but against the flying drones it was useless. Still, it was better than nothing.

More than two hours after he'd parted from Akkerman he heard yet another group of soldiers approaching. Spotting a framed panel ahead of him, he ran forward and slapped the large green button he assumed would open the door next to it.

"Access denied." The message glowed challengingly in red, and he fumbled for his norton before he remembered it was gone. The footsteps grew louder, and he looked frantically around the corridor for another means of escape. But there wasn't any.

He raised the drill in both hands, but before he could turn it on, two men in white battlesuits turned the corner and leveled their weapons at him.

"Starkiller, is that you?" one of them asked.

"Britt?" he replied, as a warm wave of relief swept through his body, so intense it was almost orgasmic. "Oh, my God," he said. "Oh, my God!"

"A simple 'Yes, Sergeant,' will do," Britt said, sounding embarrassed.

Dalton sank to his knees as twenty more LDF troopers came marching around the corner to join them. The remote, analytical side of his mind registered and wondered at the sheer number of them, but mostly he was too relieved to care. Inside his suit, he shook with an almost hysterical intensity as the fear and tension washed out of his body.

It took him a long moment to notice Jeff Mahoney pounding him on the shoulder. "Get up, Icehawk. We did it, dude! We sent those bastards running back dirtside where they belong!"

CHAPTER 16

The bedside comm unit chirped urgently. Jurgen Flanders rolled over, brushed his unruly blond hair back from his face, and fumbled around until he found his glasses. Groping for the light switch, he found his alarm clock instead. "Three a.m.? Oh, not *again*." Cursing fluently in five languages, he cleared his throat, switched on the bedside lamp, then tapped the acknowledge button.

"Yes, Señor Aguila. Sorry I don't have the weapons analysis done yet, but it's huge job. I can report, however, that there definitely *is* a pattern—"

"Never mind," Aguila interrupted impatiently. "Forget that. I've got a new job for you. The rebel team at Grimaldi has a new weapon: it's called MANTA. No one seems to know what it is, but their radio chatter is full of it, and it apparently gives them a tremendous tactical advantage."

Jurgen yawned. "And you want a full report by eight A.M.?"

"You read my mind, Jurgen."

"Sir? Where am I supposed to get this information?"

"From the battlesuit vid records, Jurgen. That's why we have those helmet cameras and black-box backpack recorders. Dozens of ATFOR troops were involved in that debacle; *someone* must have seen something."

Jurgen scratched his right armpit and glared at the comm unit. Good thing the video was off. "Those records are classified. Even if they've been uploaded to UNET, they'll be in either the ATFOR or CWP partitions, neither of which I'm supposed to have access to."

"You're right, but I won't accept that as an excuse. Don't let me down, Jurgen." Aguila rang off.

Jurgen flipped the comm unit the finger, then dragged his weary carcass out of bed and got to work.

Briefing Room, LDF Omega Company
16 November 2069
09:00 GMT

Colonel Josef von Hayek was adamant.

Sergeant Britt Godfrey was uncomfortable. "But, sir. *Starkiller?*"

Josef nodded. "Absolutely. I know, he's not much good in combat and he has the emotional maturity of a fourteen-year-old. But the little geek did volunteer for the Grimaldi Raid, after all, and he came through for me when the chips were down. I want him in my company, and I want him on Three-Card Monte."

Britt winced. "I'll try to talk 'im into it, sir. But no promises. I doubt 'e's forgotten who talked 'im into Grimaldi."

Josef shook his head slowly. "Don't *try*, Britt. There is no *try*, only *do*. I *want* him."

Britt shrugged, then saluted. "Yes, sir. As you will."

New York City
17 November 2069
6:30 P.M. EST

The coffee house off Washington Square Park was dark, smoky, and filled with the accents and smells of a dozen Third World cultures. Botschafter Heinrich Graf, head of the NDE legation to the UN, was clearly put off by the place, and pulled his trench coat tightly about him, as if to protect himself from the risk of infection by foreignness.

Aguila found Graf's reaction perversely amusing, and made a point of squeezing the little blond German through a party of arguing Pakistani students as he led him to a small round table in the back of the place.

Shi Cheng Wu, chair of the UN Committee on World Peace, was waiting for them there. He acknowledged Aguila and Graf with a slight nod. Aguila dropped into the chair to Wu's right; Graf looked around himself nervously, then squeezed into the chair to Wu's left. A waitron wandered by; Aguila waved it away.

When the androgynous thing was safely out of earshot— about two meters, in this place—Chairman Wu turned to the ambassador. "So good of you to come, Herr Graf," he said softly, speaking English with a Hong Kong BBC accent.

Graf shuddered at the sound of his name and darted nervous eyes around again. "Is this absolutely necessary?" Graf asked, his voice barely more than a sibilant whisper. "I do not approve of clandestine meetings."

"Clandestine?" Wu asked, smiling innocently. "We are simply three . . . business associates who have chosen to meet away from the office for a change. This is a charming and colorful place, don't you think? It's such a joy to be stationed in New York."

Graf shuddered. "My appointment is up in six months. If I have succeeded in doing nothing to embarrass the Fatherland, they will let me leave this pestilential dunghill and return home."

A young Rastafarian brushed up against Graf as he

staggered by, heading for the men's room. The ambassador, clearly disgusted, brushed imaginary soil from this left shoulder.

Aguila leaned in then and took charge of the conversation. "Trust us, Herr Graf. What we have in mind will bring nothing but honor and accolades to your government."

Graf looked skeptical. "I don't know. The world gets nervous when Germans make plots. Why can we not deal with this through the Security Council and formal diplomatic channels?"

Shi Cheng Wu frowned. "You heard today's session. This MANTA weapon has the Security Council spooked. And the prospect of seeing UN soldiers as prisoners and hostages always robs them of their manhood. It is only a matter of time before they vote to suspend this operation."

"Besides," Aguila added, "we have reason to believe the Security Council has been compromised. There is an intelligence leak."

Graf gasped in mock horror. "No, really? Only fifteen ambassadors and sixty staff members, and we cannot keep a secret? How shocking!"

Wu responded. "We're not sure where the leak is. It could be in my committee or in the CLD."

Aguila tapped a finger on the table. "The point is, we can still win this war if we act quickly. We are offering your government the opportunity to play a decisive role in the solution. Think about it: for the first time in two centuries, the German army will be seen as a force for *peace.*"

From the look on Graf's face, and the slow way he set his left elbow on the table and brought a finger up to tap his lips, Aguila knew he had the ambassador hooked. "I will have to discuss this with the chancellor," Graf said slowly. "But tell me, what did you have in mind?"

Halfway through the explanation, Aguila's phone chirped. He fished it out of his pocket, flipped it open, and answered.

"Sir?" It was Allegria. "Is there a vidscreen where you are?"

He craned his neck and looked around. "No. Why?"

"I suggest you get yourself to somewhere where there is one and turn it to GNN. Now."

Aguila was puzzled. "Right now?"

"Now," she repeated emphatically.

Office of the Governor, Port Aldrin
17 November 2069
23:30 GMT

Patrick Adams paused in the doorway to watch them. It was always strange to see Pieter and Josef von Hayek together. The governor and the colonel, the aging professor and the twenty-eight-year old military man. They seemed less like father and son than mentor and eager student or commanding officer and fiercely loyal underling. Both had the same aquiline nose, piercing blue eyes, and strong jawline. Both were haunted by the ghost of the long-dead Erika von Hayek, wife and mother, and both blamed the Committee on Lunar Development for her death in a dome blowout twenty years ago. Watching the two of them together, chatting, playing chess, and occasionally laughing, Adams was once again struck with the idea that this was an exquisite story of revenge worthy of a Japanese Noh play. Even now, in what should have been a touching moment of family togetherness, they were exulting in the way they had tricked the UN generals.

Operation Three-Card Monte was a success, pure and simple. The LDF now held ATFOR prisoners of war; by keeping them on the move, they prevented General Daniels and the SAS from knowing where the POWs were, so she dared not attempt a rescue mission. Thus, in exchange for informal assurances of the POWs' continued good treatment—no one had used the H-word ("hostages") yet—Daniels had informally ordered the gunships to back off and had allowed the rebels to start flying "mercy shuttles" between their domes. True enough, these shuttles did transport urgently needed medical supplies, but unknown to General Daniels they also carried a far more important cargo: MANTA disks.

And now, to look at the two von Hayeks playing chess and chatting, you'd think the project was all their idea, their personal revenge against the UN.

Pieter von Hayek laughed at something Josef said, looked up, and noticed Adams hovering in the doorway. "Patrick, do come in." He beckoned and smiled. Adams didn't realize until that moment how rare von Hayek's smile had been recently. The governor had been cold-blooded these last few weeks—almost as cold-blooded as his ruthless son.

Adams bowed slightly and walked into the room. "Governor?" He turned to Josef and nodded. "Colonel?" The younger von Hayek responded with an unreadable look that made Adams feel relieved to turn back to Pieter. "How goes the game?"

The first councillor lounged back and waved a hand over the board. "Hard fought, as always. We've traded bishops and a knight apiece, but I've still got my queen and both my rooks."

Josef chuckled and leaned forward. "Ah, but, Vati," he chided. "I outnumber you two-to-one in pawns. You have always undervalued your pawns."

Adams smiled, looked at the chessboard—which made as little sense as ever to him—then back to the von Hayeks. "Tell me: does the game of chess allow a deus ex machina?"

Josef considered the question and answered. "In a way. Just point, shout 'Look, there's Elvis!' and while your opponent is distracted, tip over the board."

"Well," Adams said, smiling smugly, "in that case, Elvis has just been sighted. Watch this." He strolled over to the UNET terminal on the wall—inactive these last three weeks—and turned it on.

"UNET is back on-line?" Pieter asked, eyes wide.

"Even better." Adams tapped through the menus and picked a real-time channel. "This report is in heavy rotation on GNN." He turned up the volume.

The face on the screen was the almost iconic Colin Covert, GNN's top investigative reporter, with his trademark black suit, serious expression, and hair so heavily sprayed it could have been white vinyl. The scene was an outdoor shot on a gray and rainy November afternoon: the familiar building in the background was the United Nations Headquarters in New York City.

"We apologize for the poor quality of this recording," Covert was saying, "but to repeat, this video was recovered from the battlesuit camera of Colonel Hamilton Bowen, which somehow miraculously survived the destruction of Volodya. GNN obtained this copy from a highly placed United Nations source, and we must warn you in advance, it is *extremely* graphic.

"The images you are about to see will speak for themselves. The voices you hear will be those of Colonel Bowen and the late General J. T. Jackson, commander of the secret UN-authorized military force code-named ATFOR."

The picture cut away from the shot of Colin Covert in front of the United Nations complex to a grainy, jerky image speckled with noise bits. What was being shown was unmistakably clear, though: heaps of tiny corpses, contorted in death agonies, their young faces smeared with vacuum-frozen blood. "The Volodyans must have been short of pressure suits," a nervous, breathy voice was saying. "They were using this as a staging area for civilian evacuation. As near as we can tell, there were about sixty children in here, mostly infants and toddlers." The voice cracked, and something that could have been a sob filtered through.

"Explosive decompression," a second voice growled, coming through a radio link. "What a hell of a way for babies to die."

First voice: "Sir? Now do you understand why we're having so much trouble pacifying Volodya? There's only a handful of rebels left alive, but they're fighting like devils. Can you blame them?"

There was silence for a bit, as the camera panned over the awful sight in the room. Then the other voice spoke up: "Burn them." The camera whirled, and came to rest on a figure in a blue battlesuit with one gold star on the helmet.

"Sir?"

"That's an order, Bowen! The minute you get air restored, get some plasma guns in here and incinerate *everything.* Not one speck of organic matter is to remain. Is that clear?"

"Yes, sir . . . I mean, no, sir. I don't—"

"This. Never. Happened." Jackson enunciated each word like a gunshot. "Got that? Find the battlesuit vid records. Grab the remote probes. Erase everything. Then burn the erased cores. If it ever leaks out that our troops did something like this, the UN won't even bother with a war crimes trial!"

The video cut back to the image of the grim Colin Covert, standing in front of the United Nations. "It is now clear that the destruction of Volodya was neither an accident nor an act of terrorism but rather a suicidal act of war. There is obviously some kind of violent revolution going on up there, to what extent we do not know, but the Security Council has clearly gone to extreme and illegal measures to cover this up.

"The fallout from these new revelations is certain to be dramatic and widespread. Already members of Congress are demanding a full investigation and threatening to cut off all U.S. funding for United Nations military operations. In Great Britian, the House of Commons has scheduled a vote for tomorrow on whether to pull out of UN peacekeeping operations, and a similar measure is currently being debated in the Japanese Diet. While Russia has expressed a cautious—"

Adams switched off the screen and turned around with a smug smile on his face. "Well, gentlemen? It looks like we've got a guardian angel down on Earth. Shall we crack that bottle of champagne we've been saving?"

Pieter von Hayek looked at Josef. Josef returned the same meaningful look. Both shook their heads, then turned to Adams.

"No," Pieter said. "Now we hit them."

Adams couldn't quite believe his ears. *"What?"*

Josef nodded. "They're in check. Let's go for the mate."

Adams started to hyperventilate. "Are you *kidding?* Didn't you just . . ." He gestured at the blank UNET screen, temporarily at a loss for words. "ATFOR is on the verge of collapse. All we have to do is sit tight and wait!"

Josef shook his head. "That's not what General Consensus says. A clear victory now would be the master stroke. We can bring the Security Council to its knees."

Pieter looked at Josef, and they exchanged that meaningful glance again. Pieter stroked his chin. "Lacus Mortis."

Josef nodded. "Exactly. Strike while they're in chaos. Destroy the gunships or capture them if we can."

Adams took a few deep, slow breaths, then tried one more time. "Look: Pieter, Josef. All we have to do—"

They turned and looked at him. "We've got a plan," one of them said.

Adams would never be sure which of them had said that.

New York City
18 November 2069
03:00 A.M. EST

The bedside comm unit chirped. This time, Jurgen was wide awake and ready for it.

"Señor Aguila! Good news. I've figured out the rebels' smuggling scheme; they've been shipping disassembled matériel up to the Moon piece by piece, disguised as mining equipment, and assembling it there, and they've been doing it for ten *years*. And this MANTA thing: it's not a weapon at all. It appears to be a portable teleport receiver."

Aguila was struck silent for a moment—but only a moment. "Very good. But I'm not interested in that now. I've got a more important assignment for you."

Jurgen's excitement and sense of achievement burst like a balloon. Again. *"Now* what?"

"Did you see that report on GNN this evening?"

"You mean last night? Yeah. Pretty ghastly, innit?"

"The reporter said the video was leaked by a highly placed United Nations source."

Jurgen shrugged. "Isn't that what reporters always say?"

"Jurgen?" Something in the tone of Aguila's voice warned the younger man, and he thumbed the comm unit volume down.

"Find me that leak!"

Port Aldrin, Luna
20 November 2069
11:00 GMT

Dalton, Britt, and Jeff Mahoney had been on the run for six days straight, bouncing from dome to dome, spoofing the computers, installing MANTA receivers, and sometimes ferrying ATFOR prisoners.

It was a dizzying job, but Dalton didn't mind. It kept him from thinking about Dara, and besides, he was finally learning to appreciate the concept of Operation Three-Card Monte.

It was the old shell game, pure and simple. If ATFOR didn't know where their prisoners were, they couldn't mount a rescue mission. And between the actual movements of prisoners, and the imaginary movements and shuttle schedules Dalton was feeding into the local airlock computers, there was no way the UN could sort them all out, even if they *had* penetrated LunaWeb—which presumably they had, since they no doubt had their own compspecs working every bit as hard as Dalton was.

He finished deleting some real transit records from the local computer and darted off to catch up with Britt and Jeff, who had just installed another MANTA disk. Much as Dalton hated to admit it, young Mahoney had been right. Once he'd gotten on Britt's good side—which, despite Akkerman's death, was something his actions during the Grimaldi Raid had managed to accomplish—the Cockney sergeant *was* willing to give him the shirt off his back. Probably the fillings from his teeth and the hair from his chest, too; Britt had an incredible tolerance for pain, which he'd demonstrated one night by biting the neck off a beer bottle.

The memory made Dalton's stomach churn. They'd been drinking TychoBrau that night, and Britt had knocked off a twelve-pack by himself. Jeff Mahoney had only made it through two bottles before he developed a compulsion to worship at the altar of the porcelain goddess, and Dalton had wisely remembered something Terrell Davis had told him years before: that TychoBrau was actually German for "urine sample."

He chased the memory away and rounded the corner, almost bumping into Britt and Jeff, who were coming back the other way. "You done already?" Dalton asked.

Jeff nodded. "Yeah."

"So what's next, Sarge?"

Britt fished a notepad out of his pocket. Paper and pencil may have been awfully low-tech way to transmit information, but it was harder to intercept than a bitstream. "Uh, next," Britt said, consulting his notes, "we report to Airlock D and pick up a prisoner sod to be transported back to Imbrium. That's—" He looked up and scratched his head.

Jeff pointed. "That way." To Dalton and Britt's questioning stares, he replied, "Hey, I used to come down here all the time with my dad. I know this particular piece of this rat's maze, like—" His sunny freckled smile failed. "Well, anyway, there's a FoodNet unit about half a klick down that way. We can grab something to eat on our way to the airlock."

The first two food selections came out blue and fuzzy, but the turkeyburgers seemed to be safe, edible, and just as appealing as on the day they were made. "Sorry," Dalton mumbled. "The peripheral systems are going a little wonky."

"Never mind." Britt took a bite out of the burger, and turned to Jeff. "So, Mahoney, what does your old man do?"

"Did," Jeff corrected. "Past tense. He's dead."

Britt looked down and mumbled, "Sorry I brought it up."

"Nah, not your fault. Dad was always getting into trouble. He was the black sheep of the family; met a girl from the wrong side of the freeway. You know the story. Dropped out of college to become a longshoreman; emigrated up here to be a spacedock worker. Mom got bored and took off when I was three; Dad got into the labor movement and became a union organizer."

Dalton finished chewing, swallowed, and wondered if he was brave enough to order up some FoodNet coffee. "So what happened to him? Accident?"

Mahoney shook his head. "No. He tried to organize a shop that some friend of Kinthavong's didn't want organized. The SAS paid us a little visit in the middle of the night. Broke Dad's arms, then his legs. Then they got carried away and busted his skull. He never even woke up."

Dalton looked down at his suddenly unappetizing turkey burger. "Sorry. I really am."

Mahoney shrugged. "You didn't know. But now maybe you understand. I'm not in this for any big intellectual reason. For me this is personal."

Britt finished his own burger and started eyeing Dalton's uneaten half. "Not to be rude, what, but why'd you stay 'ere? Moon's a 'ell of a place for a kid alone."

"Dad had family, back on Earth," Jeff said, "but we were never close. I stayed up here because"—he lifted his hands, palms up, and looked around—"well, this is my home. I was born on Earth, but I don't remember it. This is where I belong." He looked down at his unfinished turkey burger, then scooped it up and threw it in the FoodNet recycling chute.

He stood up. "C'mon, Sarge, Dalt. Let's go collect our goddam prisoner and get over to Imbrium." Without waiting for a reply, Jeff stalked off.

Britt licked his fingers and looked at Dalton's half-eaten burger. "You going to ditch that?" Dalton nodded, and Britt scooped up the burger and darted after Jeff. Dalton fell in behind.

They met up with another LDF group at Airlock D and located their prisoner. She was a woman, clearly, and judging from the back and the way she filled out her blue jumpsuit, a young and good-looking one. Reddish blond hair, in a collar-length cut; lean, muscular physique, not tall, not short. Dalton and Jeff checked her out and elbowed each other like a couple of frat boys eyeing the newest sorority pledge, while Britt took possession of the keys to her cuffs and leg irons. Then the three of them strode forward to introduce themselves.

"Captain?" Britt barked out. The prisoner turned around.

Jeff's lower jaw nearly dropped off.

"Aunt Bunny?"

MAJOR NAKAGAWA

Given that the Moon was settled primarily by scientists, engineers, and agronomists, one question naturally arises: how did the Lunar Defense Force manage to come up with so many excellent high-ranking officers?

In one part, it was simple supply and demand. Just as it is easy to make the varsity ringball team in a town of 2,000, commissioned-officer status in the LDF was pretty much there for the asking, for anyone with military experience and an honest desire to join. And as few ex-military personnel aspire to be second lieutenants, some rank inflation was only natural.

As for the other part, the LDF acquired good officers because General Jackson was right: the final frontier *was* a magnet for disgruntled veterans, cashiered mavericks, and other idealists, romantics, and social misfits. And despite the UN's insistence to the contrary, there *were* defections from the ATFOR ranks, particularly during the latter stages of the campaign.

Consider Major Yuji Nakagawa, for example, a romantic if ever there was one. The middle son of a prominent Kobe shipping family, he spent his childhood dutifully studying mathematics and engineering and sweating his way through the series of examination hells that constitute the Japanese school system. But at night, when the lights were out and his parents thought he was safely tucked in bed, young Yuji would pull the covers up over his head, switch on his forbidden flashlight, and thrill for hours to tattered old books that told him the ancient stories of brave ronin and noble samurai. Then, when he could keep his eyes open no longer, he'd switch off the light and drift into a restless sleep, his dreams filled with the sight of brave men in lacquered armor, the sound of heroically clashing steel, and the distant siren call of Bushido.

Occasionally his father caught him reading. But the books and the flashlight were easily replaced, and the bruises soon healed. And in a way, the beatings were never half so painful as that one cold, silent stare his father gave him on the day he turned eighteen and announced that he was not going to Keio University but rather had enrolled in the Naval Academy at Eta Jima. Years of estrangement and silence followed, broken only by the terse fax of congratulations he received on the day he was promoted to first lieutenant and assigned to the *Amatsukaze*.

It was, as even his father had to admit, a plum of an assignment. The *Amatsukaze* was an absolutely state-of-the-art missile destroyer, barely two years old, and a proud national symbol of Nippon's reemerging role as a great world power.

The Okinawa Incident put an end to all that, however. China, acting through the Security Council, quickly realized it did not want another Greater East Asia Co-Prosperity Sphere, and in a defanged Nippon there was no room for military machines like the *Amatsukaze* or for career officers like Yuji Nakagawa. So he spent a miserable six months in a cheap flat in Hiroshima, staring alternately at his navel and his knife blade, then decided to move to the one place where his experience in engineering and nuclear propulsion systems would be valued and welcome.

He emigrated to the Moon.

— Chaim Noguchi, *A History of the Lunar Revolution*

CHAPTER 17

Port Aldrin, Luna
Briefing Room, LDF Alpha Company
21 November 2069
20:15 GMT

A riding crop slapped sharply on the top of his computer monitor, snapping him back to the here and now. "Major? You're drifting off again."

Yuji looked up and blinked rapidly. "Sorry, sir." Colonel Emile Vachon was Gallic to a fault and, unfortunately, Yuji's commanding officer. "It won't happen again, sir."

"It had better not. You are perhaps suffering an attack of the attention deficit disorder?"

"No, sir. I was just thinking a moment about my family, back on Earth."

Colonel Vachon arched an eyebrow. "Oh? Perhaps there is some question of where your loyalties lie?"

A flash of bushido made Yuji's spine stiffen, and his short black hair bristled in anger. "Absolutely not, *sir!* I am proud to be a citizen of the Free State Selena and a loyal member of the Lunar Defense Forces, *sir!*"

Taken aback by Yuji's outburst, Colonel Vachon fumbled with his riding crop, then looked around at the other officers in the briefing room and recovered. "Yes, very good, Major

Nakagawa. Now, the sooner we do our part in this little war, the sooner we can all talk to our families back on Earth again, *n'est-ce pas?* So if you would be so kind as to resume . . ."

With a faint blush of embarrassment coloring his cheeks, Yuji settled back into his seat and lifted his lightpen. "Right. We're now at T-plus-fifteen." He touched the lightpen to his monitor panel. "If all has gone according to plan, the commando squads will have penetrated the Lacus Mortis outer perimeter and set up MANTA receivers here, here, and here." Yuji tapped three points on the screen map, and left three pulsing orange dots behind. These were echoed on the rotating holographic map hovering in the center of the briefing room. "When we receive the confirmation signal, I will lead Alpha Company First Platoon through here." He circled the third MANTA dot, the one farthest from the dome, and drew an arrow pointing upward. "We will slip under the shield and secure the south airlock here"—he drew another circle and another arrow—"and begin a diversionary thrust toward the main reactor, here." He scrawled a thick X.

Colonel Vachon nodded. "Splendid. Major Thompson?"

Major Lloyd Thompson, commander Alpha Commander Third Platoon and sitting ninety degrees to Yuji's right, picked up his own lightpen and began drawing, this time in green.

"With any luck," Thompson drawled, "the dirts'll think Yuji's gang is a sapper squad, out to blow the reactor, and they'll shut down the ion shield and scramble the gunships. Not that the gunships'd do any good against soldiers inside the complex, but they won't want to risk losing the birds if they can't shut down First Platoon." Thompson paused and grinned as if he'd just run over a big fat armadillo.

"Personally, I expect those shields'll drop faster than a cheerleader's drawers, at which point I will lead Third Platoon through here." He circled the northernmost MANTA dot. "We'll grab control of the hangar and make sure none of those gunships actually get out'n the barn door. Over to you, Terabi."

Major Benazir Terabi, commander Fourth Platoon, sitting opposite Yuji, looked to Colonel Vachon for approval to proceed and received a quick nod. "While Third Platoon is holding the north end of the gunship hangar," she began, "I will lead Fourth Platoon through here"—she circled the middle MANTA dot in yellow—"and secure the main gallery just south of the hangar area. This should prevent the Terrans from reinforcing the hangar security personnel and give Third Platoon sufficient time to seize the gunships intact or destroy them. At which point my team and I will deploy our MANTA receivers and be reinforced by two companies of colonial militia to complete the elimination of all resistance."

Colonel Vachon smiled and slapped his riding crop against his open palm in satisfaction. "Excellent! And I myself will wait with Major Chao and the Second Platoon, ready to provide reinforcement wherever it is needed. This is, I must say, a most brilliant and logical plan!"

"'Course you'd say that," Thompson grumbled, apparently not realizing anyone could hear him. "It's *your* plan."

Vachon hadn't quite caught Thompson's words. *"Comment?* You had something to say, Major?"

Thompson screwed his face up in a thoughtful scowl, then threw his lightpen down on the console and went for it. "Beggin' the colonel's pardon, sir, but this idea of sending us in in dribs and drabs all over the map strikes me as being about as bright as takin' a whiz on a fire ants' nest. We'll be spread out thin as a raccoon on Interstate 35. If just one of our teams runs into serious opposition—"

Vachon dismissed the objection with a wave of his hand. "Ah, do you not see? That is the beauty of this plan. We have the advantage of superior firepower and superior armor. If we strike them *everywhere,* we throw them into such confusion that they cannot possibly react in time."

"Confusion works both ways, sir," Thompson said, shaking his head slowly. "And besides, what about the intel reports that Lacus Mortis has been reinforced with a company of Quebecois light infantry?"

Colonel Vachon smiled. "Then we have nothing to fear. Once they find out that *I* command this battalion, my French-speaking brothers will join hands with us in solidarity!"

Major Thompson let out a deep sigh, then took off his glasses and rubbed his eyes. "Liberty, equality, insanity," he muttered, so softly that only Yuji heard.

The command briefing broke up, and the majors went back to their platoons to brief them on the final details. Then it was only a matter of waiting and trying to rest while the commando teams crept closer to Lacus Mortis and the chronometer slowly ticked down to H hour.

A loud knock on the door roused Yuji Nakagawa out of his meditation. "Enter!" he called out. "C'mon in, y'all!" The door slid open, and a somewhat haggard and sleepless-looking Lloyd Thompson plowed through.

"Sorry to bother you," Thompson said, "but I couldn't sleep and I thought you—" He stopped short, sniffed the thick incense smoke in the air, and looked around the room, wide-eyed. "Jesus, Yuji, what the hell are you doing? Holding a séance?"

As always, Yuji felt a pang of irritation at the arrival of the Texas gaijin. It was hard to tell which was worse—his complete lack of manners, his braying voice, or those cloddish *boots*. And then, as always, Yuji shrugged off his annoyance and patiently accepted the fact that Thompson, whatever his shortcomings, was the closest thing he had to a friend. "Something like that, yes. It's a Shinto thing. You wouldn't understand."

Thompson finished looking over the room and brought his gaze back to Yuji. "And how can you *sit* like that? It hurts my knees just to look at you."

"Long practice," Yuji explained, as he slowly straightened out of the full lotus position. "Can I do something for you, Lloyd?"

Thompson didn't answer. Instead, he strode across the small room and dropped to his knees in front of

Yuji's *daisho*. "Wow! Beautiful blades, man! When did you—"

"I brought them up when I immigrated," Yuji said, gently taking the razor-sharp katana from Thompson and re-sheathing it. "I kept them in storage until now." He replaced the sword on the rack.

Slowly Thompson turned around and looked Yuji in the eye. "But tonight you felt like it was finally time to pull them out?"

Equally slowly, Yuji nodded.

Thompson grinned. "Hell's bells, man! Then I'm not nuts after all! Look what *I* dug out!" With a wild flourish, he opened up his jacket and whipped out a fourteen-inch stag-handled bowie knife.

Yuji gently steered the point away from his face. "I take it you're worried about the mission?"

Thompson nodded. "Darn tootin'. I figure either Colonel Vac-head is right and I'm wrong, and this is gonna go down slicker'n an owl's wick. Or else the colonel's wrong and *I'm* right, in which case we are about to take off our trousers and jump butt first into a cactus patch."

"That would indeed be a problem," Yuji observed.

Thompson paused a serious moment and looked his friend right in the eye. "So how about it, man? Don't it bother you that we're going in without a clearly defined way of getting out again?"

"Colonel Vachon seems to think—"

"Screw the colonel! If the mission goes to hell and the feces hit the fan, what're we gonna *do?*"

"What we must do," Yuji answered. "Our duty, as soldiers. To follow our orders; to lead our men. To fight, if we can. To die, if we must."

Thompson took a long, hard look at Yuji. "That seems like kind of a fatalistic attitude."

Yuji shrugged. "But a traditional one. There is a song, you know. We Japanese put everything important into our poems and songs. I won't try to sing it for you—the translation wouldn't fit the melody—but it's called 'The

Song of the Warrior,' and it's at least a thousand years old: 'If I go to sea, I shall return a corpse awash; if duty calls me to the mountain, a verdant sward shall be my pall; thus for the sake of my fatherland I shall not die peacefully at home.'"

Thompson waited until the last word died away, then shuddered. "Jeez. Talk about morbid. No wonder you people invented hari-kari."

"It's hara-kiri," Yuji corrected. "But never mind that. It just so happens that I've been saving something else for a day like this." He gestured for Thompson to sit on the floor, placed a tiny cloisonné cup in his hands, and turned to the cooking unit. "Sake," he said proudly, over his shoulder. "A half-liter of the absolute best, brought all the way from Earth. And it should be just the right temperature now." He lifted a steaming saucepan off the burner and turned around. "Hold your cup steady." He poured delicately, somehow managing to hit the cup and not Thompson's fingers. The potent, acrid fumes brought tears to Thompson's eyes.

Next, Yuji filled his own cup, then raised it up to his face and breathed deeply. "Ah," he said, smiling broadly, "nectar of the gods!"

Thompson gulped and started to take a tentative sip.

"Wait!" Yuji called out. Thompson paused, with some relief evident. "Before we drink, a toast!"

Thompson looked into the cup, then back to Yuji. "You mean like 'Prosit'? Or 'Over the lips and through the gums, look out stomach—'"

"No. A *real* toast. To honor, glory, and battles that will live a thousand years in the hearts of men!" Yuji lifted his cup high. *"Tenno heika,* banzai!" He downed the sake in a single toss.

Thompson watched Yuji, then shrugged, and followed suit. "Remember the Alamo!"

Lacus Mortis
22 November 2069
06:30 GMT

Major Yuji Nakagawa pelted hell-for-leather down a narrow corridor inside the Lacus Mortis dome, trying to force a fresh power cell into his ACR pulse rifle as he ran. "Lieutenant Devereaux, report!" No response. "Sergeant Ganter!" Dead air.

A burst of projectile fire ripped across the plazmetal floor, and a glancing hit from behind made his shields flare. More out of instinct than thought, Yuji threw himself shoulder-first into a tiny alcove off to the right.

Ricochets spanged and spattered off the floor and walls, but the alcove offered some protection from direct fire. Yuji pulled himself up to a seated position with his back against the wall, then punched up the gain on his suit radio and tried again. "Lieutenant Devereaux! Report!" Again there was no answer beyond the faint hiss of an open comm channel.

Yuji Nakagawa swore fluently in three languages, then spared a moment for his jammed rifle. The drill was almost a reflex: clear, tap, reset, reload. All the red indicators switched to a satisfying green, and rifle hummed up to full power.

Whew. At least one thing on this mission was working right.

Yuji swung the rifle around to cover the corridor he'd just come from, then turned his attention to the suit radio. "Baker Squad!" He punched for the alternate NCO frequency. "Anyone in Baker Squad! Report!"

A hash of heterodyning signals stabbed through his ears; then the comm system signal processors sorted them out and one clear young voice emerged: "Corporal Jeffers reporting, sir. Sergeant Fong is dead." A harsh blare of static surged through, obliterating the voice. "—pinned down. Repeat: we are pinned down! Heavy full-automatic weapons fire! I count eight, possibly ten hosti—" Another blast of static; probably a side effect of Jeffers's shields taking a direct hit. "Heavy armor and at least one rocket laun—"

There was a sharp guttural noise, maybe human, maybe electronic, and then Corporal Jeffers went off the air.

"Corporal?" Yuji slammed a fist on his ACR in frustration, then punched up the Able Squad NCO frequency. "Sergeant Hegstrom! Update status!"

The Norwegian sergeant's laconic voice rolled through Yuji's helmet, speaking calmly in blatant defiance of the gunfire and screaming in the background. "It's worse, sir. Lieutenant Kirin just finished dying, and Beck and Parrant are both down. I don't think we can hold our position much longer." Something exploded with a noise that made Yuji jump, then he realized the sound had come through the comm link. "Sergeant, is that external sound I'm hearing?" he asked.

"Yes, sir, my helmet visor has been shot away. But I can still see okay out of my right eye."

Yuji sagged against wall and muted his end of the comm link. *Oh, you fickle, fickle gods of war . . .*

He thumbed the comm link back on. "Get out of there, Sergeant. Take anyone who can still walk and head north, for the hangars. Try to rendezvous with Third Platoon."

Hegstrom sounded puzzled. "Sir?"

"That's an order! Mission scrubbed. Withdraw north and evacuate."

"But, sir, you and Baker Squad—"

"Baker Squad has been neutralized, and I'm cut off and pinned down. Save what you can, Sergeant."

There was a short, poignant pause. "Roger, sir. Hegstrom out." The link fell silent.

Yuji wasted a few moments fondling the corded hilt of his tanto knife, strapped tightly to the outside of his right boot. Then a sudden realization struck him like a slap in the face, and he sat up, all senses tautly alert.

The probing fire in the corridor had stopped.

Excluding divine intervention, that could mean only one thing: the bad guys were coming down the corridor to dig him out. If they had grenades, one of those silvery, spiky red things should come bouncing around the corner any moment now. Beads of icy sweat sprang out in Yuji's short black hair, and every muscle went tight. Ten seconds crawled by like snails.

No grenade. They must not have grenades. Slowly, Yuji drew one breath, then another, and willed his arms to relax and start moving again. *They're going to do this the old-fashioned way.* Carefully, deliberately, he lifted his rifle and sighted in on the place where he expected the first head to pop around the corner. *So I'll get one. Maybe two.*

His gaze fell on the large ventilation grate set in the wall on the far side of the corridor. One tiny detail slowly stood out. *A door activator? Why would anyone put a door activator on a ventilation grate? Unless . . .*

He lowered the rifle a little. "No," he said softly. "That would be stupid." But insane as the notion seemed, it offered him the only glimmer of hope around. He got to his feet and stretched the kinks of out his leg muscles. "Crazy. Stupid." *But what the hell have I got to lose?* Rocking on the balls of his feet, he drew several deep, clearing breaths, focused on establishing a rhythm, pumped his *chi* until he felt as if his chest might explode, raised his rifle high, and—

"Banzai!" He burst into the corridor sprinting at top speed and firing like a madman, not at the enemy troops up the corridor—*My gods, how'd there get to be so many of them?*—but at that tiny bronze nubbin at the side of the ventilation grate. Some of the UN soldiers had wits and reflexes; as if in slow motion, guns opened up and lines of fire tracked across the corridor. In another instant they would catch up to him—

"HAI!" Yuji fired one last wild shot at the activator and threw himself into a headlong leap at the ventilation grate.

The shot connected. The grate flashed open to reveal the narrow secret passageway concealed behind it. Yuji hit the floor in a tuck-and-roll, came up on his feet, and slapped the door-close button as he sprinted past it. With a clang like the gates of Hell the grate slammed shut behind him.

Yuji didn't stop running. A dip in the tunnel, a left turn, a quick drop-and-roll to avoid colliding with a low-hanging beam. He hit a fork in the tunnel, took the right branch strictly on a hunch, and ran into a closed door.

The door slid open automatically, and Yuji's ACR made short work of the two enemy soldiers on the other side. He paused a second to listen for sounds of pursuit—there were none, he must have shaken them off—then knelt down to snag a spare oxygen bottle that had rolled away from one of the corpses.

Then he did a double-take. "UN troops in *black* uniforms?" he said out loud. "That's odd." He considered taking a moment to investigate the matter further, then decided it would be smarter to keep moving. Yuji set off again, this time at a fast jog.

The next corridor he emerged into was broader, better lit, and apparently empty. He shifted the rifle to his left hand, kept jogging, and tried the suit radio again. "Baker Squad?" No answer. "Able?" This time there was some kind of response, but the interference was too severe for it to be intelligible. "Alpha Company? Respond."

There was a burst of static, and then he could practically feel the Texan's warm grin through his headphones. "Yuji? Are you still alive?"

"So far. What's your situation, Lloyd?"

"Not good, little buddy. Not good. We're pretty much bottled up here in the hangars. The dirts can't get in, but we can't get out, either."

"The gunships?"

"Our compspecs couldn't crack the onboard computers, so we got 'em wired for demolition, but we'd kind of like to be out of here when that happens, y'know?"

"Roger that." Yuji came up to an intersection of corridors, flattened himself up against one wall, and edged along to the corner. Nothing to the left. Carefully, carefully, he tried a duck-and-peek. Nothing to the right.

Again, on a hunch, Yuji picked the left corridor and resumed his jog. "What about the Fourth Platoon?"

There was a pause from Thompson, a keyed mike, but no speech. "They're toast," he said at last. "We picked up a few stragglers, but—"

"Well, you'll pick up a few more lost sheep from me, if they make it. What about the Second and the colonel?"

"Word is Colonel Vachon came through right behind Terabi just before all hell broke loose. I haven't had any contact with the Second. Dirts've managed to jam all our long-range comm."

Yuji swore and shook his head.

His momentary distraction was almost fatal.

A tall soldier in a solid black uniform seemed to come out of nowhere, sweeping his heavy weapon down in a blow that knocked the ACR out of Yuji's hands and sent it spinning across the corridor floor. He followed up with a reverse to Yuji's head that threw him back against the wall and made his helmet ring like a cast-bronze gong. Before Yuji could recover, the man brought his weapon to bear and fired a burst at Yuji's head. Yuji managed to drop beneath that, but in trying to roll away from the Blacksuit, he slammed into a wall. As the air exited his lungs, he looked up to see his ACR beckoning to him from across the corridor, and one thought flashed into his mind: *It's too far away.* The killer clearly expected Yuji to go for the rifle, though, and stepped aside to get a clear field of fire.

Yuji saw his one opening. In a move he'd been preparing for all his life, he drew his tanto knife and swung it up and around in an arc that slid slowly through the enemy soldier's shields, then speeded up as it ripped deep into the man's left thigh. There was a high, inhuman scream, audible even through Yuji's helmet, as the black-clad soldier staggered back and tried to bring his weapon to bear, but it was already too late. Yuji was on his feet, willing his entire body to be a weapon, a lance of unstoppable iron, and in one fluid lunge he drove the blade of the tanto through the Blacksuit's shields, his armor, his sternum, and his heart.

Suit shields flared and flashed an iridescent blue; the feedback threw Yuji back against the wall. But something worse was happening to his attacker: his shields arced and shorted out, and thick snakes of dazzling lightning danced across his body as kilovolts of shield energy took the shortest path to ground.

The shortest path to ground was through the blade of the tanto. The soldier jerked and writhed like an earthworm impaled on an electrified hook, then dropped like a nerveless bag of meat.

"Yuji!" Nakagawa shook his head, blinked away the afterimages, and realized the ringing was in his ears, not his helmet. That, and he realized Thompson had been screaming through the open comm link for at least the last thirty seconds. "Major Nakagawa! *Report!*"

"I'm still alive," he said. He drew a deep breath, let it out, then staggered to his feet and over to the fallen Blacksuit. The corded hilt of his tanto, still embedded in the enemy's chest, was mostly gone, and what remained was still smoking. He grabbed it, and with considerable effort, wrenched it free. The blade was partially melted.

He dropped it on the floor with a clatter and turned his attention to the corpse. Until now he'd never really had a chance to take a good look at a black-suited soldier. The fallen man's uniform and insignia markings, subtle as they were, quickly told the whole story.

Yuji sat down heavily on the floor, and thumbed his comm link back on. "Lloyd? I've got some bad news for you about the fellows in the black suits: they're not ATFOR."

Thompson's disbelief was audible. "Say again, Yuji? I coulda sworn I heard you say—"

"The Blacksuits are not ATFOR," Yuji repeated, speaking slowly and clearly. "They are NDE—New German Unity Army. Sturmwehr."

"You sure about that?"

Yuji cast another sidelong glance at the corpse. "Yes. Absolutely."

"Oh, Jesus H. Christ on a Popsicle stick! No *wonder* we got our asses handed to us on a platter. We gotta get word back to—"

"Yes," Yuji said. "That would be nice. Any idea how?"

Thompson fell silent a moment, then laughed. "Well, my

news is better than yours. My techs've hot-wired a cargo shuttle! Sergeant Hegstrom and the rest of your boys have shown up, and we're gettin' ready to bust outta here. Any chance you could still make the party?"

Yuji laughed, sighed, shook his head, and tried to feel about six emotions at once. "Yes, you goddam gaijin! Yes! Give me about fifteen minutes. If don't make it by then, I never will. Nakagawa out."

"Roger and a big ten-four, little buddy. Thompson out." The comm link went dead. Yuji laughed once more, then staggered to his feet, found his ACR on the other side of the corridor, picked it up, and checked it out.

The primary emitter was smashed, useless. "Damn!" Yuji threw the wrecked rifle down, then turned around, scowling and looking for something to kick. His eyes fell on the heavy multi-barreled automatic weapon of his deceased adversary.

"Well? Why not?" He picked up the weapon—it was massive but not unmanageable—then retrieved a spare ammunition drum from the corpse. "Sorry about that, Überman." After making one last check to be sure the weapon was loaded and ready to rock, he started up the corridor—

And stopped. Turned back to the corpse. "Hey," Yuji asked, "does this mean I've lost my Honorary Aryan status?"

CHAPTER 18

Lacus Mortis
21 November 2069

Rest, the little man in the back of Yuji's head whispered. *Lloyd Thompson will hold the shuttle for you. This looks like a good place to sit down. Rest.*

"No." Yuji fought off the weakness invading his legs, picked up the railgun, and staggered on. "Keep moving."

Then drop the gun, the voice suggested. *It's too heavy. You'll go faster without it.*

"No." Yuji wrapped both hands arms around the gun, just in case one of them decided to rebel, and clutched it to his chest. The railgun went through standard blue UN battlesuits like a hot fork through tofu—there were the skeletal remains of six or eight men back there somewhere to prove it—and Yuji was not about to give it up.

Trouble was, the railgun was also more than a match for *his* armor, too, and two Blacksuits back there had almost succeeded in proving that. *Trying to slug it out with them was capital-D dumb, Yuji,* that annoying little voice said. It was starting to sound like his father. He had finally beaten the Germans, yes, but he'd drained his shields almost flat in the process. Then, when he'd run into that Blacksuit with the heavy armor and the rocket launcher—

201

Another stab of white-hot pain surged out from the jagged shell fragment buried in his left thigh. Yuji sagged against the corridor wall and bit his tongue to keep from crying out.

My stupid, stupid little samurai, the voice whispered, mocking. *Your head is full of stories, and look where they've gotten you.*

"Father," Yuji gasped, when the wave of pain let up, "there's one thing I've always wanted to say to you: Shut up. Just shut up." He fumbled for the medipack on his left bicep, and punched in the code for more endorphins.

Ha, the voice said, *weak fool. A* real *samurai would not submit to pain.*

"Eat my shorts," Yuji answered. Slowly, much too slowly, a flow of cool relief flooded through his veins, and the inner voice fell silent.

"Yuji? Come back at me, little buddy." It took him a minute to realize the new voice was not another hallucination, but Lloyd Thompson. Yuji activated his mike.

"I'm still here, Lloyd. So are you, obviously. Why?"

Thompson ignored the question. "How's the leg?"

Yuji peered at the wound, then prodded it. The endorphins were starting to work. "Bleeding's almost stopped. That fragment must have been so red-hot that it cauterized the hole."

"Good. Now, how bad's your suit? Will it hold air?"

Yuji fingered the torn fabric. "Nothing a little duct tape won't fix. Why?"

"Never mind. Just . . . You're sure you're in L corridor?"

Yuji called up his computer map of the Lacus Mortis installation. "Corridor L, Section Twenty-three, Frame D-Two." He looked around. "Just across from the power conduit, about fifty meters from you—but with two solid walls and three platoons of Blacksuits between us."

"You leave those walls to us. Are you feeling up for a little exercise?"

The endorphins had finally taken full effect. Yuji poked

his wounded leg firmly and didn't feel a thing. "As ready as I'll ever be."

"Good. If there's any cover, you might want to take it. But be ready to move out when I give the signal."

Yuji worked himself back into a narrow gap between two sections of wall. "Got it. What's the signal, Lloyd?"

"Fire in the hole!"

An instant later, twenty meters down the hall, a section of wall erupted in a massive explosion that took out half the ceiling as well. The flaming debris was still flying when white-clad LDF troopers poured through the gap and into the corridor. *"Move it, Yuji!"* Thompson screamed. Naka-gawa popped out of his hole and dashed for the Whitesuits, dropping the railgun as he ran. As soon as he reached the men they fell back through the jagged hole in the plazmetal wall.

The next room was supposed to be warehouse space, but it was an insane red-green hell of blasting lasers and clattering railguns. Almost the full remaining force of Alpha Company was in there, trading heavy fire with a squad of Blacksuits. The last trooper through the hole slapped Yuji hard on the back and pointed him at a black-scorched hole in the far wall about twenty meters away. Yuji understood instantly and took off at a run. Something hard swatted him in the legs and lower back, and knocked him flying headfirst through the hole. He felt a little dizzy. . . .

Thompson was leaning over him, shaking him gently. "Yuji? Little buddy? Can you hear me?"

"Yes, gaijin." Yuji tried to sit up. For some reason, his legs wouldn't move. "What's going on?" In the distance he could hear firing.

"We're in a hell of fix, pardner. Dirts tried to do an end run around us; they sent a rocket squad outside the dome. We got 'em, but not before they blew the hangar door."

"Yes. So?" Yuji tried to sit up and failed again. Most aggravating.

"It's now hard vacuum in the hangar. Nobody without an intact suit is gonna make it."

"What about my wounded?"

"Most of them were already on board the shuttle. The rest are dead. But we got one more wounded man we can't move."

Yuji started to suspect where this was leading. "Help me sit up!" he demanded. Gently the Texan slipped his arms under Yuji's shoulders and eased him up to a sitting position. Yuji willed himself to look.

From the rib cage down, he was a bloody, punctured, shredded mess.

He could still turn his head, though. He looked at Thompson. "Just how many boosters did you give me?"

"All of 'em. And all the icers and blood pressure stabilizers, too."

"Why?"

Thompson stood up, looked away, then turned back to Yuji. "We got one more problem, little buddy. We had to improvise some on the demolition charges. Can't detonate 'em by remote."

Yuji threw his head back and laughed. "So you need a kamikaze—"

Thompson wheeled on him. "Christ, no! You could pass out or chicken out or—" Abruptly Thompson realized who he was talking to. "No, we'll use timers. But we figure we need three minutes to start the clock and get clear, and we need someone to stay behind and make sure those black-suited devils don't disarm the charges."

Yuji made his best attempt at looking Thompson in the eye, then glanced around the room and spotted a captured railgun standing in a corner. "Give me that damn thing," he said. "Then prop me up someplace where I'll have a good field of fire." Thompson did, and they gave the remaining LDF troopers the order to fall back through the airlock, start the timers, and board the shuttle.

The Blacksuits wasted almost a minute after the firing stopped—probably wondering if it was a ruse—and didn't start moving forward until a deep rumble through the floor indicated the shuttle's engines were coming to life.

Yuji waited until he had a few Blacksuits in clear view,

then squeezed off a burst and made them all dive for cover. A change in the tenor of the rumble told him the shuttle had lifted off and was safely away.

Thompson's voice crackled softly through the remains of Yuji's suit radio. *"Tenno heika,* banzai, little buddy."

"Remember the goddam Alamo, pardner."

Off to the right he caught the furtive movement of a pair of Blacksuits trying a flanking maneuver, and sprayed a burst of fire at them. Then he checked his watch. *Less than two minutes left. I wonder if the explosion will rupture the airlock.*

He never found out.

LACUS MORTIS, POSTMORTEM

One of the historian's favorite games is What If? For example, what if the Savoy cavalry had reinforced Marlborough's right at Blenheim? What if the Luftwaffe had left the bomb racks off the Me-262, and used it as the air-superiority fighter it was clearly meant to be? What if the United Nations, in its earliest notable military action, had permitted the Americans to complete the destruction of the Iraqi army in Kuwait?

Along with these intriguing but ultimately unanswerable questions, one may as well ask this: what if the lunar rebels had forgone the raid on Lacus Mortis? The coalition that made up ATFOR was already in its death spiral. The Danish Duma had voted to pull its troops out. The fourth week of the conflict saw two minor mutinies among the Ivory Coast troops, both of which were repressed brutally. And now, with the covert insertion of New German Unity troops into the situation—a development that appalled many permanent members of the Security Council — it was only a matter of time until the war ended and the negotiations began. Victory — as measured by survival, and the achievement of at least some of the LDF's demands — was there for the plucking. *Why didn't the rebels wait?*

The answer lies with Pieter von Hayek and Josef von Hayek and, most of all, with General Consensus. The general was not, as SAS intelligence had theorized, a dishonorably discharged ex-American officer with the battle skills of Erwin Rommel and a sociopathic streak a kilometer wide. Rather, General Consensus was the Port Aldrin Central Computer chess program as adapted by Pieter and Josef to accept input from the Council of Lunar Governors and to output strategic decisions.

Few in the Lunar Defense Force knew the true nature of their commanding general. Also, considering the amount of time and money the United Nations put into trying to locate and capture "General Consensus," and given the fact that a warrant for his arrest remained open well into twenty-second century, it's apparent that the Security Council never got the joke either.

But when seen in this light, the decision to attack Lacus Mortis does make a sort of sense. In a chess game, the raid would have been a brilliant gamble, a master stroke that could have ended the game in one move.

In the sticky world of human emotions, however, it was an unmitigated disaster. Not only did the rebels suffer a costly defeat, but they also gave certain factions within the Security Council a new and grim resolve and figuratively drove the generals of ATFOR and the New German Unity into each other's arms. For General Consensus, brilliant tactician though he may have been, was completely unable to understand hate and the dangerous decisions and alliances it could cause humans to make.

After Lacus Mortis, the Security Council declared a unilateral cease-fire. Few in the colonial leadership deceived themselves, however: they knew the United Nations was only buying time to prepare for the final assault. And when that assault came it would be led not by the blue uniforms and indifferent conscripts of ATFOR but by the pitiless Blacksuits of the NDE.

The only questions were when, and where.

— Chaim Noguchi, *A History of the Lunar Revolution*

CHAPTER 19

Captain Eileen "Devil Bunny" Mahoney squared her shoulders, took a deep breath, and repeated herself. "You heard me correctly, sir. I want to defect."

Josef von Hayek leaned back in his chair, stroked his chin, and considered this novel turn of events. "Are you out of your mind, Captain?"

"No, sir!"

Josef arched an eyebrow and looked at Jeff. "Private Mahoney, do you think Captain Mahoney is sincere?"

Young Jeff Mahoney gulped, took a step forward, and nodded. "Yes, sir. I think Bunny, er, Captain Mahoney is serious about tossing in with us, sir."

"I see." Josef swiveled in his chair and looked at Britt. "Sergeant Godfrey? You've had the pleasure of the captain's company for four days now. What do you think?"

Britt scowled and considered the two Mahoneys. "I think, sir, they're going to drive me barmy if they don't stop bickerin'. First she says something, then 'e contradicts 'er, then she snaps back, and pretty soon there's a bleedin' *row* going on."

"I do not contradict her," Jeff blurted out.

"Yes, you do," Bunny retorted.

"Just stay out of this, Aunt Bunny. I was handling it just fine."

"You're just like your father!"

"Knock it off!" Josef ordered. Both Mahoneys fell still and looked a little embarrassed. Josef swiveled in his chair and looked at Dalton. "Starkiller? What's your take?"

"Sergeant Godfrey's got it nailed, sir. If those two weren't related, they'd be married."

Bunny lifted her chin. "Sir? I'm sorry, but it's just that Private Mahoney here is a dead ringer for my brother Sean."

"Dead is right," Jeff snorted.

"That's not—"

"Stop it!" Colonel von Hayek counted slowly to ten, then turned to Britt again. "Sergeant Godfrey, have you had a chance to get them DNA-scanned?"

"Yes, sir. It's not as accurate as matching parent and child, but they *are* related. First cousins or closer."

"Very good." Von Hayek nodded. "Now, Captain Mahoney," he waggled a finger at Jeff, "and I'm speaking *only* to Captain Mahoney. Why is it, exactly, that you want to turn traitor and join the LDF?"

Bunny shuddered at the word "traitor" and pursed her lips slightly. "Because—" she began in a hoarse voice. She stopped, swallowed hard, and tried again. "I am a loyal officer in the American army, sir. I am *proud* to be an American. And to tell the truth, if the LDF were fighting the American army, I don't think I could do this." She blinked. Her eyes were starting to look a little moist.

She stole a glance at Jeff. "But blood is thicker than words, sir. And Jeffrey's all the family I have left. I thought he was dead ten years ago. I'm his godmother, you see, sir, and I promised Sean I'd look out for him."

"You're kinda late, Aunt Bunny," young Mahoney grumbled.

"Private?" Josef said, in a low and menacing growl.

Bunny took a deep breath and blinked away her remembrances. "Besides, Colonel, you need me. I've fought the NDE before, during the Vienna Airlift in 2065."

Von Hayek perked up sharply. "NDE? Who said anything about the NDE?"

"C'mon, Colonel, the scuttlebutt's all over. Your guys didn't hit ATFOR at Lacus Mortis; they ran into Sturmwehr. I don't know how the Germans got there or what the Security Council is trying to pull, but you're going to need all the help you can get to beat those blacksuited bastards."

Josef von Hayek leaned back in his chair and went back to stroking his chin. "So you're just going to keep an eye on Private Mahoney, then?"

Bunny swallowed nervously. "Well, I've also seen those news reports about what happened at Volodya. I . . . I just can't feel any loyalty to the murderers who did that. I never swore allegiance to an army that would kill noncombatants. If you and the LDF don't stop the UN, who will?"

Colonel Von Hayek reached a decision. "Okay. Private Mahoney, escort our guest outside and wait in the hall with her. Godfrey, Starkiller, you stay here." He waited until the door had closed behind the Mahoneys, then turned to Britt. "Well?"

The sergeant shrugged. "Well, 'er reasons check out. And she was a capture, not a walk-in. I don't think she's a plant."

"I see. Starkiller?"

Dalton smiled coldly. It was not a nice sight. "It wouldn't be hard to jimmy the shields on her suit. We use a phase inverter and give it to her watchdog. If we get into a situation and she tries to turn on us, *splat!* Her shields will invert, and we'll clean her up with a mop and bucket. Jeff'll think it was an accident."

Von Hayek nodded thoughtfully. "Who'll control the inverter?"

Britt glanced at Dalton, then answered. "Dalt. I'm gettin' a wee bit soft on the chickadee, and I might hesitate. But 'e's still lookin' to get even for that Dara of 'is. Oh, 'e'd pull the trigger on 'er all right. No sweat."

Von Hayek took in Dalton's impassive demeanor. He nodded. "Okay, that sounds workable. Do that thing with her shields, then put her in your squad. If nothing else, we'll learn something about the way the ATFOR troops are trained." He stood up and opened the hall door. "Captain, in here, please. No, Private Mahoney, you stay put."

When Bunny had reentered the office, Josef sat down. "Okay, Captain, here's the story. Your offer is accepted, but you're on probation. You'll be issued a uniform and allowed to train with one of our units, but you will not be issued a weapon. And if we so much as suspect you're an intelligence plant, you will die. Is that clear?"

Bunny nodded crisply. "I expected nothing more, sir. Will I be in the same unit as my nephew?"

"Yes."

"Then I am satisfied, sir."

"Very good. Sergeant Godfrey and Specialist Starkiller here will see to getting you your equipment, and then they'll get you checked out on MANTA."

There was a slight but noticeable reaction out of Bunny, which was exactly what Josef was seeking. She clearly recognized the word, but didn't want to admit to it. "MANTA, sir?"

Von Hayek considered how to play this. If she was a mole . . . "Surely you must have heard of it. It's our tele-port system. That's how we beat you at Grimaldi. It's no secret anymore; your people at Lacus Mortis must have recovered at least five MANTA receivers—not that they're of any use without transmitters."

Bunny shrugged. "Don't tell me any more, sir. I'm not a tech, and I wouldn't understand anyway."

Well, *that* was an unexpected response. Josef considered her a moment longer, then nodded. "Right. Dismissed." Bunny wheeled around and marched toward the door.

"Oh, and, Bunny?" Josef added, as if as an afterthought. She stopped and turned around. "Yes, sir?"

"Sorry, but you're being temporarily demoted to lieutenant. Right now we need good platoon commanders more than we need captains."

"Understood, sir." If she was disappointed, she didn't show it. She left, and Dalton and Britt followed her.

ENDGAME

The rebels' last-ditch defense strategy was simple to describe but complex to execute. Since the question of when and where the New German Unity would attack was completely open, and as fortifying every known vulnerable point was quite impossible, the von Hayeks, junior and senior, adopted a doctrine of rapid response, which involved using the MANTA teleportation system to move LDF and militia units instantly where needed. For as everyone realized, even as they continued the pretense of negotiations with the Security Council, the forthcoming battle was one that would be won or lost in the colonial dome airlocks and the corridors immediately adjacent thereto.

The implementation of this plan called for a considerable amount of training. Not that there was much to learn in order to use the MANTA system — one simply stepped onto a transporter pad and reappeared microseconds later on a receiver pad — but because humans have an innate resistance to being dematerialized. The smooth operation of the rapid-response concept required, more than anything else, that troops be conditioned to *get off* the receiver pad before the next transportee came through.

The lunar technicians never came up with an adequate word to denote the condition that existed when two teleportees tried to occupy the same place at the same time. They simply knew that the results were unmistakably bad for all parties involved, and that it left a nasty stain on the receivers.

— Chaim Noguchi, *A History of the Lunar Revolution*

CHAPTER 20

Patrick Adams sat tensely in his chair, watching Pieter von Hayek talk. The governor was looking bad these days: haggard, and worn out. Sometimes Adams thought it was sheer force of will that kept the man going. That and pure anger at the UN.

He watched Von Hayek nod to the five Security Council members on the wall-mounted UNET screen and bring the video conference to an end. "Sirs, madam, I thank you in the name of the Free State for your thoughts and your time. I trust that you will consider some of the matters we have discussed today, and I hope we will be able to find more common ground as these discussions continue. Good day." Von Hayek tapped a button on his desk, and the link to Earth was broken.

Adams was on his feet, moving to the governor's side.

"My God," von Hayek said as he sagged back in his chair and ran his hands through his thinning gray hair. The hands, Adams noted, came away dripping with sweat. "It's like the mating dance of some kind of crane. One step forward, two steps back, squawk once, crap twice."

Adams handed the governor a paper towel. "I thought you did well. You're becoming quite the slippery politician."

Von Hayek glared. "That was not a compliment, Patrick."

"I agree." Amalia Trelstad, governor of Kepler Colony and silent up to this point, entered the conversation. "We don't need a canny negotiator now. We need a *leader*. Far be it from me to question your priorities, Pieter, but did we really need to waste two hours discussing the shape of the negotiating table?"

"Jaw-jaw is better than war-war," von Hayek said, quoting Churchill. "No, you're right, today's discussion did give new meaning to the word 'pointless.' But as long as the UN is still talking, they're not shooting, and every moment we prolong these discussions increases the chances of a peaceful settlement. One of these mornings they're going to wake up and realize they're in bed with the NDE, and on the day that happens, this war will be over."

Trelstad looked unconvinced. "I sincerely hope you're right, Pieter."

"Frankly, so do I." He stood, bowed slightly, and waved a hand toward the door. "I trust you'll inform the rest of the council of today's discussions?"

Trelstad took her cue and collected her things. "Yes, of course. And I trust you will remember to attend the council meeting tonight? Eight o'clock, Picard B. And you'll bring Josef?"

Von Hayek was slightly surprised. "The colonel? Why?"

"We need to make it clear to the hard-liners just how precarious our military situation really is and what we'll face if these negotiations collapse. Otherwise . . . well, some of the governors are getting impatient."

"I understand. Very well, I'll see if I can pry Josef away from his duties. See you then." Von Hayek squeezed Trelstad's hand, then smiled as Adams escorted her out the door.

The moment the door was safely shut, von Hayek collapsed rather than sat in his chair.

Adams darted to his side. "Pieter?"

"Patrick, I don't know who's worse, the Security Council or my own—" Von Hayek's desktop alarm pinged. *"Now* what?" he said, with some irritation.

Adams read the alert message upside down, a skill he had long ago cultivated. "Personal e-mail, for you. Looks like another bogus technical report."

Von Hayek looked at Adams narrowly. "Oh, so you've figured that much out?" He sighed. "Hell, then you may as well know the rest. Watch this." Von Hayek acknowledged the message, grabbed the report file, and dragged it over to his desktop compression processor. Covering his hand to hide his fingers, he punched in the decryption key, and a few moments later the real contents of the message were displayed: "Something wicked this way comes; the storm is rising. Advise you castle posthaste. Concerned, Beacon."

Patrick and Pieter's eyes met. "Oh, hell," Adams whispered. Von Hayek blanched a ghastly shade of white, and the vein in his forehead started to throb. "I'll call the Tycho Research Station and tell them we're coming," Adams said.

Von Hayek shook his head. "No," he gasped out. He seemed to be having trouble breathing. "Alert Josef first." He gulped hard, then fumbled open the center drawer of his desk and fished out a medicine vial. Adams caught a glimpse of the label: cardiac nitroglycerine.

Von Hayek got the vial open and dumped out some tiny pills.

"I'll get you a glass of water," Adams said, as he started to turn toward the door. Von Hayek caught his sleeve with surprising strength.

"No. Tell Josef!"

UN Headquarters, New York
26 November 2069
9:17 A.M. EST

Jurgen Flanders burst through the oaken double doors, causing Allegria Saldana to look up with a start. "Where's Aguila?" Jurgen demanded. He hadn't slept in days and was in no mood to negotiate.

Allegria darted a glance at the closed inner door, which gave the game away. Jurgen swept past her. "You can't go in there!" she called after him, as she tried to rise from her desk and got tangled in the headset wires. "He's in a meeting!"

"I don't care!" Jurgen got to the inner door and threw it open before Allegria could hit the power-lock button.

Three faces turned to greet him: Aguila, obviously annoyed; Heinrich Graf, obviously surprised; and Shi Cheng Wu, obviously . . . unreadable.

"I broke their code!" Jurgen shouted.

Aguila still seemed annoyed. "Jurgen, can't this wait until—"

"I know who the mole is!" That made even Aguila shut up. Everyone looked at Jurgen; tense, expectant.

"It's Haversham," Jurgen said softly. "He's been setting the rebellion up for ten years—papering over the weapons and armor shipments, handpicking radicals for important posts on the Moon, and tipping von Hayek off to your every move."

The silence hung a moment longer. "How . . . interesting," Shi Cheng Wu said.

"Are you certain of this?" Heinrich Graf asked.

Jurgen turned to him. "Did you just launch a raid from Lacus Mortis on Port Aldrin?"

The little German paled. "The rebels know about it," Jurgen said. "They're ready."

"*Damn!*" Aguila slammed a fist on his desk. "That deranged old *fool!*"

"I could have him arrested," Wu offered.

"No," Graf purred in an oily voice that made Jurgen shudder. "He would post bail and hold a press conference. I suggest that he's about to have a medical emergency."

Aguila looked at Graf, his mind obviously working through the implications. "You can arrange that?" Graf nodded. "Good." Aguila turned to Wu. "We need to get through to Leighton-Smythe. The Germans will need reinforcements if the Loonies know they're coming."

Later it would occur to Jurgen that he'd just seen a turning point in history, and he was amazed that they'd let him out of that room alive. But at the moment he was simply too exhausted to care.

Port Aldrin, Warehouse District
26 November 2069
15:20 GMT

Bunny's squad was moving forward in a two-four-two leapfrog pattern, practicing an assault. First Britt and Stahl would step out into the corridor, laying down covering fire as Oshikatta and Jeff moved forward. Then with Oshi and Jeff providing cover, Britt and Stahl moved up, followed closely by Bunny and Dalton.

"Closer to the wall, Jeff!" Bunny shouted as she ran by, her shoulders hunched to make a lower profile. "You don't want your butt sticking out and getting shot off!" Then she slammed up against Dalton, forcing him back against the closed door as she attempted to fit both their bodies into a niche barely deep enough to hold one. "Always keep flat, Starkiller. You never know when one of your squaddies might need to share your cover."

Dalton nodded. They weren't wearing battlesuits for this exercise, and the warmth and smell of Eileen Mahoney's body against his made him tremendously conscious of how uncomfortable he was. He squeezed back closer to the wall. "Yes, sir."

"Go!" she shouted, and again they dashed forward,

twelve meters to the next cover, where another corridor intersected the one they were in. As he'd been trained to do, Dalton took the left side and kept his pistol pointed down the intersecting corridor as he went around the corner. When he saw someone in a battlesuit charging toward him, he reflexively jerked the trigger.

He almost screamed when he saw the blue flare of shields around the man and realized he'd just shot someone in white LDF armor—with a gold eagle on the helmet.

"Colonel!" he shouted. He dashed forward and helped Josef von Hayek to his feet.

"My mistake," the colonel said as he shut down his shields and opened his faceplate. "I should have warned you I was coming down. Nice shot, by the way—center chest. But next time take your weapon off the low setting."

"Sorry." Dalton blushed, reset his pistol's power setting to high, then engaged the safety and holstered the weapon.

Bunny joined Dalton and Josef. Britt and the rest weren't far behind. "Come down to inspect us, Colonel?" Bunny asked, smiling. "It's going pretty well. I think my boys'll give you some surprises in that scrimmage with Captain Berghoff's squad tonight."

Von Hayek shook his head. "Sorry, Mahoney. Game's canceled. I came down here to tell you that we've just scanned two squadrons of hopshuttles leaving Lacus Mortis on a heading for here. ETA is twenty-five minutes."

Bunny's smile faded. "Blacksuits."

Von Hayek nodded. "Yeah."

Dalton objected. "Wait a minute. What about the ceasefire?"

"That's with the UN," Bunny pointed out. "This is the NDE. Maybe ATFOR is trying something slippery, or maybe the Germans have gone freelance."

Von Hayek nodded again. "Right. In any event, I want you suited up and ready to go in ten minutes. Observe comm silence; that's why I came down here to tell you myself. That, and I'll be tagging along with you."

"Maybe it's a bluff," Stahl mused hopefully.

"Maybe," Von Hayek said. "The governor is trying to contact the UN right now. But if it's for real, we'd better be ready."

"Right," Bunny said firmly. "Rock and roll in ten, boys!"

First Division Forward HQ
USN *Schwarzkopf*, CNV (S) - 93
26 November 2069
15:27 GMT

"General Daniels?" the tech sergeant said. "We scan six armored shuttles on course from Lacus Mortis to Port Aldrin."

Marcia Daniels looked up from the report she was reading. "That's odd. Nothing was authorized. You sure they're not our gunships?"

"No, sir, they're definitely troop shuttles."

Daniels frowned. This didn't smell right. "Very well—"

"General Daniels?" This was another tech, the long-range telecomm officer. "Sir, I've got an urgent message for you from Chairman Wu of the CWP."

"Wu?" Daniels weighed the two events, then decided the mystery shuttles could wait and opted to receive the message. "Put him through." A few seconds later the calm, unreadable face of Shi Cheng Wu popped up on one of her smaller viewscreens. "Chairman Wu," she said, nodding slightly. "What can I do for you?" Out of habit, she waited the three seconds for the light-speed lag.

"General Daniels," Wu said curtly, "by now you should be tracking a flight of troop shuttles en route from Lacus Mortis to Port Aldrin. They are not to be hindered in any way, and you are to stand by to render them assistance, if needed."

Marcia Daniels's surprise quickly turned to anger. "With all due respect, Chairman, I take my orders from Field Marshal Leighton-Smythe and General Buchovsky, not from you."

The light-speed lag seemed to crawl by.

"Bernard Leighton-Smythe and Fyodr Buchovsky have been relieved of their duties for insubordination, General. Do you also wish to be relieved?"

Daniels shook her head emphatically. "No, sir."

Seconds ticked by.

"Very good. Then I suggest you follow my orders. Those shuttles are carrying commandos from the New German Unity. They are operating under my authority. You are to do nothing except stand by to assist them if they request help. Is that clear?"

Daniels nodded. "Yes, sir."

"Good. Wu out." The screen went black.

Baldwin, the general's adjutant, stepped up beside her. "Bit of an icicle, isn't he? What do you make of it, General?"

"I think someone is trying a power play, both on the Moon and in New York. Maybe in Berlin, too."

"So what do we do, sir?"

Daniels drummed her fingers on the arm of her chair, then came to a decision. "Call Colonel Houston. No matter what's going on, we've got POWs down on the lunar surface, and I don't want our people falling into NDE hands. I want Houston and a platoon of ATFOR heavies on the ground five minutes after the Blacksuits land."

"But, sir," Baldwin protested, "Wu told us to stand by and do nothing."

"No," Daniels corrected him. "He told us to stand by to assist if the Blacksuits need help. *I* clearly heard a call for help. Didn't you?"

"I absolutely did, sir." Baldwin saluted and dashed away to find Colonel Houston.

CHAPTER 21

"Get down!" Bunny screamed on the broad band as a squad of LDF militia came running toward her. "Down!"

The retreating fighters dropped to the ground, and immediately Stahl fired two grenades toward the end of the hallway. The lethal silver balls spun slowly through the air, exploding against the far wall just as two Blacksuits came around the corner. The double impact tore the first soldier to shreds, and hurled the other one back down the corridor to the left. Even as the explosion faded, Bunny's squad of regulars was moving forward, stepping over the militiamen.

"Get up!" Josef shouted at the prone militia, most of whom were too frightened to move. "Fall back to the central shield generator. There's some ACRs there!"

Dalton knew that even with the laser rifles, the militia would be outgunned by the NDE regulars, and the NDE heavy infantrymen, with their standard grenade launchers, would brush the commandos aside without even breaking a sweat. But at least the ACRs would give them a fighting chance.

Ahead of him, Britt was pointing at the fallen Blacksuit, who was still moving. Dalton couldn't hear what Britt was saying, but he checked his oxygen sensor, and guessed the oxygen generator hadn't been shut down yet. Dalton switched off his internal tank, trying to stretch his resources, knowing the suit would warn him when the dome's atmosphere became unbreathable.

Britt fired a burst from his plasgun into the wounded Blacksuit's head.

". . . been there by now," Britt was saying as Dalton moved into range. "If the Blacksuits are not goin' for the oxy, they must be goin' for the shields." He pointed to the weapon of the man he'd just killed and indicated that Dalton should pick it up. Without hesitation, Dalton obeyed.

The railgun was a strange weapon, looking more like an industrial device than a traditional gun. But it had more in common with the machine guns of the previous century than modern energy weapons in that it fired rapidly bursts of long, thin metal projectiles meant to quickly overload an enemy's shields, then penetrate his armor. In low- or no-atmosphere combat, a railgun was a lethal weapon. It required two hands, though, so Dalton strapped his ACR to the tanks on his back.

"No, that doesn't make sense either," Bunny was saying to Colonel von Hayek. "They can't teleport in; they don't have the disks."

"The council!" Josef exclaimed. "They think the Council of Lunar Governors is here! They don't realize we do everything by teleconference."

But before anyone could suggest a plan of action, they heard the clattering of a railgun just around the corner. Oshikatta, Jeff, and Stahl were already in position, and Dalton leaped back behind the corner, seeking cover with Britt and Bunny.

"Hold your fire!" Bunny commanded via the suit-computer comm system. The squad waited as the first four Blacksuits came around the corner, moving quickly in a leapfrog formation. Dalton couldn't see what was happening, but he forced himself to wait until the order to fire appeared on his display.

"Fire!"

The first two Blacksuits were felled by Stahl's grenades, and the general barrage accounted for a third. Dalton popped out from behind the corner a bit late, but apparently the last Blacksuit's shields had been weakened, and the first burst from his railgun killed the man. He started to move forward, but Bunny waved him back.

"More coming." There was a flash at the far end of the corridor, then another, and suddenly the hallway seemed to be filled with deadly silver balls. "Christ, they're heavies!"

Tycho Research Station
26 November 2069
16:30 GMT

"What is the meaning of this blatant violation of the cease-fire agreement?" Pieter von Hayek was practically frothing at the mouth as he raged at the screen, but the two faces on the screen reflected nothing but surprise at his words.

"Am I correct in assuming that you are imputing responsibility to the United Nations for an attack of some kind?" Shi Cheng Wu asked. "Governor von Hayek, none of our troops are currently involved in any sort of action on the Moon. If they were, rest assured that I would know about it. We have not violated the agreement in any way." Chairman Wu was unflappable, and his placid black eyes revealed no sign of emotion.

"You're lying, Wu. Who sent those fascists up here in the first place? You know as well as I do that the NDE has no space capability. And where's Haversham?"

Antonio Aguila raised a finger. "Lord Haversham took ill earlier this morning. I am authorized to act in his place." He allowed himself a slight smile, showing a glint of white teeth. "I assume you are referring to the New German Unity?"

"NDE troops are attacking Port Aldrin right now!" von Hayek shouted. "Call your dogs off, Wu, or tear that peace treaty into shreds! We'll blow the launchers!"

The chairman raised his hands. "I assure you, Governor, I will investigate this matter immediately and take the facts to the Security Council. If the NDE has indeed taken it upon itself to attack Port Aldrin, rest assured they will suffer appropriate sanctions. I do hope you are not in any immediate personal danger?"

The governor shook his mane of white hair. "Of course not. But that's not the issue. Once again Earth forces are violating the sovereignty of the Free State, and we will not stand for it! This time you've gone too far, and your little charade doesn't fool me at all!"

When neither Wu nor Aguila dignified his outburst with a response, von Hayek continued, his voice much calmer. "You have ten minutes to call those troops off. I don't care whether they're yours or the NDE's. Either way, if they don't leave Port Aldrin within ten minutes, you can consider yourselves at full war with us."

Von Hayek slammed a fist down on the comm console and terminated the conversation.

"He is intelligent," Chairman Wu commented after the screen went dark. "But he is worried."

"Not worried enough," said Aguila. "He's not at Port Aldrin."

"What do you mean? Our intelligence very clearly placed him and the rest of the council there."

"No. You heard him speak. Did he sound like a man who's got half a battalion of soldiers on his doorstep? He's somewhere else. They've fooled us, Wu, and our big surprise strike is missing the target." He stood up to leave and bowed slightly. "With your permission, though, I believe I can soon find out where he is."

"How?"

"I'll bet Haversham knows," snarled Aguila. "And I'll rip his spine out with my teeth if I have to, but I'll get the truth from him."

Undisclosed Location
26 November 2069
11:45 A.M. EST

"Ah, Antonio. I was wondering when you might get around to visiting me." Although his face was badly bruised and caked with dried blood from the NDE beating, Haversham's voice was as light and cheerful as ever. He was bound harshly to the steel-framed hospital bed and his arms were restrained, but he clearly continued to keep the traditional stiff upper lip.

When Aguila didn't answer, Haversham went on. "All the same, I must say: a 'medical emergency?' And then you had me whisked away to this ghastly private Lubyanka? Really, how . . . *Soviet*. I expected something far more creative out of you and Graf."

Aguila looked down at him with contempt and hatred, his well-formed face almost glowing with barely suppressed fury. The rage in his black eyes made him look like an avenging devil returned to Earth to pay back an evil tenfold.

"It wasn't enough for you, Edward, was it? It wasn't enough to be a living anachronism, a fossil from an earlier age. You wanted to restore the old system, return to the time when insignificant little nations like yours raped and pillaged the rest of the world!"

"You can't prove anything," Haversham said mildly. "There's simply nothing to prove. I never conspired with any of the Lunar leaders. I never even had any contact with them."

"But I know you, Edward! Your very thoughts condemn you! I see how you look about you and sneer, thinking you're superior to everyone and everything else. And with your outdated ideology, you and von Hayek are simply two sides of the same coin!"

"Liberté, egalité, fraternité," Haversham said ironically. "Your problem, lad, is that you simply can't bear the thought that others might not share your priorities or your

values. The people of the Moon simply want to be left alone, and you can't even allow them that right."

"That right does not exist! They have a duty to the rest of the world."

"I understand. The group is all, and there are only duties for the individual, never rights. It's the same old dream, Antonio, cloaked in different terms. But it has never worked, and it never will. That's the problem you face, Antonio. Because at the root of your system is simply raw force, and some people will never submit. You'll have to kill them, and in doing so, you will become the very monster that you claim so much to hate. Open your eyes, my dear boy. You're not a bitter little child in Chile anymore. Stop thinking like one."

"Enough!" Aguila was barely containing his anger now. "Where is the lunar leadership? I know you know where they are! They're not at Port Aldrin, so where are they?"

"It won't make any difference."

"Tell me!" Antonio looked over his shoulder towards the door and called out. "Dr. Schwartz, bring the equipment now, please." He turned back to Haversham. "You're an old man, Edward. You can't keep secrets from us. It'll take Schwartz only a few minutes to rip the truth from your mind."

"That won't be necessary, Antonio. I'll tell you where they are, but the information won't do you any good. There are factors at work here that go far beyond you, me, and von Hayek."

"Tell me anyhow!" As the younger man loomed threateningly over the frail figure on the bed, a nurse entered the room pushing a cart laden with syringes, vials, and other ominous-looking apparatus.

"Tycho," Haversham said sadly. "They're at Tycho."

"Thank you, Edward." Aguila knew instinctively that Haversham spoke the truth. Then he turned away from his former mentor and addressed the nurse. "Tell Dr. Schwartz that the truth serum is no longer necessary." He tapped a black vial. "Use this instead."

"Yes, sir," she replied without looking at him.

"Good-bye, Edward," Aguila said as he strode from the room without looking back.

Haversham smiled faintly and shook his head with regret. "Good-bye, you poor wretched boy," he whispered. "I had such high hopes for you."

Then he looked up at the nurse, who was studiously avoiding his gaze as she prepared a syringe. *"Et tu,* my dear? Though I should consider myself fortunate to be graced by so fair an Angel of Death. Might I enjoy the comfort of one cigarette? I do believe there are some in my briefcase." He gestured toward the other side of the room with his angular chin.

"Sorry," she said. "This is a smoke-free building."

Aboard UN Gunship SC-23v
26 November 2069
16:47 GMT

Chuck Houston surveyed his troops as the two gunships sped toward Port Aldrin. Although a single armored shuttle could have ferried the whole platoon down from the *Schwarzkopf,* Houston had chosen to use gunships instead. If his men had to shoot their way in, he reasoned it was best to go in with all the speed and firepower he could manage. It didn't look as if the landing zone would be contested however. The Loonies were already in a hand-to-hand fight for their lives; they weren't likely to be manning space defense stations. Houston wasn't worried about that.

The colonel *was* worried about was the morale of his platoon, though. These soldiers were from the New Guinean contingent; they were ill-trained, unfamiliar with the heavier Nonex battlesuits, and worst of all, unhappy at being thrown into a risky combat situation when they'd thought the war was over. Houston had hoped they'd be hyped up at the prospect of rescuing other UN soldiers, but most of them were simply alarmed at the prospect of facing the business end of the Blacksuits' railguns. Not that he could blame them for that, of course. He himself wasn't feeling too sanguine about surviving that possibility.

A beeping in his ears shook Houston from his worrisome thoughts, and he accepted the comm link before realizing it was a relayed link from Earth.

"Colonel Houston?"

"Roger. This is Houston," he answered. The voice sounded familiar, and he wondered who it was as he counted down the light-speed lag.

"General Daniels tells me you are heading for Port Aldrin to support the NDE forces attacking the rebels there. This is Antonio Aguila, acting chairman of the Committee on Lunar Development."

The slick one, Houston thought. *I knew that voice sounded familiar.* "That's correct," he lied.

Light-speed lag.

"Your orders have been changed. The rebel leadership is at Tycho, not Port Aldrin. Change course for Tycho immediately and take Governor Pieter von Hayek at all costs. I don't care if you take him alive or dead, but take him. The only way to end this is to cut the head off the snake. Literally, if necessary."

"I understand, sir. But what about the UN prisoners being held at Port Aldrin?"

"The information we received about the hostages being held at Aldrin was from the same source that led us to believe the leadership was there too. At this point we don't know where the POWs are, but if you nail von Hayek, you'll be able to find out."

Houston nodded inside his helmet. For once, a politician was making sense. "Understood, sir. I'll have the pilots change course immediately. Will we have any backup?"

Light-speed lag.

"Of course. Our allies from the NDE have the situation at Aldrin under control, and I've already ordered Colonel Starkenburg to pull out as many troops as he can spare and send them to Tycho. He's promised one platoon immediately and another platoon ten minutes from now."

"What's the first platoon's ETA at Tycho?"

"According to General Daniels's estimate, they're fourteen minutes behind you. We can't afford to wait for them, though. There's also an ATFOR platoon being sent down from the *Schwarzkopf,* but they'll be twenty minutes behind."

"Understood, sir." Houston didn't at all like the haphazard nature of this operation, but he wasn't paid for his opinion, he was paid to get the job done. He understood that the appearance of even a small unit in the right place at the right time could turn the tide of a battle, and sometimes a war. But he also knew that such maneuvers were usually hard on the men in that particular unit. "We'll be there. Just tell those damned reinforcement pilots to keep the pedal to the metal."

Surprised, Aguila laughed shortly. "I will do that, Colonel. We're keeping a link open to General Daniels, so please keep us informed."

"Yes, sir."

On the relay, there was no audible click, but somehow Houston knew that the voice in his helmet was gone. After giving the new orders to the pilot of his gunship, he told the pilot of the other ship to set up a comm relay so he could address the troops on both gunships at once.

"I've got good news and bad news," he told his men. "The good news is, we're not gonna fight the Blacksuits after all. The bad news is, our prisoners aren't at Aldrin. It turns out the Loonie leaders are at Tycho, and we figure they know where our POWs are, so we're gonna get old man von Hayek and beat the information out of him."

There was a brief cheer, which heartened Houston, although he suspected it was due to the prospect of not having to face the NDE rather than to the chance to bring the war to a close. But it was a start. Settling back against the cabin wall, he called up a 3D map of Tycho on his display and began to work out a plan of attack.

Port Aldrin
26 November 2069
In the Fog of Battle

"Where's Stahl?" Bunny asked as they fell back toward the center of the dome. Only five of them were still together: Dalton, Britt, Jeff, Josef, and Bunny. "I saw Oshikatta go down. Did anyone see what happened to Stahl?"

"He got hit," said Britt, sounding short of breath. "Too much shrapnel and his shields went."

"Dammit!" Bunny swore. "We should have fallen back as soon as I saw how many there were. Now we don't have the damn grenade launcher. We'll have to try to ambush a heavy squad and steal one from them."

"No," said Josef, holding up his hand. Since they'd begun to fall back, he'd been silent. Now Dalton realized the colonel had been in communication with someone else the whole time.

"We've got to go to Tycho," Josef said. "Somehow the dirts've figured out that my father's there, and they're sending gunships. We've got to get to the transports."

"We can't do that," protested Jeff. "There are people here who need our protection. The militia will get slaughtered without us!"

"Shut up, boy," replied Britt. "Without the governor, we have no reason to keep fighting."

"But there's regulars at Tycho."

Before the argument between Jeff and Godfrey could erupt into a full-fledged conflict, Josef spoke up.

"This isn't a matter for discussion. CenCom says a whole company of NDE Blacksuits has broken off of the attack and is being loaded back onto transports. One of the ships has taken off and is on a heading that may be . . . Yep, they're heading for Tycho too."

Josef slowed down to a fast walk, and the others followed suit. "Tycho's gonna need all the help we can give them. Now, which way is the transport room?" He looked around.

"Oh, damn!" he exclaimed when Dalton pointed back toward where they'd lost Oshikatta and Stahl to the Blacksuits. "It *would* have to be that way."

Dalton ducked another burst from a Blacksuit's railgun. He almost laughed aloud as he recalled how naive he'd been just three weeks before. Back then, wandering alone through the corridors of Grimaldi, he'd been sure he was as scared as any human could possibly get. *Ha!* He snorted bitterly as he responded to the Blacksuit with a burst of his own.

In comparison with this, Grimaldi hadn't been so bad. There he'd just been wondering if there were troops around the corner, whereas now he knew beyond any shadow of a doubt that there were. Not to mention the fact that these same troops had kicked butt on his squad not fifteen minutes before. He fired again, a longer burst this time, and howled with glee as the blacksuit finally fell.

"Mayday, Mayday. This is Colonel von Hayek. We need support in section two, level three, corridor seventeen, just past the intersection with corridor N. This is a priority one. Repeat: priority one." Von Hayek was broadcasting across the spectrum, not caring if the invaders heard him. If he and his commandos stayed here much longer, they'd be dead anyway.

"Colonel? Come in, Colonel. This is Lieutenant Smirnov, Aldrin Militia, Beta Company. We're down five halls from you, to the west. I can hear a firefight going on ahead of us. Is that you, Colonel?"

"Right, Lieutenant. Now, here's the deal. We have to get down hall seventeen, but these two squads of Blacksuits are blocking our way. Can you create a diversion?"

"Yes, sir. We'll hit them from behind, and you can get past while we keep them occupied."

"Crude, but it'll work. How many men do you have?"

"Two squads, sir. We've even got a couple ACRs, sir."

Dear God, thought Josef. *Nothing but ACRs against Blacksuits with railguns. They'll get slaughtered.* "Okay, Lieutenant. When we hear you hit them, we'll move. But keep your heads down and your butts covered. They'll have you outgunned." Josef knew he was about to condone something that would haunt him for the rest of his life, but he also knew where his duty lay, and so he was forced to content himself with the brief warning.

At his first opportunity, he darted across the corridor to the alcove where Bunny knelt, firing her captured railgun methodically down the smoky hallway. It was hard to see any farther ahead than five or six meters, even with infrared boost, but the occasional shield flare cut through the gloom and told him that at least some of the Blacksuits were still in position.

"The militia will be cut to pieces!" Bunny protested after he told her of his plan.

"Not in time. It'll only take us two minutes to burn our way past the Blacksuits. The NDR will need more time than that to shut down two squads of militia."

"Is it really *that* important for us to get to Tycho?"

"If we don't get there, everything's over and the NDE wins. I assure you, it's that important!"

"All right." As Bunny spoke, they both heard shouts and screams coming from down the hallway.

"Do it right now, Colonel," the voice of Lieutenant Smirnov shrieked on the broad band.

"Go, dammit, go!" Bunny shouted, as Von Hayek led the sprint down the hallway. Not all the Blacksuits had turned to deal with the new threat from their left, but enough had, and Britt and Josef cut down two strikers with searing plasma gobbets before the Blacksuits even realized the commandos were advancing.

A large Blacksuit raised his weapon and fired a burst at Bunny, catching her square in the chest. Blue light exploded around her, and she fell as her shields ablated, but just before they collapsed before the furious metal onslaught, Dalton blew the Blacksuit into pieces with the launcher he'd just picked up. He had emptied it, and he didn't have any more grenades, so he cast it aside as he extended a hand to Bunny, fumbling at his back for his ACR as he helped her up.

"Grab your weapon later. Just run," she screamed at him, and together they ran down the corridor as railguns chattered and lasers illuminated the hallway with neon streaks of green and red. As they ran, they saw to their right the militia in rapid retreat, forced back before the fury of the German counterattack.

We got through, but at what cost? Bunny thought. "Stop," she ordered Dalton once they were clear of the immediate combat zone. She unsnapped his ACR from his oxy tanks, handed it to him, and then slapped him on the rear. "Do you know where the transports are?"

"Around that corner, then a left and a left."

Knowing Dalton's general tendency to be unobservant in matters directional, Bunny worried that they were lost, but for once his memory was correct, and they reached the transport room just as the lights dimmed and began flashing red.

"Oxygen's down," said Dalton. "Seal your suit."

"It is sealed, you moron." She pressed the access button. "Dammit, the door's locked."

"No problem." Dalton grinned and pulled out his new norton with a flourish worthy of an Old West gunfighter. Slipping it into the slot, he set happily to work.

"Um, Dalton . . ."

"Hang on. I've almost got it." The numbers flashed by his display at speeds too fast to read, but the patterns were starting to emerge and repeat as the virus sorted out the correct access code. "Just a few more digits."

"Okay," Bunny said as she leveled her railgun at the approaching Blacksuits. "But you might want to hurry it up just a bit."

CHAPTER 22

Tycho Research Station
26 November 2069
17:00 GMT

In no hurry to go back inside after his hour-long surface patrol, Lloyd Thompson sat gingerly down on a ledge that appeared stable enough to hold his Moon-weight, and looked out over the rocky bottom of the massive depression left by an asteroid's chance encounter with the Earth's lonely satellite.

The crater was supposedly one of the Moon's youngest, though Thompson couldn't remember if "recent" meant thousands or millions of years in lunar time. He wondered how big an asteroid had to be, and how fast it had to be moving, to make a hole this big. Big as it was, it still wasn't as large as the newly made crater at Volodya, but he doubted anyone would be building a dome there anytime soon. Not unless somebody developed a way to scrub radiation out of the rocks.

His suitcom bleeped at him, and a radar map appeared on his display. It showed two objects moving slowly toward him, and he raised his ACR and glanced wildly around the vicinity until he realized the radar was zoomed out as far as it would go. The units were in hundreds of kilometers, and he whistled when he saw how fast the objects were approaching.

He knew hopshuttles didn't fly that fast, and wondered why space defense command hadn't warned him that hostile craft were heading toward the dome. Unsure whether he should contact AtCon or the on-duty central security officer, he began to walk toward the nearest airlock. But after he had taken only three or four bounding steps, the objects disappeared from his radar.

Puzzled, he stopped and adjusted the map controls, but the objects didn't reappear. He walked back toward the ledge, as if moving physically closer would make any difference. He was shocked when the objects reappeared.

Thompson was an experienced vet, but he'd never before seen anything like this. He stepped back and forth in an impromptu test to see where the signals appeared and disappeared. After marking the invisible line of demarcation by gouging a furrow in the regolith with his toe, he began to measure how far around the Tycho dome the anomaly extended.

He'd walked more than fifty meters and detected the anomaly's existence every step along the way before he realized that the entire dome was surrounded by what he was mentally referring to as the blindness effect. Then the truth hit him like a cheetah, and he looked up at the black sky.

"AtCon, this is Major Thompson, on surface patrol. We've got two incoming craft, presumed hostile, at a range of one hundred twenty kilometers, ETA seven minutes."

"What? I'm not seeing that on our screens, sir."

"Yeah, I didn't think you would. We're getting hit by some kind of electronic mask that's suppressing our radar. Probably getting laid down by that damn USN ship up there. Fifty meters out, I can pick 'em up clear as day on my suit radar, but I take a step or two in, and nothing."

"I don't know . . . I'm still not getting anything, Major. I've run through all the frequencies, and there's nothing out there."

"Listen here, boy. You just call a code red right now! We're gonna be under attack in less than ten minutes, and with only two squads to protect the brass, we'd better be ready! That's an order, soldier. Now do it before I come in there and cut your *cojones* off!"

"Y-yes, sir, Major." There was a brief pause as the AtCon sergeant pressed a button and spoke a few urgent words into an open mike. "You got your code red, sir."

"Good work, boy. Now go get yourself a gun."

Major Thompson breathed a sigh of relief as he lifted his ACR and checked the status indicators. Time to get his boys ready, because it sure looked like the Blacksuits were coming. In a way, he was almost glad. He had a score to settle with those bastards. Grinning ferally, he drew his bowie knife and saluted the sky. Somewhere, he knew Yuji Nakagawa and the spirits of other samurai, dead many centuries ago, were nodding with grim approval.

Port Aldrin
26 November 2069

"Hurry, Dalton!" Another blacksuit popped up and risked a wild shot at them, and Bunny sent him back to cover with a burst from her railgun. "I'm almost out."

"Hold on," Dalton said, as he worked the norton in the door lock just as fast as his gloved fingers would let him. "I've almost . . ." The door beeped and a set of status indicators switched from red to green. "Got it!" Dalton crowed. He pulled the norton out of the slot and slipped it back into his belt. As the door began to slide upwards, the blacksuits surged forward, and Bunny rolled under the door and into the room. Dalton dove after her.

"Shut the door!" he shouted, as he rolled over onto his back and began firing at the pursuing blacksuits. Bunny desperately punched every button she could see, hoping one of them was the right one. Apparently one was, as the door slammed shut.

"Hit the red button. No, the other red one!" Still lying on

his back with his weapon leveled at the closed door, Dalton breathed a sigh of relief. "Okay, it's locked now. We better hurry, though. It won't take them long to cut through it."

"So which one do we take?"

He looked at the transporter pods—three rectangular structures, each with a central disk above and below radiating an eerie, alien blue light. One led to Tycho, one to Grimaldi, and the other to Kepler, but Dalton couldn't remember which was which.

Was it Tycho, Kepler, Grimaldi, left to right? He thought so, but he vaguely remembered that the order was the opposite of what he thought it would have been. Or maybe that was the Picard transporters. He couldn't remember. Either way, he was pretty sure Kepler was in the middle.

"It's not the middle one," he said finally.

Bunny stared at him for a moment. Although he couldn't see her features, he was pretty sure they were showing disgust at the moment. Behind them she could hear scraping noises as the NDE soldiers worked at the door. "Pick a number," she said. "One or two."

"Two."

"Okay." She pointed to the pod on the right. "That one." Without waiting for a response, she jumped into the rightmost transporter and disappeared without a flash. Dalton stared at the eerie device for a long second, then closed his eyes and leaped into it—a scant moment before the door to the room exploded inward, spraying lethal shards of metal through the space where he'd been standing.

Tycho Research Station
26 November 2069
17:15 GMT

Lloyd Thompson had never subscribed to the myth that life was fair. He'd been kicked in the teeth often enough to realize that sometimes a man just had to endure. He'd regretted having to leave Yuji Nakagawa to his death at

Lacus Mortis, but he hadn't doubted the necessity of it, and he wasn't the sort of romantic fool who wished that he could have been the one left behind.

But standing around out on the lunar surface, doing nothing while the bluesuits attacked the two surviving squads of his platoon inside the dome, made him want to scream at the stars at the unfairness of it all. But then again, as the young captain in the control center had put it, there just wasn't anybody else outside. So he sat and waited, watching the map display on his suit.

The sitting and waiting wasn't too bad, not to a soldier who'd laid down thirteen or fourteen ambushes in his time; he wasn't sure of the exact number, but it was something like that. No, the hard thing was watching the gunships cut down the two young fools who'd come out to be his backup, who had more bravery than sense. They were glorious in their own stupid, tragic way, he thought. Two young men who thought they could outshoot a gunship with their ACRs. And now that he thought about it, he wasn't sure how smart those Texans at the Alamo had been, either.

He shook his head sadly at the two white-suited corpses lying near the airlock. It was a pity and a waste, but he knew that Death had quite a few more hands to play. The gunships he'd first seen had dropped their ATFOR troops five minutes ago, and those troops were now inside, engaging his strike teams. The gunships themselves were overhead somewhere, darting around like giant venomous insects, hunting for more stragglers like himself.

His suit beeped a warning, and he glanced at his display. Much as he hated to admit it, the control captain had been right in pleading with him to stay outside, beyond the boundaries of the blind zone where radar was suppressed. There were two more ships coming toward Tycho at a speed that suggested armored transports. Two platoons worth, he guessed, and from Port Aldrin if remembered the relative directions correctly. Those would be the Germans, he figured: ETA eight minutes.

Lloyd Thompson opened a broadband comm link.

* * *

For Dalton, the experience of teleporting was neither as thrilling nor as terrifying as he'd expected. There was no magical glimmer as he disappeared from Aldrin, nor was there a blinding flash of green light, just a weird throbbing whine as he reappeared stumbling off the yellow receiver disk at Tycho. Opening his eyes, he managed to regain his balance before falling and saw Bunny standing at the far side of the room facing him, with her railgun pointing at his midsection.

He looked around and saw that Josef, Britt, and Jeff were there too, along with two battlesuited guards from Alpha Company, and all of them had their weapons drawn.

"Get out of the way!" Josef commanded. "Those black-suits'll be coming through in a minute. Bunny said they were right on your ass."

Dalton nodded, but instead of moving to the side, he turned and examined the MANTA receiver. Unlike the transmitter pods, built later, the Tycho disk wasn't a large device, it was simply bolted to the floor by four screws driven into the plazmetal.

"Do these things have a top?" he asked thoughtfully. "And a bottom?"

"Dalt, what the hell are you doing?" Britt screamed. "You're in the goddam line of fire!"

"Shut up, Britt," he responded absently, as he dropped to his knees in front of the disk and withdrew an autoscrewing device. Working methodically, without rushing, he removed the four screws, then lifted the disk and began to flip it over.

Just as it reached an angle perpendicular to the floor, a Blacksuit appeared in midair above the disk's "top." The NDE slammed into the floor with such force that his shields flared explosively.

Surprised nearly out of his wits, Dalton dropped the disk as the Blacksuit, stunned by the impact, lay motionless on the floor. The others in the room were stunned too, but Britt was the first to react, killing the NDE soldier with a burst from his plasgun.

Another Blacksuit appeared just as Dalton desperately

crawled toward the disk, lying two meters away with the yellow receiver pointed up.

"Flip it over!" Bunny shouted as her railgun roared and blasted the Blacksuit's shields away. Dalton's own shields flared as bursts of energy ricocheted off the Blacksuit onto him, but he ignored them as he gripped the rubbery sides of the disk and finally turned it over.

Each of the LDF fighters in the room watched the disk and waited expectantly. Dalton didn't know what to expect—perhaps a scream or a bang or at least some other noise as the NDE invaders materialized into solid rock and metal. But there was nothing, just two square meters of rubbery material, six centimeters thick, lying upside down on the floor.

"May as well make sure it doesn't go anyplace," Dalton said finally after a long moment of silence. He shoved the receiver disk roughly back into position with his foot, then knelt and lined the corners up with the mounting holes in the floor. After screwing the first three screws down, he looked around for the last one.

"Here it is, Dalt." Bunny handed it to him. He screwed that one in too, then stood up. No one said anything. It was too bizarre, standing there doing nothing as men and women died undetectably, almost within reach.

Finally Britt broke the morbid silence. "Well, that's one way of doing it. Not all that dramatic, though, is it."

But while the others were staring at the MANTA receiver, Josef had been in communication with the Tycho Central Computer. He closed the link, then slammed his armored fist against the wall. "Damn! They've already got two squads in the south side, and more transports are on the way. We've got to get to the governor's office and move my father to Farside!"

"Who's 'they'?" Britt asked. "NDE?"

"No, ATFOR. Two squads of heavies. Looks like it's not the NDE behind this after all." Josef pointed a threatening finger at Bunny. "You've done well by us so far, Lieutenant, but don't forget, you're still on probation."

"I never forget, Colonel." She spoke coldly, but Bunny couldn't blame him for being a little paranoid. Von Hayek had no way to know what she was really thinking. And even now, if she was honest with herself, she really didn't know which side she would come down on when the moment of truth arrived. Killing Blacksuits was one thing, but gunning down her own former comrades was another. She shrugged as she followed Britt out of the transport room. She'd find out soon enough.

Patrick Adams didn't like the way the governor's hand kept returning to his chest. Pieter von Hayek looked haggard, and his face seemed wan and gray once the confrontation with the Chairman Wu was over and his anger had begun to fade. Now he looked desperate and old.

"This doesn't change anything," Amalia Trelstad snapped. "We're better equipped to fight now than we were three weeks ago. Our troops are rested, and the militias have been training nonstop since the cease-fire was declared. We fought them to a standstill once before. Why should anything have changed?"

Adams ignored her protestations as he circled the table and offered support to von Hayek, who was grimacing with pain and clutching at his chest. "Pieter, are you okay? Do you think you're having a heart attack?"

"No, no. I'm all right. It's just—my chest feels tight." He reached out blindly for a chair and sat down hard. "Just give me a moment to catch my breath. Where's Josef?"

"He's at Port Aldrin, directing the defense, no doubt." Adams turned to the second councillor. "Governor Trelstad, could you call the medics? Tell them we need a paramedic team immediately."

No stranger to crises, Amalia nodded quickly and ran to the controls at the other side of the room.

"Get me a link—to Graf, in New York," von Hayek gasped.

"Not now, Pieter. Wait for the paramedics."

But before the emergency medical team could respond,

Governor Trelstad turned her head and called for Adams. "Patrick, we're getting some kind of message here. A UNET channel just opened up Earthside from the New German Unity. It's a diplomatic channel, marked priority one urgent."

"Play it," von Hayek said, wincing as another wave of pain hit him.

Amalia looked quizzically at Patrick, and he nodded. She pressed a button, and a haughty Aryan face filled the screen. The woman's cold blue eyes seemed to glare at them out of the display as she began to speak, in German. *"Ich bin Katja Buhtsbach von der Neue Deutsche Einheit."* Her harsh, guttural accent was both unpleasant and impossible to understand, but fortunately, English subtitles began to appear on the screen below her.

"This is Katja Buhtsbach of the New German Unity. As first ambassador to the Free State Selena, it is my duty to inform Governor Pieter von Hayek and the people of the Moon that, as of null nine hundred hours, the people of the New German Unity officially declare a state of war between our two nations."

The woman's face disappeared, replaced by the full English text, displayed in white with red highlights on a black background. No one spoke for a moment.

Then Pieter, with some difficulty, cleared his throat. "Well, at least someone's finally recognized us," he rasped.

Despite the severity of the moment, Adams couldn't restrain a chuckle. "It's a start, I suppose."

Governor Trelstad regarded the two of them with disbelief, but before she managed to say anything, the door opened and Josef von Hayek burst into the room, followed by Dalton, Britt, Bunny, Jeff and two Alpha commandos. Right behind them was the paramedic team.

"Blacksuits are coming!" Josef cried. "We've got to get you out of here, Dad!"

UN Headquarters, New York
26 November 2069
12:30 P.M. EST

The comm system chirped. Aguila answered. Shi Cheng Wu's face was, as always, calm and unreadable. "Antonio? It appears we have made a significant miscalculation. The NDE has just recognized the Lunar government."

Aguila was stunned. "And reached a separate peace?"

"No. They've declared a separate war."

The implications of this were immediately clear to Aguila. "Have they claimed any of the territory they've taken?"

"Not yet. But it is only a matter of time."

Aguila nodded and bit a finger. "Thank you for telling me this." Shi Cheng Wu rang off.

I was a fool to think this was almost over, Aguila thought. *It's hardly begun.*

Tycho Research Station
26 November 2069
17:30 GMT

Both Patrick Adams and Amalia Trelstad were shocked by the sudden arrival of Josef and his companions, but the most severe response was provided by Josef's father. Upon the colonel's entry into the room, the governor slumped back in his chair, one hand reaching for his son, and the other clutching at his heart.

"Vati!" Josef cried, reverting in a moment of panic to the German of his childhood. He leaped across the room and dropped to his knees before his father, covering the old man's hand with both of his own. He turned back toward the paramedics, and although his visored face was unreadable, there was fear in his voice.

"Help him!" he pleaded, and the two women rushed forward, moving the distraught Josef out of the way. Over on the far side of the room, Bunny and Britt were briefing Trelstad and Adams and on the situation.

"Only two squads of ATFOR troops are attacking now, and the garrison here could push them back, with our help, but at least two platoons are heading this way, and we suspect that they're NDE regulars." Bunny spoke rapidly, hoping no one would question her too closely or ask who she was.

"When will they get here?" Adams asked.

"ETA five minutes. We've got to get out of here now. Aldrin is going to fall, and there's nothing we can do about that." Britt's helpless anger showed in his voice.

Adams nodded. "The teleports here lead only to Farside and Port Aldrin. Aldrin's out, so we'll have to go to Farside. That's better anyway, since it'll be harder for them to reach us there."

"It's no harder to send gunships to Farside than anywhere else," Governor Trelstad pointed out.

"True, but in the mines it's hard to find someone who doesn't want to be found. We'll just go underground for a while. As long as the leadership is free, the people will have hope. That above all has to be our concern."

"And we have our . . . resources," said Trelstad, with a significant look at Adams.

"Yes, but they haven't made a difference so far. Still, you never know." Adams shot a look of concern at Pieter, who was lying on a table with his eyes closed as the paramedics administered to him. "How is he?" he called.

"Not good," the taller woman called, her eyes never leaving the digital readout of the little machine connected to von Hayek's bare chest. "We need to get him to a hospital."

"Four minutes," Bunny called. "If we're going to Farside, we've got to suit up now, everybody."

"Where are the suits?" asked Britt.

"Behind you, in that suit locker," said Trelstad, pointing.

"Three of you?" the shorter paramedic whirled around. "You can't take this man anywhere! He'll die if we don't take him to a hospital immediately."

"You're not taking him anywhere," Josef shouted angrily, as Patrick threw a suit toward the table. "Goddammit, he's going to the hospital!"

"Josef . . ." said the elder von Hayek. His voice trailed off before he could say more, but his eyes opened briefly.

At the sight of the powerful emotions contained in that momentary look, Bunny had to turn away. There was sorrow, pride, and even joy, she thought. But most of all, there was *command*.

Patrick had finished putting on his suit, as had Amalia Trelstad. After sealing his helmet, Adams walked up to the younger von Hayek and placed a hand on his shoulder.

"The people must not know," he said. "Your father realizes that." There was a pause, and the colonel nodded. Adams gestured to Britt, and he and Jeff began to slide the now unconscious Pieter into a vacuum suit.

"You can't put a suit on this man. He'll die if you do. I won't permit it!" The taller woman tried to physically force Godfrey and Jeff away from von Hayek. But Josef interceded, grabbing her by the lapels and throwing her back against the wall. He drew his pistol, then pointed to the suit locker.

"You have two choices: put on a suit and come with us, or I will kill you now."

The shorter woman hurriedly complied, but the taller paramedic continued to argue. "Aren't you listening? Your father is going to *die*—"

"I know," said Josef, as he pulled the trigger. "And so are you." The laser burned a precise hole through the center of the paramedic's forehead, and she slumped, dead before she struck the floor.

"Josef, no!" cried Adams.

"My God," gasped Trelstad.

Bunny was horrified too, but she was even more concerned as the counter she'd set dropped to zero. "Party's over, gang. Blacksuits are on the ground as of *now.*"

"Let's get the hell out of here," Josef said. "Patrick, and you, medic, carry my father. Amalia, take this." He tossed her the pistol, and she caught it instinctively, but held it away from her body as if it were a soiled diaper. "Who knows the way to the transmitters?"

"I do," said Patrick, desperately hoping Josef hadn't gone completely over the edge. He wrapped his arms around Pieter's chest and nodded to the paramedic. "Ready? Okay, follow me."

As Houston had expected, the fighting was bitter once they got inside the Tycho dome. The landing had been much easier than he'd anticipated and after the gunships had eliminated a few Loonies on surface patrol, they'd dropped down and gone in without a scratch or even a shot fired at them.

Once inside, though, they hadn't covered twenty meters before encountering a squad of determined LDF regulars. After a fierce firefight, they'd managed to force the Loonies back a little, but not much.

"We need reinforcements," a lieutenant called. Houston ducked reflexively as another laser burst flashed silently past his head, even though it would have been too late.

"Yeah, I know. I'm working on it." He moved back around a corner and tried again, broadcasting on the ATFOR wide band. "This is Colonel Chuck Houston, calling all NDE units. Calling all NDE units."

"Colonel Houston, this is Oberleutnant Moesser of the NDE Fifth Battalion, Nordpol Company. What is your situation?"

Houston breathed a sigh of relief and switched to a secure channel. "Where are you, Lieutenant?"

"We are on final approach, sixty kilometers out."

"Good. The landing zone should be fine; we faced only light opposition, which we neutralized easily. We're just inside the north airlock; I'll upload you our location now." He tapped his wrist pad. "Got it? Okay. As far as I can tell, they don't have more than a squad or two defending here, but they're equipped with heavy lasers and the occasional plasgun. They're mostly packed heavy in the central corridor, the one marked red, but I don't have enough men to risk an end run."

"Just hold your position, Colonel. I am assuming these yellow marks are enemy units?"

"That's right, Lieutenant."

"Good. I see from your map how we can enter from the east and trap them between us. This we will do."

"Then I look forward to seeing you soon, Lieutenant." Houston closed the link and sent word to his men. "The Germans will be here in five or six minutes. All units, hold your positions, but don't stop shooting. When they hit the Loonies from the side, we move."

As a hailstorm of laser fire erupted from the guns of the troops around him, Houston sat back and examined the Tycho map he'd called up on his display. Third left, then second right, fourth left, and then an immediate left; he memorized the directions to the central control room. He knew that time was critical, but getting his men killed in a mad rush to where he hoped the rebel leadership was holed up wasn't going to do any good either. Waiting, he thought, was always the hardest part.

Secure channels weren't always secure, however, especially when the eavesdroppers knew your routine. Knowing the standard UN protocol, Bunny had left a channel open to the ATFOR wide band, and as the small band of Free State leaders and LDF personnel left the governor's office and headed for the teleporters, she was stunned to hear a voice she recognized calling over the frequencies.

"Colonel Houston, this is Oberleutnant Moesser," she heard. Then the voices dropped out, no doubt as Houston switched the link to another channel. She tried three different channels that Houston had used before at Grimaldi and Imbrium, then finally a fourth, and was relieved to hear the harsh, distorted sound of a scrambled conversation.

She'd asked Josef if she could keep her ATFOR comm unit, but not trusting her, he'd refused the request on the grounds that he didn't want her able to converse with her former comrades undetected. However, she did manage to convince him to let her keep the descrambler, just for this very purpose. She tried the 82nd's standard code and was immediately rewarded as the warped, distorted sounds metamorphosed into normal speech.

"Just hold your position," the German was saying. Bunny listened to the rest of the conversation as she ran and called up her own display. It wasn't hard to tell where the ATFOR troops were pinned down, but she froze as she realized that the path her group was taking to the transporters would intersect the entry point of the NDE force at the east side airlock.

"Stop!" she cried, and quickly filled Josef and the others in on what she'd learned.

"Dammit," said Patrick. We don't have time to double back and take the other elevator up to the first floor. We'll just have to fight our way through."

"Through Blacksuits? With you and her?" Josef indicated Trelstad. "We'll never make it."

"So what do you suggest? The only other path would take us right by the north airlock. That's where our guys are keeping ATFOR pinned down." Adams wasn't a military man, but it didn't take a genius to know that running through the middle of a firefight was a bad idea.

"We instruct our fighters to fall back toward the core; then we can make a run behind ATFOR. It's our only chance. Besides, we can't just leave our guys where they are. They'll get hit by Blacksuits in a few minutes."

"Risky," Bunny warned. "If we time it wrong, we're screwed."

"Yeah, well, the other choice is to surrender, and that's no option either," Josef said. "We're going for it and that's final. I'll upload a redline to everyone's maps. Patrick, who's in charge of our forces inside the dome?"

"Major Thompson, sir," said one of the Alphans.

"No, he's stationed outside. Damn. Well, I'll just signal retreat on the wide band."

"Alphans should be used to retreating," Britt said, drawing nasty glares from both Alphans.

One of them spoke up. "Sir, you might try contacting

Lieutenant Asari. If Thompson isn't there, she'd be in charge."

"Okay," said von Hayek. He looked at the paramedic, who was kneeling over his father's body, checking his vital signs. "How's he doing?"

"Not good. I'm sorry, but there doesn't seem to be a heartbeat. Maybe the indicators are defective, but—"

"No, they're not." Josef's voice was icy and determined. "Just make sure you don't drop him. Now let's go!" Without looking back at his father or anyone else, Josef began to run toward the elevator at the end of the hall.

The Loonies were starting to fall back, Houston noticed, and he could almost feel the tension in his men as they waited for the order to pursue and turn the retreat into a rout. But something wasn't right; it was a little too soon for the NDE forces to have arrived, and besides, the Loonies' withdrawal was orderly and methodical.

"Forward, but watch it." He decided to play this one carefully. "Leapfrog it slow, and keep an eye out for booby traps." Dome combat inevitably turned into this slow, deadly game of careful hopscotch played for keeps, very much like the house-to-house drill back on Earth.

He kept his ACR up and wished he dared to turn on his suit's radar. Then he laughed. What the hell. The Loonies already knew where they were, and by turning on the tight radius he could avoid getting ambushed before the Germans arrived.

When he activated his radar, he was confused. Six isolated yellow dots were scattered about the corridors before him. But just *behind* his location was a clump of eight or nine dots, moving rapidly—

Houston whirled and fired from the hip at the white-suited figures running through the hallway he'd just vacated. There was a blue flash, and he knew he'd hit one of them, but he didn't wait to see more, instead diving and rolling to avoid the laser beams that were sparking down the corridor toward him.

One beam nicked his shields, but he was otherwise

unscathed, and he shouted to his men on the wide band. "Squad Two, hold your position. Squad One, follow me. They're behind us!"

"Rearguard action!" Josef shouted to Bunny. "You and your squad cover us, then withdraw! Britt, Chen, with me!" Josef kept running toward the teleporters, followed by Adams, Trelstad, and the medic, carrying Pieter. Bunny dropped into a defensive position and signalled Dalton, Jeff, and the other Alphan to find cover on either side of the hall. A moment later, the pursuing Bluesuits came into view.

For five furious minutes, Bunny's squad managed to fight Houston's men to a standstill and halt the ATFOR advance, losing only the Alphan and killing at least two overconfident Bluesuits. But then, in the red flash of a laser burst exploding against a wall, Dalton caught sight of a black battlesuit.

"Bunny, Blacksuits are here," he shouted. "Time to bug out!"

"Right. Fall back, everyone. To the teleports." Bunny turned and ran as fast as the servomechanically enhanced suit would take her. It wasn't until they reached the transport room and slammed the door behind them that Bunny realized she had no idea which of the two transporters went to Farside.

"You want me to pick a number again?" Dalton asked. "Worked pretty well last time."

"We've got at least a little time," Bunny said. "Can't you use that gadget of yours to figure out how these things are programmed?"

Dalton held up his norton. "If you can tell me where to put it, sure." Bunny looked at the units but saw no slot or anything that even looked like a data readout. As she went over the transporter on the left, Jeff was busily examining the other one. Dalton sighed and withdrew another object from his utility belt, then tapped Jeff on the shoulder. It took him only seconds to complete his task.

"Okay, we're done. We'll take the left pad." Dalton drew his ACR from his utility belt.

Bunny looked up. "Done with what?"

"We set a grenade next to this pad. Now jump before it goes off."

"But we don't even know if the teleports can be destroyed!" Bunny protested.

"Yeah, well, tell you what. I don't plan to stick around to find out. If you want, you can wait thirty seconds and tell me." He politely gestured to Jeff, who quickly leaped into the first teleporter and disappeared. Surprised, Bunny stared at Dalton for a moment, then hastily followed Jeff.

Twenty seconds later, a team of NDE engineers examining the MANTA receiver units at Port Aldrin were suddenly surprised by a violent explosion in their midst. The sole survivor later told his commanding officer the blast had come out of nowhere.

Chuck Houston heard the explosion, but fortunately his shields held up against the fragments of the metal door that were hurled against him. He entered the transporter room cautiously and eyed the remaining teleporter with some misgivings.

He contacted the NDE commander.

"Yes, Colonel Houston?" came the polite response.

"Lieutenant Moesser, a group of rebels has escaped through one of these portal devices. I suspect the defense forces engaging us to the south were a diversionary tactic and the rebel leaders may have escaped this way. My belief is that we should follow them."

There was a brief pause. "My orders are to secure this dome, not to pursue. You may do as you wish, Colonel, but none of the NDE forces will leave Tycho until I receive direct orders to that effect."

"I understand. Then we will pursue on our own. And thank you for your timely assistance, Lieutenant."

"It was my duty, nothing more, Colonel." The NDE officer closed the link, leaving Houston to gather his thoughts as he ordered Squad Two to break off their attack and join him at the transports.

UN Headquarters, New York
26 November 2069
1:00 P.M. EST

The chairmen of two of the most powerful United Nations committees were sitting together in Aguila's new office, both feeling rather helpless in the face of the German treachery.

"We should have known better than to trust them," said Chairman Wu. "We should have used Chinese troops."

Antonio, who had successfully argued against that option, didn't say anything. He might have said something about hindsight being twenty-twenty, but he thought it best to remain silent.

"Of course, had things gone wrong then, the blame would have fallen on my shoulders," Wu said. "At least this way, we can lay the burden at Edward's feet. He won't mind, I'm sure." Wu leaned back in the expensive genuine leather chair and withdrew a cigarette from a gold case. "Do you mind?"

"Not at all," said Antonio, making a mental note to have the office fumigated as soon as the crisis was over. Normally he didn't allow anyone to smoke in his offices, but he didn't think this was the time to make a fuss about it. Instead he opened his liquor cabinet and withdrew a bottle of Haversham's best scotch. "Care for a finger?"

"Two," said the Chinese official. "The question is, how do we break the news to the Security Council. It would be best if we had a solution to offer them."

"I agree." Antonio closed his eyes and took a delicate sip. "There's only two hundred and fifty NDE soldiers up there. They have no means of reinforcement except through us. How many low-G trained troops could we draft into ATFOR in the next, oh, week or so?"

"China has five thousand. America has more, but their House of Representatives has already voted to pull out of ATFOR. The president remains on our side, as does the

Senate, but I predict that they'll cave to their constituents' pressure."

Antonio nodded. "Yes, you're right, no doubt. But the obvious question that will come up in the Security Council meeting will be whether China won't simply attempt to do the same thing the Germans have done. I think the Americans will veto."

Wu shrugged. "Then the pressure to provide a solution will be off of us, at least. The fact is it will take either the Chinese, the Russians, or the Americans to fight the Germans. No one else can do it."

"You're right." Then the familiar chirp sounded. "Excuse me, I have a call."

General Daniels appeared on his screen. "I have a relay for you, Chairman Aguila. One of my colonels believes he is close to capturing von Hayek and the rest of the rebel leadership. Will you speak with him?"

"Send him through, by all means!" Aguila turned and smiled at Chairman Wu. "Perhaps we may find an easier solution, using the troops we already have." He turned back to the comm screen. "Greetings, Colonel! I hear you have interesting news for us!"

CHAPTER 23

Dalton glanced wildly about as he materialized in a small dark chamber. The walls looked as if they'd been carved out of stone, and ahead of him he could see Bunny walking down the corridor to join Jeff at the entrance to another room. He quickly joined them near two large pillars that framed a path leading to a metal door at the end of the hall. On either side of them, he could see bronze panels that seemed to indicate some kind of human activity here, but there were no other signs of life, or of Josef and the other rebels.

"What do you think?" Bunny asked them.

"We could just keep going, I guess," Jeff said.

"Yeah, we'd better not wait here, just in case that grenade didn't blow up the transport that brought us here," Dalton added.

"Good point," Bunny said, and she walked toward the end of the hall.

The door opened, and they saw another door just a few meters ahead. They opened that one too and entered a large

257

chamber with yellow warning strips lining either side of a red pathway that led to an elevator at the far end of the room. Bunny and Jeff started forward, but Dalton stopped, noticing some large black computers on a ledge to the right.

"Hey, guys, check this out!" He leaped up onto the ledge and examined the leftmost panel closely. Something didn't look right about it, and he pressed one of the buttons. Sure enough, the false panel slid upward to reveal a small arms cache containing a plasma gun and some ammo. He checked the charge on the plasgun and, seeing that it was full, tossed the extra canister to Jeff as he attached the gun supports to his utility belt.

"Man, these things are heavier than they look!" Jeff said, catching the canister.

"There's more!" Bunny said, stepping back and pointing out the cache she'd just found. "There's another railgun in here, if anyone wants it." She ejected her half-spent magazine and snapped in the new one. "Let's see if this last panel is fake, too."

Bunny disappeared into the rightmost cache and returned with a grenade launcher cradled in her arms. "Bingo!"

"Hey, can I have that?" Jeff said.

"Find your own," she replied. "But you can have my railgun. Besides, we'd better get moving." She hopped off the ledge and turned north, toward the elevator.

Dalton could see a large computer control center beyond the columns to the east, but there didn't appear to be anyone there. If Josef and the rest had come this way, it appeared that they'd traveled below, to the bowels of the mine, or whatever this place was.

They stepped aboard the elevator, and Bunny pressed the button to take them down. It was a tight fit with the three of them, and Dalton wondered what use a mining team could possibly have for such a small lift. The elevator took them down deep—at least forty meters, he estimated—finally depositing them in an empty, unlit room carved from the lunar rock.

"What now?" he asked.

"Just keep going," Bunny said. "Somebody on our side left those caches up above and carved this place out, so there must be something at the end of this tunnel."

They wandered for what seemed like hours in the dark, although his display told Dalton it had been only ten minutes. Finally a greenish glow appeared in the distance. Relieved, they increased their pace, only to find nothing except some strangely broken rocks that gave off an unearthly green light.

"What the hell is this?" said Bunny, nudging one of the rocks distastefully with her foot. "Radioactive material?"

"My Geiger isn't picking up anything," Jeff replied. "This stuff is weird—I've never seen anything like it before."

Dalton had to agree. Then, out of the corner of his eye, he he saw something scuttling around in the shadows cast by the rocks. He leveled his plasma gun and stepped toward the movement.

"Hey, I thought I saw—" He screamed suddenly as something the size of a medium-sized dog leaped out at him. It looked like an armadillo on steroids crossed with a piranha, and its razor-sharp teeth flashed white as its jaws gaped wide. But it didn't try to bite him. Instead it vomited forth a green globule, which fortunately evaporated on his shields.

Still screaming, he fired two long bursts from the plasgun, killing the thing immediately. Bunny and Jeff came racing to his side and stopped, stunned by the sight of the unearthly corpse.

Its hide was a mottled gray, and it was covered with a hard carapace of overlapping V-shaped plates that began at the top of its head and ran the length of its body. It had four limbs, and the two front legs ended in lethal-looking twenty-five-centimeter claws. Its blood looked green, a darker shade of the color that glowed from the rocks.

"*Ugly* little brute," said Jeff. "Those claws could rip an unarmored suit in half."

Bunny looked back at the glowing rocks. The fragments

were scattered about, but not randomly. It was almost as if they'd been blown apart from a central location. "You don't think those rocks could be eggs, do you?"

"Yeah, I think they could be," said Dalton in a tight voice. "And I think the mama-monster is pretty pissed off!"

Bunny turned around, and what she saw nearly made her wet her suit. Something was illuminating the rocky walls of the giant cavern to the south with a deep reddish light, and as the light grew brighter, they could see just what that something was.

It was a giant reddish orange version of the monster Dalton had killed, but where the little one had claws only twenty-five centimeters long, the giant's appeared to be three meters or more. It scrambled toward them on its armored knuckles, its massive, razor-lined jaws yawning open.

Undisclosed Location
26 November 2069
18:30 GMT

Pieter von Hayek lay in state on a crudely carved platform as Adams and Josef stood beside his body. Josef was holding his dead father's hand and grieving openly. Patrick Adams placed his arm around Josef's shoulder.

"The medic did everything she could," Adams said. "His death couldn't be prevented. We don't have the equipment here."

"I know that," Josef snapped, shrugging Adams's arm off. Tears streaked his face, but there was still a fire in them that no amount of weeping could conceal. "My father always gave everything he had. If he had known that the cause of freedom would require him to be buried in an unmarked grave, he'd have erased his name from the tombstone himself."

He looked around the empty chamber, angry, but not knowing why. Maybe it was because he was ashamed to be seen crying, but even so, he was determined to shed tears for his father, although he'd be damned if anyone else would.

"First of all, he is *not* dead. Only six people know otherwise, and they're all sworn to secrecy. I want his body incinerated, and I'll personally scatter his ashes. I don't want a trace of him to be left anywhere but in the people's minds."

"Four," Adams said.

"What?"

"Soon only four will know the truth. Britt and Chen teleported back to Tycho. They're going to shut down the transporter there."

"They can't do that! What if they get captured?"

Adams smiled sadly. "Britt told me to tell you not to worry, that he guarantees they won't be. He also said to say good-bye."

Josef worked his jaw, unwilling to believe Adams. "I can't believe he didn't tell me." He felt betrayed and would have been furious if he hadn't already been emotionally drained.

"He knew you'd order him not to go. So he didn't ask."

"Did you put him up to this?" Josef was suspicious. He knew Adams was just cold-blooded enough to arrange the removal of two of the only witnesses to his father's death.

"No." Adams's tone was cool and self-assured. "I don't like it either, but the risk of leaving the portal open is too great. The men we left behind might be able to hold the Blacksuits off for a while, but they can't hold forever."

"Right." Josef felt a momentary pang at the loss of yet another friend. But he was finished grieving, at least for now. There was too much to be done. Bending over the table, he gathered his father in his arms and carefully lifted him, then walked over to the far side of the room. Gently, he laid Pieter down on the bare rock on the far side of the room, then returned to the other side and began to put his battlesuit back on.

"What are you doing?" Adams asked.

"We don't exactly have a crematorium here, Patrick," Josef replied as he checked the charge on his plasma gun.

Tycho Research Station
26 November 2069
18:40 GMT

It hadn't seemed that difficult, deciding to try pulling off an insane stunt like this, Britt thought. The trick was simply not to let yourself think about it until it was too late. Until you were committed, with no way back. He felt like the man who'd just swallowed a bottle of sleeping tablets and now wasn't so sure that he wanted to die.

Of course there *was* an easy way out. He could just march around the corner with his hands above his head. But Britt knew that with what was in his memory, surrender was a price too high to pay. He wasn't willing to buy his life at the price of the cause. He just hoped the team at Farside had done as he'd asked and cleared the transport room there. If not, well, they were in for a hell of a surprise.

He looked over at his companion kneeling next to him and grinned, not that Chen could see him. As far as he could tell, the little Taiwanese commando was as insane as he was, which was apparently saying something. But their plan had worked—so far, anyway—and they were now within ten meters of the teleport room, according to his map. A left and a left and then: *kaboom.* If you're gonna go out, do it with style, Britt thought. One of his biggest fears was that he would die old and drooling and begging for his life. Bravery, he'd figured, was really just fear of cowardice.

He touched his visor to Chen's. "Switch on your radar when we move, laddie. I'll take the left side, you got the right. If there's fewer than four of them, we'll try to take the room and dismantle the teleport before we blow it. No sense wreckin' the Farside receiver if we don't 'ave to." Hell, they might even make it out alive somehow.

"Right," Chen said. "Got another nitro?"

"Sure, why not?" They'd already shot up two apiece, but at this point, what difference did it make? "Too 'igh to die!" He slipped a Syrette into Chen's shunt, then into his own. A few seconds later the adrenaline rush hit him and he closed his eyes as he rode the initial wave.

"Now!" he shouted and switched his radar on as he rose from his knees. He felt as if he was moving in slow motion, so heightened and drugged up were his senses, and he saw on the heads-up that only three guards were positioned outside the teleport room. But as quickly as he moved, Chen still rounded the corner first, firing a rapid series of three bolts into the midsection of the leftmost ATFOR guard, sending the man sprawling backwards.

Britt had emptied and dumped his plasgun a few corridors back, but the railgun he'd picked up was perfect for his present need to move the bastards out of his way. He fired a long burst at his first target, snarling gleefully as the Bluesuit's shields collapsed. A shorter burst smashed into the middle guard just as a red bolt from Chen's ACR ablated the man's shield, and the dead Bluesuit was hurled back like a rag doll.

Only steps from the door, Britt's own shields flared and he was knocked off-balance by a volley of lasers fired by a team of troopers stationed down the hall. He rolled with the blow and fired a wild one-handed burst that didn't hit anything, but forced the troopers to take cover. By the time he'd scrambled to his feet, Chen was already in the room, wiring a grenade to the frame of the transporter.

"Can we get the pad off?"

"I don't know," Chen said. "I think there's bolts on the bottom of the frame. I'll get the top."

Britt dropped his weapon and fell to his knees, fumbling at his belt for his autoscrewer. Finally he got it unhooked and began to remove the bolts, one at a time. He managed to get three out before an ATFOR trooper appeared in the doorway, holding his ACR pointed at Britt's head. A moment later three more shock troopers arrived.

"Put your hands on your heads—slowly, now," one of the Bluesuits commanded. Britt caught Chen's eye, then gave him a peek at the grenade in his hands.

* * *

Fifteen thousand kilometers away a small explosion ripped through an empty, shielded room at Farside. At the sound of the concussion, Josef von Hayek and Patrick Adams looked at each other and gravely nodded. They were safe now.

Josef handed Patrick a glass, then reached for a bottle of champagne. He poured Adams a glass, then one for himself, and corked the bottle up again. It was cheap synthetic stuff, but it was made on the Moon, and in this case, it was only the symbolism that mattered.

"To Britt Godfrey," Josef said solemnly.

"To Britt Godfrey," Adams repeated. "And Chen Wang. May they never be forgotten."

The giant red alien roared as it rushed toward them, eager to avenge its young. Jeff snapped a quick burst off with his railgun, but the metal projectiles just bounced off the thick plated armor. The beast moved much faster than its huge bulk would seem to permit, and the three LDF commandos barely managed to dash into a small alcove before the monster smashed into the wall, showering them with dust and small rocks as the ceiling shook with the force of the impact.

Bunny and Dalton managed to get behind a bend in the alcove, but Jeff, a little behind them, was hit in the back and knocked over by a massive green glob spat at him by the monster. It was apparently energy-based, as the glowing stuff evaporated upon striking his shields but, in doing so, burned them down nearly to nothing.

Dalton dropped the barrel of his plasgun and pulled Jeff toward them, managing to drag him around the corner just as another glob, nearly three feet in diameter, came hurling toward them. It splattered against the wall, and there was a faint hiss as some of it struck Dalton's shields.

"God, what *is* that stuff?" he exclaimed, disgusted.

"I don't know, but damn, that was too close!" said Jeff, still clinging to his arm. There was a loud scraping, scrabbling noise, and Dalton disengaged himself from Jeff to see what was happening around the corner. He was horrified to discover that the monster was clawing away at the wall protecting them, its long talons carving through the hard rock almost as easily as a miner's laser.

Although Josef von Hayek owed her his life, he'd never laid eyes on Dr. Marjorie Gillen before. Upon meeting her, he was surprised to see that the chief of Farside Station and the head of MANTA research was a short, chubby woman of around sixty, with a grandmotherly air about her. He wasn't sure what he expected her to look like—this scientist who'd just made what might turn out to be humanity's most significant scientific development in centuries—but it surely wasn't the woman standing in front of him.

"I have to thank you, Doctor," he began, ducking his head in a short bow. "I—"

"No time for this—what are you, a colonel? Colonel, then." She turned toward Patrick. "The Estrons are going *nuts.* What's happening in the mines? You didn't let anyone down there, did you?"

"I don't think so." Adams thought about it. "No, not that I'm aware of. Amalia?"

"No, certainly not."

The doctor frowned and pushed her glasses higher on the bridge of her stubby little nose. "Well, something has them upset. Tara's been trying to talk with them, but we can't make head or tail out of anything they're saying."

"Wait a minute," Josef interjected. "Who are the Estrons?"

"Why, the aliens, of course. You didn't think we developed MANTA on our own, did you?" She laughed at the expression on his face. "My God, you did, didn't you?"

"But I heard that you, Doctor . . . *Aliens?*"

"Yes, of course. They traded us the matter transport technology. I'm a xenolinguist, not a physicist or a quantum mechanic. Talking to the aliens is my job. And right now they're really upset about something."

Josef's mind, reeling and desperately seeking something

familiar to latch on to, suddenly filled in an earlier blank. "You mentioned the mines. Did you mean the Highland Mines, the ones that were abandoned?"

"Yes. One of the Estroni hive mothers is there. She was pregnant, you see, and we let them have the mine as a birthing place for her."

"Oh no," said Josef slowly. "The left teleporter pad in the transporter room back at Tycho." A stricken look appeared on Adams's face.

"I don't understand," said Dr. Gillen, and Trelstad shrugged. She was confused too.

"Some of the soldiers who stayed behind to cover our retreat never followed us through to Darkside," Adams explained. "We thought they'd been captured or killed, but maybe they took the wrong teleporter."

Dr. Gillen nodded. "Yes, the other teleporter does lead to the mines, now that you mention it." She rubbed her hands together. "Dear Lord, we're going to have to try to explain this to the Estrons. You'd better come with me, Colonel. I hope you can talk fast, because without the aliens' help, it's all over."

"We can't stay here," Dalton shouted above the noise of the alien's giant talons tearing at the rock. "And we can't outrun it." He started at the sound of a railgun firing two long bursts behind him. "What the hell's going on back there?"

"Sorry," Jeff said, wiping green gunk off the barrel of his weapon. "One of those little suckers was hatching back here, and I got carried away."

Bunny, meanwhile, had slipped past Dalton and raised the grenade launcher to her shoulder. "Stay back," she warned Jeff. "We're gonna get some shrapnel in here, and your shield power-level is too low to take it."

She fired a round directly into the monster's face and, seeing how the beast bellowed, fired another. The force of the explosion knocked her back, but her shields held, and she shouted when she saw the monster retreating in pain and confusion.

"It doesn't like grenades! Maybe it's not so tough after all." Bunny stepped out of the alcove and fired again, and again the monster roared in agony.

"Let's see if it likes the plasgun any better," Dalton yelled. He joined Bunny outside the alcove and squeezed off two streams of plasma. Both hit, and though the result was not quite as dramatic, they clearly did some damage.

But the monster wasn't through fighting. It spat a blob of plasma at the two commandos, forcing them to scatter, then charged Bunny. At such close range, she didn't dare to fire a grenade, and she closed her eyes as the beast rose up on its hind legs before her, its head nearly touching the cave's ceiling seven meters from the floor.

Before the monster could bring its mighty claws down on Bunny, though, Dalton had recovered and fired a long stream of plasma into its chest. The ferocious heat forced the wounded monster back far enough that Bunny could risk a shot, and she quickly fired another round at its head.

"Dammit, how much damage can this thing take?" Dalton swore, but he grimly set his jaw and continued to fire. They pursued the alien around the cavern, dodging its occasional dripping green projectile and forcing it into a protective crouch every time it seemed ready to gather itself for a charge. As his shields recovered, Jeff joined them, snapping off an occasional burst from his railgun whenever the monster's seemingly vulnerable chest presented itself.

Bunny was down to her last few grenades when finally, after absorbing at least thirty direct hits, the monster uttered a noise that sounded like a moan and collapsed on its side. It shuddered briefly, then its eyes closed and vomited forth a large mass of glowing green ooze.

"Do you think it's dead?" Dalton asked wonderingly.

"I sure as hell hope so," Bunny said. "I've only got two more grenades."

Jeff didn't say anything. While Bunny walked over and prodded the dead alien with her foot, he dropped his railgun and slowly put his hands on his head.

From the northern entrance to the cavern, a squad of ATFOR troops had emerged. Seeing Bunny's grenade launcher, they immediately spread out and pointed their ACRs at her.

"I'm pretty sure it is dead," Bunny called. When she didn't get a response, she turned around to face the others. "Dalt—"

"Drop the launcher," Chuck Houston's voice grated in her ears. She quickly complied, and one of the Bluesuits stepped forward and retrieved the weapon. "Now tell me: what the hell is *that* thing?"

Josef gazed at the alien in wonderment. It was both frightful and beautiful; standing more than two meters high, it towered over the tall colonel. It had two legs and two arms, a head with two eyes, a mouth, and what appeared to be a nose ridge. But there the resemblance to anything even remotely humanoid ended.

The Estron was covered with a thick reddish orange hide. Its eyes were a bright solid green and lacked pupils but had a clear nictating membrane, like that of a snake. Between the eyes began a series of V-shaped overlapping plates that ran over the top of the head and down the back, terminating in a short tail. It clearly understood the use of tools, as it wore a utility belt not unlike the one around Josef's battlesuit, from which hung several strange devices.

Its hands were clawed, with four digits, two of which were opposable. Other than the belt, it wore no clothing, but Josef couldn't see any sexual characteristics. It regarded him calmly, without making any movement or sound.

"H-hello," Josef said.

The doctor pushed a button on the small box-shaped device she was holding, and a weird ululating sound came out. The alien cocked its head to the side and opened its lipless mouth, revealing sharp triangular teeth. Then it made a series of noises that sounded vaguely similar to those emanating from the doctor's box.

"What's it saying?" Josef asked.

"Just a minute," the doctor said. "It's processing the data. Sometimes this takes a while."

The synthetic voice of the translator box spoke. "Greetings, Warrior God-King. New mother dead. Why kill?"

"Holy moley!" Josef couldn't believe he was actually talking with an alien! For a moment the shock of it threatened to overwhelm him, till he realized the seriousness of the alien's words. "I—We didn't kill the new mother. We are your friends." He looked anxiously at the doctor, as he waited for the translation.

"See new mother dead. See warrior plural." The next words were undecipherable, possibly a color reference. Then: "Kill."

Josef puzzled it out and answered. "Those warriors who killed the new mother—did they wear this color?" Josef pointed to a blue cloth of a shade similar to UN armor.

"Negative response."

"This color?" He pointed to his black belt.

"Negative response."

"This color?" He pointed to his chest.

The alien seemed to grow agitated, bobbing its head and making noises. "Strong affirmative response."

Josef shook his head. He never found it easy to apologize for anything, but this was impossible. He looked at Dr. Gillen. "Any suggestions? You're the xenolinguist, not me."

"I don't know what to do, Colonel. After all, we've never actually been in contact with aliens before, so all I've had to go on so far is theory, which to be honest, looks more like bullpuckey every day. Go with your gut, Colonel. Wing it. That's what I've been doing since the Estrons first came through the dimension gate six months ago."

"Fair enough." Josef turned back to face the alien. "I don't suppose you've ever read Arthur Conan Doyle?"

CHAPTER 24

UN Headquarters, New York
26 November 2069
2:30 P.M. EST

"I don't understand this," said Chairman Wu via the video screen. "You say you received a message saying Tycho had fallen but von Hayek and the other rebels had fled to some other location? Whom did the research station fall to? My sources tell me the NDE troops were in control of both Tycho and Port Aldrin."

"That's correct," Antonio assured him. "But two squads of ATFOR troops arrived at Tycho first, and I understand they pursued the rebel leaders through one of those teleport devices during the conflict. That's the last we've heard of it thus far, though I've instructed General Daniels to relay any links immediately."

Wu nodded. Though his face was still grave, he had lost the worried look he'd been wearing for the past twelve hours. "At least the Germans didn't capture von Hayek. That was my primary fear, that he would fall into their hands and they'd stage a formal surrender. Fortunately, that doesn't appear likely now."

"No. I'd heard they'd announced the capture of General

Consensus, but it turns out they just got some major, an ex-Texan."

"That doesn't surprise me," said Wu. "The Americans are a rebellious people still. I see it every day in the streets."

"Yes, well, they haven't had the benefits of two thousand years of civilization and culture." Antonio grinned. "You must be patient, my friend." A tone sounded, and Chairman Wu's image disappeared momentarily, replaced by a text message.

"It appears that link I've been waiting for has just been relayed. I'll call you after." Wu nodded, and Antonio broke the link as he switched to the relay.

As he expected, there were no visuals, but the audio came through loud and clear. "Chairman Aguila?"

"Aguila here," he responded.

There was the usual time lag. "This is Colonel Houston. I'm afraid we haven't found von Hayek yet, but I thought you'd better know about this first." There was a pause.

"Yes? What is it?"

Three-second time lag.

"We've captured some of the rebels we were chasing. And . . . well, this is going to sound crazy, but we've discovered a dead alien."

"An alien? Are you sure?"

The seconds crawled by like handicapped snails.

"Yes, I'm afraid I am, sir. Unless you know of something that looks like a giant red bug the size of an elephant."

Aguila was nonplussed. It was hard to know even where to start. He had to admit, though, the creature didn't sound like anything he'd ever heard of. "And you say it's dead?"

Time lag.

"Yeah, it's dead, all right. The Loonies killed it; they said it took thirty or forty grenades before it died. There's green blood all over the place, so I think they're telling the truth, but they don't know any more about the creature than I do. Hang on a second, and let me see if I can get my cam working again."

After a seemingly interminable wait, Antonio was rewarded with a wobbling image of the dead alien. Not knowing what to say, he settled for hitting the record button.

"So what should I do?" the colonel asked. Then: "What the *hell?*"

The image on the screen whirled away from the monstrous corpse and focused unexpectedly on a group of about twenty figures. Some were humans in white battlesuits, but there were other, taller figures that bore a vague resemblance to the dead monster. Suddenly the screen went black.

"Colonel? . . . Colonel Houston?" Antonio smashed his fist against his desktop. "Dammit, Colonel, don't do this to me!"

But the link was broken, and even repeated attempts to relink through General Daniels failed. Antonio ground his teeth in frustration and called Chairman Wu again.

"What's going on, Antonio?" Wu asked with anticipation.

"I have absolutely no idea," he replied.

Highland Mines, Luna
26 November 2069
17:32 GMT

When she'd heard Chuck Houston's voice commanding her to drop her weapon, Bunny had known terror unlike any she'd ever known before in her life. Giant aliens with claws longer than her body vomiting explosives were bad enough, but the thought of being captured and tried as a traitor had reduced her to a two-legged mass of quivering panic.

Fortunately, Houston and the other ATFOR soldiers were obsessed with the alien, and Dalton—who, with his curious mind, was quite willing to let bygones be bygones in light of the situation—had answered all their questions about the killing of the monster.

Houston was standing off to the side, apparently deep in conversation with someone, while two of the other ATFOR troopers attempted to perform a crude dissection with a

laser pistol. The weapon didn't make for a good scalpel, but
they were just beginning to make progress when Bunny
noticed movement at the northern entrance to the cavern.

"Murderer! Blasphemer!" she heard a synthetic voice
pronounce judgment like the voice of God over the wide
band, and a motley assortment of battlesuited LDF troopers, civilians in vacuum suits, and giant two-legged *things*
came rushing at them.

One of the ATFOR troopers managed to squeeze off a
shot from his ACR, but it ablated without much effect on
the shields of an LDF trooper, and in less than ten seconds
all of the ATFOR men were on the ground, held down by
the clawed hands of the aliens. Dalton, Bunny, and Jeff were
all knocked down too, but at the apparent command of the
alien standing near Colonel von Hayek they were released
and helped up by their LDF comrades.

"New mother dead. Blue warrior plural kill?" asked the
synthetic voice.

"No," said Bunny, indicating Dalton, Jeff, and herself.
"We killed it."

"Oh, dammit, Bunny," said Josef. "Why'd you have to
say that?"

"Bunny?" said a startled Chuck Houston. "Bunny
Mahoney?"

"Yeah," she replied. "Sorry to disappoint you, boss, but I
kind of switched sides."

Houston snorted. "And to think I came down here to
rescue you!" He turned away from her, and Bunny knew he
was shaking his head inside his helmet.

"White warrior plural kill new mother," stated the alien
leader. The other aliens began to ominously circle the three
guilty parties.

"Wait, it was an accident!" Josef cried as the armed LDF
troops began to point their weapons at the Estrons. "They
didn't mean to do it! Accident. Do you understand accident? Dammit, we don't want to fight you too!"

"Understand negative. Wait, think, talk." The creature's

next words were undecipherable, possibly a reference to itself. Then: "God-King."

"Doctor, what's he saying?" Josef asked as the barrel of his ACR moved back and forth between Houston and the Estron leader.

"He wants to think about what he's heard."

"Good . . . I think." Josef turned to Houston. "Now, what do we do with you? We don't have the supplies or the time for prisoners. Not to mention the fact that I don't particularly want word of this incident to reach Earth."

"It already has," Houston said nonchalantly, as if unfazed by the implied threat. "I established a cam link to Earth not five minutes ago. They already know about the aliens. Teleporters too. Before the cease-fire, we picked up three of your transporter disks at Lacus Mortis."

Josef regarded him thoughtfully. "I'll have to speak to my father about this. The governor should be the one to decide what to do with you." He turned and addressed several of the LDF troopers: "Take them away."

Houston shrugged away the hand of the first guard to reach him, then looked at Bunny. "Don't think you've gotten away with anything, traitor. The UN will crush this little rebellion soon, and you with it, honey bunny."

"Whatever, Chuck." Bunny yawned. She was really too tired for this; she'd had too much high weirdness for a single day. "Say hi to Sara if you see her."

"Say hi to her yourself when you're dragged in to face the court-martial," he spat as two LDF men frog-marched him away. "Before they hang you!"

"Oh, shove it," she replied.

Dalton started laughing, then stopped when he realized he was laughing all alone. "What's wrong?" he asked, looking around, bewildered. "Did I say something wrong?"

"No," Josef said. "You *did* something wrong. Really wrong. So wrong, in fact, that it may go down in the history books as the biggest screwup of all time." Josef was tired too, weary to the depths of his soul. "So congratulations and come with me. We'll figure something out."

Josef turned to Dr. Gillen and pointed to the Estron leader. "Tell him we'll talk about it tomorrow, okay?" He strapped his ACR to his back and led Dalton and Bunny toward the southern end of the cavern, toward the transporter to Farside Station.

THE ESTRONS

It was always assumed that if mankind ever did meet an intelligent alien species, it would result in a paradigm shift of unimaginable proportions. All bets would be off; all wars would stop instantly; no doubt the stock market would crash in flames. The presumption was always that the reality of alien contact would force humanity to collectively reevaluate its place in the universe and that all the people of the world would immediately join hands and hold their breath, overwhelmed by the awe of it all.

How disappointing, then, to find that despite radical differences in biochemistry, anatomy, technology, and familial organization, the Estrons in fact understood our political situation perfectly, for it mirrored their own. And not only did the encounter with the Estrons *not* produce an immediate end to global conflict; it in fact exacerbated it, as the Estrons were quite willing to take sides.

And prisoners.

— Chaim Noguchi, *A History of the Lunar Revolution*

CHAPTER 25

The three ambassador-prisoners rose as their final mission briefing at last came to an end. Tara Beckman, Dr. Gillen's assistant, smiled and repeated her final instruction. "Just remember not to throw up on anyone—or anything, since you probably won't be able to tell the anyones from the anythings, at least at first. No matter how sick you feel, try to hold it until you're sure you're alone. Vomiting is seen as a mortal insult, like waving a gun in someone's face."

"Well, it's not like we're going to throw up on anyone with our suits on," Dalton said, grinning.

"Right, but as far as we've been able to understand, some kind of habitat has been prepared for you that, theoretically, should allow you to take your suits off. But you'll be okay even if the habitat doesn't work out, as we're sending plenty of oxygen recyclers and two generators through the D-gate with you, but the Estrons may decide to join you in the habitat, so it can't hurt to be reminded."

"How can they join us?" Jeff asked. "They're impervious to vacuum, too, aren't they?"

Tara shrugged. "Who knows? The Estrons don't seem to have any formalized science, at least not in the sense that we do. And yet look at their advances in matter transport. Maybe it's like Arthur Clarke said: advanced science just *looks* like magic. That's part of what we're hoping you'll find out."

The door slid open and Josef von Hayek walked in. "The suits are ready, gang. Ready to make history for the second time in a week?"

"Josef, I wish you'd stay here," Bunny said. "We three have to go, but you don't. I don't know why you're doing this. The Free State needs you."

"Exactly," he said. "We have no money, no resources, few weapons, and about three hundred people left to take on an entire planet. Our domes are all occupied by the enemy, and troops'll be arriving here just as soon as the UN and the NDE can come to terms. We need allies, and we need them fast." He grinned darkly. "Besides, somebody has to bring back the news if the Estron god-kings decide they want your heads on a platter."

"Very funny," Dalton replied sourly. He started to say more, but a buzzer sounded, and Josef clapped him on the shoulder.

"It's time," he said, clearly excited. "Time to go."

Shuttle "Atlantis IV," Final Approach
1 December 2069
08:15 GMT

Chuck Houston checked the straps on the acceleration couch one last time before the transport entered the Earth's atmosphere. He should be feeling lucky to be alive, he supposed, but instead he just felt empty. What had started out as a simple police action had turned into something both mysterious and awesome, and suddenly he wondered if the things he'd been fighting for really mattered anymore.

What were a few paltry lunar colonies compared to the brilliant opportunities available among the stars? For the first time in history, human beings knew they were not alone in the universe, and suddenly the scramble for resources appeared to be nothing more than the squabbling of children fighting over mounds of sand in a sandbox.

He folded his hands together and pursed his lips, thinking. Eileen Mahoney had always been a good soldier of unquestionable loyalty. But she'd found something on the Moon that had compelled her to cast away everything—career, friends, and even Earth itself—in its favor. He could feel that thing she found, somehow, as if it were just on the tip of his mind, but he could not tell what it was. He envied Bunny, not for the choice she'd made, but for having been given opportunity to make such a decision. He couldn't find it in his heart to blame her now, and he wished he could take back his last angry words.

Oh, well. What was done was done. Chuck Houston was never a man to waste much time on philosophy or on thoughts of the past. He turned his mind from the strange events on Luna and thought about his upcoming meeting with the chairman of the Committee on Lunar Development. Speaking of opportunities, he could smell one waiting for him there, and with the tension high in the air between the United Nations and the New German Unity, there was plenty of room for a warrior.

The transport suddenly began to slow as it entered the atmosphere, and Chuck Houston smiled as he felt the pull of the Earth's gravity for the first time in a month. It was good to get back to the mother planet, he thought. It was very good.

UN Headquarters, New York
1 December 2069
3:00 A.M. EST

Antonio watched the ATFOR colonel's one-minute vid for the four hundred and eleventh time as Allegria lay sleeping next to him on the king-sized bed. He didn't know why, but it was a never-ending source of fascination to him, and he found himself almost excited at the prospect of meeting the colonel in person tomorrow.

The vid wasn't a fake. He knew that, having had its authenticity verified separately by two of the foremost specialists in the field. But still he needed to speak with the colonel himself. Only then could he allow himself to be convinced that there were in fact aliens on the Moon.

We are not alone. It was an intimidating thought to some, but Antonio saw it as both an opportunity and a confirmation. Now, in the face of a potential alien threat, surely mankind would recognize that the one-hundred-twenty-four-year experiment was not a waste and that Woodrow Wilson's dream of a world government was in fact the only way. There would always be those who were blind, who could not or would not see the cohesive beauty of the dream. That he recognized clearly, but those people did not matter.

Through his doing, the lunar rebellion was, for all intents and purposes, crushed. The current impasse with the NDE was, admittedly, a major irritant, but nothing more. He had no doubt that he and Wu would soon convince the German chancellor that he'd overplayed his hand. The settlement might cost the CLD a dome, perhaps even two, but it was really just a matter of time. The Germans simply didn't have enough troops up there to hold on to what they'd grabbed so greedily.

Tomorrow morning the colonel, and tomorrow afternoon the secretary-general, Aguila decided. The day after, perhaps the world. He walked over to the window and looked up at the stars. *We will unite,* he thought. *We will learn to unite, and then you'd all better watch out for us!* Let others fear, but Antonio would dream on the promise of a new world.

He looked tenderly at the beautiful woman, still sleeping soundly with the moon casting rays of light across her face so that her dark hair appeared to be frosted with silver. Tomorrow the colonel, Aguila thought. And the next day the world. But tonight Allegria.

Farside Station, Luna
1 December 2069
08:30 GMT

The Estron leader, whose name or title sounded something like "Zzheer'ach'ill," bowed formally to the four humans. Each of the humans wore a powered battlesuit, but beyond that they were unarmed. Behind them were the large boxes of equipment and supplies that would be transported after them.

"Warrior plural, warrior god-king, make peace Estron god-king plural." Undecipherable words followed, possibly a benediction, and then it said good-bye.

The humans bowed deeply, and the Estron stepped back, making way for Patrick Adams and Amalia Trelstad.

Trelstad stepped forward. "Josef, are you sure about this?"

He smiled. "Of course. Look at it this way. If I succeed, we'll be able to continue the war. If I fail and we all die over there, then at least we eliminate four more people who know our dirty little secret."

"Four?"

He indicated Bunny, Dalton, and Jeff. "They were there. If they don't realize it yet, it's just because they haven't thought it through." He grinned at Trelstad. "Besides, Amalia, you'll make a better head of a government-in-exile than I ever would."

She nodded. "True. But you're still the spiritual leader of the revolution."

"No, I'm not. Pieter is, and you'd better not let anyone forget it, including yourselves." He looked at Patrick. "You'll broadcast the speech day after next?"

Adams nodded. "Yes. The vid will be done later this afternoon, and the audio techs tell me they should be able to wrap things up by tomorrow morning. Plenty of time before the hearings begin in the General Assembly. Fortunately, your voice is very much like Pieter's, and they can enhance the audio enough to make the voiceprints match."

"That's not your only similarity to your father," Amalia said dryly. "I think I've seen this certain muleheaded stubbornness before."

Josef took her hand and shook it. "Thank you, Amalia, and good luck." He gripped Adams's hand firmly. "Keep the fire burning, Patrick."

Adams's voice grew thick. "Always, Josef. But . . . come back. We need you more than you know." He cleared his throat with some difficulty. "Do you have . . . *him?*"

"Right here." Josef patted a small container on his utility belt. "Maybe someday we'll be able to tell the world. But he'll be happy whether anyone ever knows or not. The first human to have his ashes scattered over a new world."

"I agree." At some unseen signal, Amalia and Patrick stepped back, and one of the MANTA techs pressed a button, sliding back the panel that covered the dimension gate. The portal was twice as wide as the teleport disks and bore a different symbol on the bottom, but otherwise it looked reassuringly familiar.

Dalton glanced at Bunny. Somehow her hand had found its way into his. He couldn't see her face, but he guessed she was smiling behind the mirrored visor.

"You don't think I'm scared, do you?" he said.

"Oh, no. Of course not."

"Are you?"

"Of course," Bunny admitted. "Anyone with any brains or sense would be."

"Oh," he said, surprised. "Well, I'll admit I'm a bit nervous. This is the kind of thing Britt should be doing, not me!"

Bunny laughed. "So let's do it!" she cried, and together they leaped through the gate, followed a moment later by Josef and Jeff. There was a brief flash of light, and they were gone.